If I
Were
You

If I Were You

Lisa Renee Jones

Gallery Books

New York   London   Toronto   Sydney   New Delhi

G

Gallery Books
A Division of Simon & Schuster, Inc.
1230 Avenue of the Americas
New York, NY 10020

First Gallery Books trade paperback edition March 2013

GALLERY BOOKS and colophon are registered trademarks of Simon & Schuster, Inc.

For information about special discounts for bulk purchases, please contact Simon & Schuster Special Sales at 1-866-506-1949 or business@simonandschuster.com.

The Simon & Schuster Speakers Bureau can bring authors to your live event. For more information or to book an event contact the Simon & Schuster Speakers Bureau at 1-866-248-3049 or visit our website at www.simonspeakers.com.

Designed by Ruth Lee-Mui

Manufactured in the United States of America

1   3   5   7   9   10   8   6   4   2

Library of Congress Cataloging-in-Publication Data
Jones, Lisa Renee.
If I Were You / Lisa Renee Jones.—First Gallery Books paperback edition.
   pages   cm
1. Erotic fiction.   2. Mystery fiction.   I. Title.
   PS3610.O627I38 2013
813'.6—dc23   2012041926

ISBN 978-1-4767-2604-5
ISBN 978-1-4767-2606-9 (ebook)

To Diego—this story is for you

Happy Birthday!

Acknowledgments

Happy Birthday to Tina, who is my lucky angel and dear friend. Without her love and support I would not have survived my nerves during this very special project. And thank you to all of my Underground Angels who have shown so much support. You ladies really are my wings. Thanks to my readers who make it possible for me to do what I love and to many of you who helped me spread the word about this story. And thanks to the many bloggers who helped spread the word about this story as well!

One

Wednesday, March 7, 2012

Dangerous.

For months I've had dreams and nightmares about how perfectly he personifies the word. Sleep-laden, alternate realities where I can vividly smell his musky male scent, feel his hard body against mine. Taste the sweet and sensuous flavor of him—like milk chocolate with its silky demand that I indulge in one more bite. And another. So good I'd forgotten there's a price for over-indulgence. And there is a price. There is always a price. I was reminded of this life lesson on Saturday night. And I know now, no matter what he says, no matter what he does, I cannot—will not—see him again.

It started out as any other erotic adventure with him. Un-predictable. Exciting. I barely remember where it all went wrong. How it took such a dark turn.

He'd ordered me to undress and sit on the mattress, against the headboard, my legs spread wide for his viewing. Naked before him, open to him, I was vulnerable and quivering with need. Never in my life had I taken orders from a man; most certainly I had never thought I would quiver with anything. But I did for him.

If Saturday night proved anything, it was that once I was with him, under his spell, he could demand anything of me, and I'd comply. He could push me to the edge, to unbelievable places I'd never thought I would go. Exactly why I can't see him again. He makes me feel possessed, and what is so disconcerting about this feeling is that I like it. I can hardly wrap my mind around allowing such a thing, though I burn for it. But when I saw him standing at the end of the bed Saturday night, all broad and thick with sinewy muscle, his cock jutting forward, there was nothing but that need.

He was magnificent. Really, truly the most gorgeous man I've ever known. Instant lust exploded inside me. I wanted to feel him close to me, to feel him touch me. To touch him. But I know now not to touch him without his permission. And I know not to beg him to let me.

I've learned my lesson from past encounters. He enjoys the vulnerability of a plea far too much. Enjoys withholding his pleasures until I am nearly quaking with the burn of my body. Until I am liquid heat and tears. He likes that power over me. He likes full control. I should hate him. Sometimes, I think I love him.

It was the blindfold that should have warned me I was headed toward a place of no return. Thinking back, I believe it did. He tossed it on the bed, a dare, and instantly a shiver chased a path up and down my spine. The idea of not being able to see what was happening to me should have aroused me—it did arouse me. But for reasons I didn't understand at the time, it also frightened me. I was scared and I hesitated.

This did not please him. He told me so, in that deep, rich, baritone voice that makes me quiver uncontrollably. The need to please him had been so compelling. I put on the blindfold.

I was rewarded by the shift of the mattress. He was coming to me. Soon I knew I would come, too. His hands slid possessively up my calves, over my thighs. And damn him, stopped just before my place of need.

What came next was a shadowy whirlwind of sensation. He pulled me to my back, flat against the mattress. I knew satisfaction was seconds away. Soon he would enter me. Soon I would have what I needed. But to my distress, he moved away.

It was then that I was sure I'd heard the click of a lock. It jolted me to a sitting position, and I called out his name, fearful he was leaving. Certain that I'd done something wrong. Then relieved when his hand flattened on my stomach. I'd imagined the sound of the lock. I must have. But I couldn't shake the subtle shift in the air then, the raw lust and menace consuming the room that didn't feel like him. It was a thought easily forgotten when he settled heavy between my thighs, his strong hands lifting my arms over my head, his breath warm on my neck—his body heavy, perfect.

Somehow, a silk tie wrapped around my wrists and my arms were tied to the bed frame. It never occurred to me that he could not have done this on his own. That he was on top of me, unable to manipulate my arms. But then, he was manipulating my body, my mind, and I was his willing victim.

He lifted his body from mine, and I whimpered, unable to reach for him. Again silence. And the whisk of fabric. More strange sounds. Long seconds ticked by, and I remember the chill that snaked across my skin. The feeling of dread that had balled in my stomach.

And then, the moment I know I will die remembering. The moment when the steel of a blade touched my lips. The moment that he promised there was pleasure in pain. The moment when the blade traveled along my skin with the proof he would be true to his words. And I knew then that I had been wrong. He was not dangerous. Nor was he chocolate. He was lethal, a drug, and I feared . . .

A knock on my apartment door jolts me from the seductive words of the journal I've been reading to the point I darn near toss the notebook over my shoulder. Guiltily, I slam it shut and set it back on the simple oak coffee table where it had been left by my neighbor and close friend Ella Ferguson the night before. I hadn't meant to read it. It was just . . . there. On my table. Absently, I'd opened it, and I'd been so shocked at what I found that I hadn't believed it could really be my sweet, close friend Ella's writing. So I'd kept reading. I couldn't stop reading, and I don't know why. It makes no sense. I, Sara McMillan, am a high school teacher, and I do not invade people's privacy, nor do I enjoy this kind of reading. I'm still telling myself that as I reach the door, but I can't ignore the burn low in my belly.

I pause before greeting my visitor and rest my hands on my cheeks, certain they're flaming red, hoping whoever is here will just go away. I promise myself if they do, I won't read the journal again, but deep down, I know the temptation will be strong. Good Lord, I feel like Ella seemed to feel when living out the scene in the journal—like I am the one hanging on for one more titillating moment and then another. Clearly, twenty-eight-year-old women are not supposed to go eighteen months without sex. The worst part is that I've invaded the privacy of someone I care about.

Another knock sounds, and I concede that, nope, my visitor is not going away. Inwardly, I shake myself and tug at the hem of the simple light blue dress I still wear from today's final tenth-grade English class of the summer. I inhale and open the door to have a cool blast of San Francisco's year-round chilly night air tease the loose strands of my long brunette hair that have fallen from the twist at my nape. Thankfully, it also cools my feverishly hot skin. What is wrong with me? How has a journal affected me this intensely?

Without awaiting an invitation, Ella rushes past me in a whiff of vanilla-scented perfume and red bouncing curls.

"There it is," Ella says, snatching up her journal from the coffee table. "I thought I'd left it here when I came by last night."

I shut the door, certain my cheeks are flaming again with the knowledge that I now know more about Ella's sex life than I should. I still don't know what made me open that journal, what made me keep reading. What makes me, even now, want to read more.

"I hadn't noticed," I say, wishing I could pull back the lie the instant it's issued. I don't like lies. I've known my share of people who've told them, and I know how damaging they can be. I really don't like how easily this one slipped from my lips. This is Ella, after all, who in the past year as my neighbor has become my confidante, the younger sister I'd never had. Together we are the family neither of us has or, rather, neither of us wishes to claim. Uncomfortably, I ramble onward, a bad habit brought out by nerves, and guilt, apparently. "Long day of classes," I add, "and I had piles and piles of paperwork to finish up for the summer. Lucky you got to avoid that this year, though I had some great kids I enjoyed." I purse my lips and tell myself I've said enough, only to find I can't help but continue. "I only just got home a few minutes ago."

"Well, thank goodness you have some time off now," Ella says, lifting the journal. "I brought this over last night when we'd planned to watch that chick flick together. I wanted to read you a few of the entries. But then David called, and you know how that went." Her lips tilted downward, guilt laden in her tone. "I deserted you like a very bad friend."

David being her hot doctor boyfriend. What David wanted from Ella, he got. Now, I know just how true that is. I study Ella a moment. With her dewy youthful skin, and dressed in faded jeans and a purple tee, she looks like one of my students rather than a twenty-five-year-old teacher herself. "I was tired anyway," I assure her, but I'm worried she's over her head with this man ten years her senior. "I needed to get to bed to be ready for today's classes."

"Well, they're over now and yay for that." She indicates the journal. "And I'm so glad to get this back before my date with David tonight." She wiggles an eyebrow. "Foreplay. David is going to love this. This thing is scorching hot."

6

I gape in utter disbelief. "You read him your journal?" I'd never have the courage to read a man such intimate personal thoughts—especially not about him. "And it's foreplay?"

Ella frowns. "This isn't my journal. Remember? I told you last night. It's from the storage units I bought at that auction at the beginning of summer."

"Oh," I say, though I don't remember Ella saying anything about the journal. In fact, had she, I'm 100 percent sure I'd remember. "That's right. The storage auctions you've been attending since you got obsessed with that *Storage Wars* show. I still can't believe people store their things and then default and let it go to the highest bidder."

"And yet they do," Ella says. "And I'm not obsessed."

I arch a brow.

"Okay, maybe I am," she concedes, "but I'm going to make more than double what I would have teaching summer school. You should really consider going to the next auction with me. I've already turned around two of the three units I bought for big money." She holds up the journal. "This came from the last unit I bought, and it's the best yet. It has artwork I know is going to sell for big bucks. And so far I've found three journals that are absolutely spellbinding. My gosh, I can't seem to stop reading them. This woman started out like you and me, and somehow got pulled into this dark passionate place that is terrifyingly exciting."

She's right, and I can feel that burn in my belly as I recall the words on those pages. I can almost imagine the soft, seductive voice of the woman whispering her story to me. I try to focus on what Ella is saying, but I'm wondering about that woman instead, wondering where she is, who she is.

"Oh my!" Ella exclaims. "You're blushing. You read the journal, didn't you?"

I blanch. "What? I . . ." Suddenly, I can't talk. I am so not myself right now, and I sink helplessly into an overstuffed brown chair across from Ella, stuck in the trap of my earlier lie. "I . . . yes. I read it."

Ella claims a couch cushion, narrowing her green eyes on me. "Did you think I wrote that stuff?"

I cast her a tentative look. "Well . . ."

"Whoa," she says, clearly taking my reply, or rather lack of reply, as confirmation. "You thought . . ." She shakes her head. "I'm speechless. You couldn't have read the good parts or there's no way you would think she was me. But you're sure blushing like you read the good parts."

"I read some parts that were, ah, pretty detailed."

She snorts. "And you assumed I wrote them." She shakes her head again. "And here I thought you knew me. But heck, I so wish I could live up to that assessment for just one hot night. There is a mysterious eroticism to that woman's life that's just . . ." She shivers. "Haunting. It, she, affects me."

In some small way it comforts me to know she is as affected by the words on those pages as I am, and I don't know why. What in the world do I need comfort for? It isn't logical. Nothing about my reaction to this unknown woman is logical.

"Once David and I finish with the journal," Ella continues, drawing me back into the conversation, "he's going to take pictures of a few intimate pages for potential buyers and we're listing the journals on eBay. They're going to bring in big money. I just know it."

I gape, appalled at this idea. "You can't seriously intend on selling this woman's personal thoughts on eBay?"

"Heck yeah, I do," she says. "Making money is the name of the game. Besides, for all we know, it's fiction."

Her words are cold, and she surprises me. This is not the Ella I know. "We are talking about a woman's private thoughts, Ella. Surely, you don't want to profit off her pain."

Her brows dip. "What pain? It sounds like all pleasure to me."

"She lost everything she owns at auction. That isn't pleasure."

"I'm guessing her rich man flew her off to some exotic location and she is living life in a grand way." Her voice turns somber. "I have to think like that to do this, Sara. Please don't make me feel guilty. This is money I need, and if I didn't do this, some other buyer would have."

I open my mouth to argue but relent. Ella is alone in this world, with no family aside from an alcoholic father who doesn't know his own name most of the time, let alone hers. I know she feels she has to have money for emergencies. I know that feeling myself all too well. I, too, am alone. Mostly, but I don't want to think about that right now.

"I'm sorry," I tell her, and I mean it. "I know this is good for you. I'm happy it's working out."

Her lips curve slightly, and she nods her acceptance before she pushes to her feet. I stand with her and give her a hug. She smiles, her mood transforming into the instant sunshine I so often find she brings into my life. I love Ella. I really do.

"David and I are looking forward to a bit of that spellbinding action ourselves tonight," she announces mischievously.

"I have to run." She laughs and waves a few fingers at me. "Enjoy your night. I know I will."

I sink back into my chair and watch the door close.

The sound of pounding on my door once again takes me from bliss to panic. I sit up in the bed, disoriented and groggy, and eye the clock. Seven in the morning on my first day off from classes.

"Who the heck is pounding on my door?" I grumble, throwing the blankets off me and sliding my feet into the pink fuzzy slippers one of my students gave me last Christmas. I grab my long pink robe that is not fuzzy, but does say PINK across the back. More knocking has begun.

"Sara, it's me, Ella!" I hear as I shuffle my way toward the living room. "Hurry! Hurry!"

My heart flutters not only because Ella is clearly in some sort of panic but also because, unlike me, who doesn't like to waste a second of any day, Ella doesn't get up before noon on days she doesn't have to. The instant I yank open the door, Ella flings her arms around me and announces, "I'm eloping!"

"Eloping?!" I gasp, pulling back and tugging Ella inside, out of the chill of the early morning. She's still wearing her clothes from the night before. "What are you talking about? What's happening?"

"David proposed last night," she exclaims excitedly. "I can hardly believe it. We're flying to Paris this morning." She eyes her watch and squeals. "In two hours."

She shoves something into my hand. "That has the key to my apartment. On the kitchen table, you'll find the journal and the key to the storage unit. If it's not cleared out in two weeks, it has to be rented, or it's auctioned off yet again. So take it and sell the stuff. The money is yours. Or let it go. Either way, it doesn't matter." She grins. "Because I'm eloping to Paris, then honeymooning in Italy!"

Protectiveness fills me for Ella. I don't want her to get hurt, and I've never even heard her say she loves David. "You've known this man for only three months, sweetie. I've met him only once." He always, conveniently, got called away when we'd been planning to get together.

"I love him, Sara," she says, as if reading my mind. "And he's good to me. You know that."

No, I don't know that, but while I try to find the right way to say it, she is already reaching for the door. "Ella—"

"I'll call you when I arrive in Paris, so keep your cell handy."

"Wait!" I say, shackling her arm. "How long will you be gone?"

Her eyes light up with excitement. "A month. Can you believe it? A whole month in Italy. I'm living a dream." She hugs me and gives me a kiss on the cheek. "Since we high school folks don't go back until October, thanks to the longer school days, I'm going a full month! Can you believe it? I'll never complain about our longer school days again. A whole month in Italy—I'm living a dream! I'll call, and when we get back we'll have a reception."

Her eyes soften. "You know I wanted you with me for this, don't you? But David knew I had no family. He wanted to whisk me away so that it wouldn't be painful." She pokes at the puckered spot that always appears between my brows when

I frown. "Stop making that face. It'll be wrinkled when you get older. And I'm fine. I'm perfect, in fact."

"You better be," I say, attempting my best teacher voice, but my throat is too tight to do much more than croak out the warning. "Call me as soon as you arrive so I know you're safe, and I want pictures. Lots of pictures."

Ella smiles brightly, "Yes, Ms. McMillan." She turns and rushes away, giving me a last-second wave over her shoulder before she rounds the corner. She is gone, and I am fighting unexpected tears I don't even understand.

I am happy for Ella but worried for her, too. I feel . . . I'm not sure what I feel. Lost, maybe. My fingers curl around her keys, and I am suddenly aware that I have just inherited a storage unit and the journals I swore I wouldn't read again.

Two

And then, the moment I know I will die remembering. The moment when the steel of a blade touched my lips. The moment that he promised there was pleasure in pain . . .

Those words written in the journal replay in my head early the next evening, the same day of Ella's rapid departure. They haunt me to the point I feel downright icy every time I think of them. They are why I'm here, standing inside a temperature-controlled storage unit the size of a small garage, that at some point I assume the journal writer leased. Thankfully, there is a dim light and the neighborhood is good. I stand here, unsure of what to look at first, uneasy about digging through a stranger's things.

The moment that he promised there was pleasure in pain.

Unbidden, the words replay in my head again. I shiver, and not just because the journal is explicitly arousing. I shouldn't be aroused. Not by painful pleasure and bondage. I refuse to be aroused. I am worried about this mysterious woman. Besides, I am my father's daughter, just as my mother had been my father's wife, which translated to his puppets who didn't dare walk in the same shadows he did. My mother had escaped him in death, and I'd chosen to leave him out of my life since. Despite five years without him, I remain all too aware that the lingering effects of his heavy hand are far too present in my life.

I grind my teeth at the memories. I have no idea how my mind has gone to places I try never to go. Forcefully, I refocus on the neatly stacked furniture and boxes lining the walls, as well as what looks like well-packaged artwork. A life left behind, forgotten. Who did that? Who left behind things that they'd clearly cared about enough to neatly pack and organize? I'm not buying the idea that some rich boyfriend had whisked this woman away to some exotic life. No one who hadn't seen bad luck, or maybe even tragedy, did this. I'm not about to be a part of adding to this woman's troubles by selling off her things. Not this woman, I corrected myself. Rebecca Mason is her name. That's what the paperwork said, and as per the management they couldn't give me her phone number and "it's disconnected anyway."

"I'm going to find a way to contact you and return your things," I whisper to the room, as though I'm speaking to Rebecca, and a chill races down my spine. I feel as if she is here, as if I'm talking to her . . . and it's downright creepy. Somehow, it makes me more determined to find her.

I sigh with grim realization at what my vow means. I have to invade her privacy and dig through her things to find a way to contact her, a way to return what was left of her life. If she's alive, I think grimly, hugging myself.

"Stop it," I murmur, chiding myself. The grim reaper mentality isn't me. I don't even like horror movies. The world has enough real monsters without creating fictional monsters.

There really could be a happy reason Rebecca left her life behind. Winning the lotto. There. Yes. There was a good reason to leave all your things behind. Unlikely, but still possible. Ten million to one or so, I imagine, but possible. So why does the idea do absolutely nothing to dismiss the eerie, hollow feeling of the room?

Eager to get this over with, I drop my purse to the ground and run my hands down my soft faded jeans, scanning the items around me until my gaze catches on a box neatly labeled PERSONAL PAPERS. Seems a good place to find contact information, if I ever saw one.

Two hours later, I am sitting against a wall, thumbing through information I have no business seeing. School records, bills, legal paperwork that amounted to pennies of inheritance from the death of Rebecca's mother and last living relative, three years before. I think of my own mother, of the woman who'd tried so hard to shelter me from my father but would never do anything to shelter herself. I squeeze my eyes shut, wondering if the pain of losing her will ever go away. If it will ever go away. She'd been my best friend, my closest confidante. I wonder if Rebecca was close to her mother, as I was to mine. If she'd hurt, as I did with my loss, as I still do.

With effort, I refocus on the paperwork and realize I'm not

going to find any family connections to reach Rebecca. But thankfully, the mail and a bunch of bank statements have, at least, given me her address, though I'm not overly certain it will be accurate.

Feeling not much closer to finding Rebecca, I shove everything back in the box and stand up, feeling stiff and cramped in a way that defies my morning jogs.

"Try the dresser," comes a male voice from behind me.

I yelp and whirl around to find a man wearing a staff shirt standing in the doorway. The hair on the back of my neck prickles; my nerve endings hum with warning. He is a handsome man in his midthirties—blond, clean-shaven, with short, spiky hair, but it's the dark interest in his deep-set eyes that sets me on edge. The already small room seems to shrink and close in on me, that eerie feeling I've been unable to shake no longer hollow but focused on me, like an invisible weight on my shoulders and chest.

"Dresser?" I manage to croak despite the dryness in my throat.

"Everyone has a secret bedroom drawer," he says. His voice lowers, takes on a husky quality. "A place almost as personal as their soul."

I stiffen, a new rush of discomfort slicing through me. He's been in here. I knew it with every piece of my being. He'd gone through Rebecca's things. He knew what was in that drawer. I don't like this man, and I'm suddenly immensely aware of the fact that I am alone with him, miles from the highway, not another customer anywhere near—at least not that I've seen or heard thus far.

"I don't want to know her secrets," I say firmly, keeping my voice remarkably steady considering my knees are wobbly. "I want to find her and return her things to her."

He studies me a long moment, his gaze as sharp as the slice of discomfort digging deeper inside me. Then finally, when I am about to choke on the silence, he says, "Like I said. Check the drawer." His lips hint at a sardonic smile, and he pushes off the doorjamb. "I'll be back to lock the exterior building at nine. You won't want to be inside when I do." Without another word, he is gone.

I don't move. I can't move. I want to slam the door shut but don't dare, not when it locks from the outside, a thought that terrifies me. Seconds tick by, and I wait as the man's footsteps fade away into the distance. Away. Yes. Away. I have to get away from this place. I rush to the glossy mahogany dresser against the wall and yank open the top-right drawer. God, my heart is in my throat, threatening to choke me. I have to stop and force myself to inhale and slowly exhale. I am shaking and irrationally frightened. I count to thirty, and I can breathe again. I'm okay. Everything is okay. I open the left drawer, and the breath I'd finally found again hitches at the contents. A twelve-by-eight black velvet box with a lock. A red silk scarf. Three red leather-bound journals.

My teeth worry my bottom lip. I dart a look toward the hallway and then back to the drawer. I am intrigued despite my nerves, but afraid the creepy man will return.

I quickly refocus on the drawer and search for a key to the box, telling myself there might be contact information inside. That I am not caving to carnal curiosity. I flip open each of the journals, shaking them for loose papers, for a key. A brochure falls from inside one of them, and I start to shove it aside, exposing several more brochures in the process.

I pick one of them up and read "Allure Art Gallery," San Francisco. They are all Allure brochures. Allure is the largest, most prestigious gallery among San Francisco's many. I remember Ella mentioning art she'd found in the unit. It appears that despite our vastly different love lives, Rebecca and I share a common thread in our interest in art. I love everything about art, from the history to the creative process. There was a time when I might have cut off my right arm to work in the art world. It's what I went to school for, what I'd dreamed of. A dream I'd given up years ago when life, bills, and responsibilities took precedence.

A loud crash sounds somewhere outside, and I nearly jump out of my own skin. My hand balls on my chest, willing my heart not to jump right through it. Thunder. The sound had been thunder. It is about to storm. Another loud rumble radiates through the walls, echoing as if I am in a cave—almost like an omen of warning telling me to hurry the heck up. Oh good grief, my imagination is running wild, but I won't ignore this feeling of unease.

I grab my purse, stack the journals in my arms, which I justify taking because they are my only hope of finding a clue to Rebecca's recent whereabouts. I am about to exit the room, but I hesitate for a moment before turning back and rushing to the dresser to retrieve the box. My hands are still shaking as I manage to juggle the items I'm holding and attach the lock to the storage unit.

Quickly, I head down a narrow, dimly lit hallway, past rows of locked units like the one I've just left. I feel like I am Alice in Wonderland about to be sucked down the rabbit hole. I exit the garage-style main doorway to find a dark parking lot made darker by the brewing storm. How has time gotten away from me so quickly?

I fall into a half run, half walk in stealthy silence thanks to my light blue Nike cross-trainers, closing the distance between myself and my silver Ford Focus. My keys are still in my purse, and I don't know why I haven't pulled them out before now. I set the items I'm holding on top of the hood with the intent of digging in my purse and manage to drop one of the journals. I reach for it and drop another.

"Dang it," I mumble, and squat, scooping them up, but the hair stands up on my neck again, and despite the cold droplets of water smacking my forehead, I don't stand. My gaze shifts to a shadow near the open garage door, and I search to find no one there. I jerk myself upright, stomach lurching. Get in the car. Get in the car. Why are you outside the car?

Hands shaking now, I dig out my keys and curse the out-of-character paranoia I can't escape. I yank open the car door, throw my purse inside, and get in, the journals and the box awkwardly on my lap. I can't lock the door fast enough. A heavy breath escapes me at the sound of the clicks that seal me inside, and I haphazardly stack the journals and box in the passenger seat.

I'm about to start the engine when a trickle of awareness draws my gaze to the side of the building I've just exited, and I gasp. Standing in the shadows, beneath a slim awning, one leg propped against the wall, is the man who'd visited me a few minutes before. Watching me.

I turn on the engine and say a silent prayer of thank-you when it starts. I can't get out of here fast enough.

I'm halfway home when the storm explodes on the city in a fury of pounding rain and vivid lightning, no doubt the reason why, despite its being Friday night, there isn't a nearby parking spot at my apartment complex. Thankful that a boatload of schoolwork to grade had motivated me to buy a purse the size of a small suitcase, I cram the box and the journals inside to protect them from the downpour. A wet run later, with water dripping from my hair and clothes, I flip the lights on in my apartment. I can't shut the door and lock it any faster than I could get away from that storage facility.

Maybe my imagination is running away with me over the mystery of Rebecca Mason, but I feel like I am being stalked. That man back at the storage unit gave me the creeps. I shiver just thinking about him. Well, that and I'm dripping wet and despite the fact that it's August, it's a chilly fifty-one degrees outside according to the news.

Water is puddling at my feet, and I quickly pull the box and the journals from my drenched purse, setting them on the dry carpet before stripping right there in the entryway. My tan carpet is a dirt magnet, but renting means you take what you can get. I start for the bathroom and hesitate, backtracking to grab my cell phone because it just makes me feel better to have it in hand, but I tell myself it's to call Ella. I start a hot bath and dial her number, hoping she might know where to find Rebecca and to hear she is safe and happy. Her phone rings with a fast busy signal that tells me she is out of service range, but I still feel worried. I am one big ball of nerves and it's making me insane.

Forty-five minutes later, freshly showered and dressed in pink boxers and a matching tee, my hair soft and dry and smelling like my favorite rose-scented shampoo, I am chiding myself for being so paranoid. I head to the fridge for my answer to all troubles—a pint of Ben & Jerry's Boston Cream Pie ice cream.

My gaze slides to Rebecca's personal items still sitting by the door with my discarded clothes. I should have stayed at the storage unit until I found her information. Now, I have no choice but to seek what I need in between the pages of those journals. Or in the box . . . that I can't open. I'm not even sure why I'd brought it with me.

A few minutes later, I sit down on the couch with my good friends Ben and Jerry, the stack of journals, and the box on the coffee table. The box that I still see no way to open without potentially damaging it.

With no other option, I reach for a journal and flip it open. In delicate female writing, it reads 2011. No month. I wonder if this was written before—or after—the journal Ella had left in my apartment last night.

Thumbing through pages, I try to scan for words that might relate to a place of employment and catch little pieces of Rebecca's life along the way. The night was hot and my body thirsty. I inhale and turn the page at the clear indication of something far more private than a place of work. This woman wrote with such flowery, exotic words. Who writes like that? My life changed the day I walked into the art gallery. Okay, that has my attention for the right reason. The gallery is clearly where I need to look for Rebecca. But did she work there or shop there? Or maybe she was an artist?

I keep reading, looking for my answers. I've changed. It's changed me. This world has changed me. He says he's simply helped me uncover the real me. I don't even know who the real me is anymore.

"He who?" I whisper at the text.

The places I go now, both emotionally and physically, are dark, dangerous places. I know this, yet where he leads—where they lead—I follow.

I frown, thinking of the journal entry I'd read the night before, that someone had entered the room while Rebecca had been blindfolded and tied to the bed.

How can fear be arousing? How can fear make me need and burn and want? But yet I want, I need, I dare things I never believed I was capable of doing. Is this the real me? That idea scares me deep down to my core. This can't be me. I am not this person. But even more than that fear that I am, indeed, someone I do not recognize, I fear the idea of not being that person. Of going back to the past. Of once again being the good girl with a boring life, pushing paper in a nine-to-five job. Never happy, never satisfied. At least now I feel something. The rush of fear is far better than the defeat of boredom. The high of not knowing what comes next, so much better than always knowing one day will be like the last. Never anticipation, never feeling anything. No. I cannot go back. So why am I so terrified of going forward?

Thunder rolls overhead, jolting me momentarily from my absorption. Glancing at the window, where rain is pattering on the glass, I absently curl up into the corner of the couch, thinking about what I've just read. I am so different from this woman writing the journals, yet I have an odd connection with her words. I love the kids I teach, but I feel the ache of encouraging them to follow their dreams and knowing I haven't followed mine. Knowing my words to them are hypocritical. I understand what it feels like to have each day pass, knowing I'm no closer to my dreams. Jobs in the art world are just so few and far apart, and they pay so little that I cannot justify my passion as my job.

A heavy breath of regret trickles from my lips, and my gaze returns to the page. I am lost in a world that isn't mine and never can be, but somehow, right now, it is.

Three hours later, the rain has calmed to a drizzle, and I am no longer lounging on the couch. Somewhere along the way, I've read all three journals, which have gone from erotic and thrilling to downright frightening. I'm sitting up now, hanging on the words of the final entry.

I want out. This is no longer a rush anymore. No longer exciting. But he won't let me out. He won't let me go. And I don't know how to escape him. He was at the showing tonight, watching me, stalking me. I wanted to run. I wanted to hide. But I didn't. I couldn't. One minute I was talking to a customer, the next I was in a dark corner with him buried deep inside me. When it was over, he stroked my hair and promised to see me later. Tonight. The minute I was alone, I rushed to the camera room to take the tape, to keep him from possessing it, and me with it. But it was gone. He'd taken it before I could. And now . . .

That was it. Nothing more. As if she'd been interrupted by something or someone and quit writing. I stare at the blank page, my heart thundering in my chest. Were these journals before or after the one I'd been reading the night before? I wonder again. Because if they were before, I would know Rebecca was okay. I dial Ella and once again am greeted by the fast busy signal I don't want to hear.

Frustrated, I jump to my feet and pace, shoving my fingers through my already tousled hair. Rebecca Mason must have left town, that's why her things were in that storage unit. But why hadn't she come back for them? Or paid the storage fee? I ball my fists at my sides and then slowly force them to open, force my shoulders to relax. I will myself to calm down with logic. There is no reason to jump to conclusions. I'll simply call the gallery and locate Rebecca, discover all is well, and return Rebecca's things to her. End of story. Right. Perfect. Then I'll get on with my summer tutoring.

I snatch my phone off the coffee table, intending to make that call and immediately stop myself. It's after midnight, and I've tried to call Ella even though I have no idea what time it is in Paris, and now I am trying to call the art gallery. So much for calm and collected.

Something about Rebecca Mason has reached past the pages of that journal and become personal. I'd become Rebecca while I was reading those journals. I feel a connection so intimate to this stranger that it is downright eerie. Or maybe, I think wryly, my own life is just so darn boring I'm desperate for a little excitement. Like Rebecca had been, before she met him.

With that thought, I hug myself and head for bed. But not before I grab the journals and take them with me.

Three

~~~~~~~~

"Rebecca isn't in."

That is the same reply the man who always answers the phone at the gallery had given me the last time I'd called. And the time before that.

"She's on vacation," I reply. "So I've been told all week. It's Friday. Will she be back Monday?"

Silence filters into the line. "I can take a message."

I'd already left several and I see no point in leaving another. "No. Thank you." I hang up and sip my vanilla latte from the Barnes & Noble café, where I'd just finished tutoring a football player hoping to impress colleges with more than his playing skills.

This entire Rebecca situation is driving me nuts. I've already double-checked the time I have left to clear out the storage unit, considering Ella hadn't exactly been a wealth of information, and it is a short window—one more week. After that, it would be two hundred dollars for another full month. A hard blow to my cash flow on an already tight budget. The manager has given me one extra week free for which I am grateful, but I have to deal with Rebecca and do it now.

With my laptop already open and powered up, I key in the Allure Art Gallery website, intending to search the staff listing to be sure Rebecca's name still appears. Sure enough, Rebecca is listed as marketing director. Hmm. Well, that's good. That has to be a sign she's okay. Doesn't it?

An event banner on the side of the page catches my eye and I click on it. There's a showing at the gallery this Wednesday night and not for some unknown artist, either. A thrill goes through me at the realization that the highly acclaimed artist Ricco Alvarez is doing a showing. I adore Ricco Alvarez's depiction of his homeland, Mexico, and though it's rather well-known in an artsy city like San Fran that someone of his stature owns a home here, he rarely makes appearances. But then, this is a good cause, a black-tie charity event with both ticket prices, and a piece of Alvarez's art, being auctioned off as donations to a local children's hospital. Surely, with such an event, Rebecca will be at the helm.

Tapping my nails on the wooden table, I consider my options. If I can't reach Rebecca before the show, I'll attend the event. Silently, I laugh at myself. Who am I kidding? I'm going to see Ricco Alvarez, even if I have to eat ramen noodles for two weeks to do so, and since the tickets are a hundred dollars a pop, I will. But I never, ever splurge. I bite my bottom lip and fret, and then before I can stop myself, click on the BUY TICKETS button. I won't be able to get a refund if I reach Rebecca before then, but I'll just have to rough it. I can't stop the smile from sliding onto my lips. It's not like it will be torture to have to meet Ricco Alvarez. I feel better with a plan. Now, if I can just get through to Ella and hear she is okay, I might actually sleep tonight.

Wednesday evening arrives and Rebecca is still "not in" per the Allure staff. So, I am off to the Alvarez event, but my excitement over the showing has been doused quite effectively by the feeling that something is really wrong. The entire situation makes me anxious, and while I would have preferred some company and moral support at the night's event, I had dismissed the idea. I wasn't about to try and explain why I was hunting down Rebecca Mason, whom I didn't know, and who I feared had met an untimely . . . something. I'm not going to even let my mind elaborate on that thought. And I won't justify my worry by letting anyone else read Rebecca's private thoughts.

I pull my car into a parking spot several blocks away from the gallery, by both necessity and preference. As I open the door, the chilly evening wind lifts off the nearby ocean, blowing loose strands of my long hair astray. Goose bumps form on my arms, and I gather my cream-colored shawl over my matching simple but elegant knee-length sheath dress. Okay, Ella's dress and shawl actually, but we were always borrowing each other's clothes. As a formality, I'd have asked if she minded, but I still can't get ahold of her. I lock the car and slide my keys into the dainty cream-colored shoulder purse that I'd bought on the pier last summer.

I inhale the air, embracing the sounds and sights, the action of the SoMa art district, bustling with people enjoying the stores, museums, and array of art galleries. I don't come down here often. I just can't. It reminds me of those dreams I've never chased. It's been too long, though, I realize, nearly a year since I've enjoyed the market street scene. The architecture, ranging from newly developed shiny glass structures to old warehouses converted into home and work spaces, was as much art as the sculptures and drawings on the concrete walls of the random buildings. I feel something special here. I feel alive here. It's what I feel when I leave that I dislike.

When the gallery comes into view, I pause to watch a group of elegantly dressed visitors pour through its double glass doors, which are lined in shiny silver for the black-tie affair. Artsy swirls of red letters, displayed above the entry, spell ALLURE.

Nerves flutter in my stomach, though I can't say why. I love the contemporary art Allure specializes in, love their mix of local new artists who I can discover, as well as the established names whose work I already appreciate. My nerves are ridiculous. I'm uncomfortable in this world, but then, this isn't my world. It's Rebecca's, and Rebecca is the real reason I'm here.

A glance at my dainty, handmade, gold wristwatch, also bought at the pier, confirms I have plenty of time to spare. It is seven forty-five, fifteen minutes until Alvarez will be unveiling a new painting that will be displayed in the gallery and up for silent auction through the end of the week. Oh, how I'd love to have an Alvarez original, but they don't come cheap. Still, a girl can dream.

Excitement filters in with nerves as I rush toward the door. A young brunette woman in a simple black dress holds it open for me and offers me a smile. "Welcome."

I return the smile and enter the gallery, noting the nervous energy bouncing off the twentysomething girl as I pass, an energy that seems to scream "I'm new and don't know what I am doing." This isn't Rebecca, who I know will be daringly bold and confident. In fact, the hostess brings out the schoolteacher in me, and I fight the urge to give her a hug and tell her she's doing fine. I'm a hugger. I got it from my mother, just like I did my love of art, only I wasn't talented with a brush as she had been.

The girl is saved from my mothering when the sound of a piano playing from a distant corner filters through the air and draws my attention to the main showroom. I am in awe. This isn't my first time visiting the four-thousand-square-foot wonder that is the Allure gallery, but it doesn't diminish my excitement at seeing it again.

The entryway opens to the main showroom of glistening white wonder. The walls are snow-white; the floor glistens like white diamonds. The shiny divider walls curve like abstract waves, and each of them is adorned with contrasting, eye-popping, colorful artwork.

I turn away from the showroom, attending to business before pleasure, and present my ticket to a hostess behind a podium. She is tall and elegant with long raven hair. "Rebecca?" I ask hopefully.

"No, sorry," she says. "I'm Tesse." She holds up a finger as she glances through the glass doors at an approaching customer she needs to attend. I wait patiently, hoping this young woman can connect me with Rebecca. I listen attentively while she directs the new guest to a short stairway that leads toward the music and, apparently, the location where Ricco Alvarez will be unveiling his masterpiece.

"Sorry for the interruption," Tesse finally says, giving me her full attention. "You were looking for Rebecca. Unfortunately, she isn't attending tonight's event. Is there something I can help you with?"

Disappointment fills me. To miss an Alvarez event is not something someone in Rebecca's role is likely to do. I just want to know, for certain, that Rebecca is safe. Painting myself as a stranger doesn't seem the way to do that. "My sister's an old friend of Rebecca's. She told me to be sure and say hello to her and pass along her new phone number. She seemed to think Rebecca worked big events like this one. She'll be disappointed I missed her."

"Oh, I hate that you missed her," Tesse says, looking genuinely concerned. "I'm not only new, but I also only work part-time, on an as-needed basis, so I don't hear much of what's going on internally, but I think Rebecca took some personal time off. Mr. Compton would know for certain."

"Mr. Compton?"

"The manager here," she says. "He'll be tied up with the presentation soon, but I can introduce you to him afterward if you like?"

I nod. "Yes. Please. That would be perfect."

The piano stops abruptly. "They're about to start," Tesse informs me. "You should grab a seat while you still can. I'll be sure to help you connect with Mark after the presentation."

A thrill shoots through me. "Thank you so much," I say, before I head toward the seating area. I can't believe that I am about to see an Alvarez original presented by Alvarez himself.

A tuxedo-clad usher greets me at the bottom of the stairs and offers me some help finding a seat. And boy did I need help. There were at least two hundred chairs lined up in front of a ministage, set in front of a bay window that was essentially the entire wall, and almost every single chair was taken.

I squeeze into a center row, between a man that has artsy rebel written all over him from longish light blond hair to his jeans and a blazer, and a fifty-something woman who is more than a little irritated to have to let me pass. I can't help but notice the man is incredibly good-looking, and I've never been one to be easily impressed. I know too well that beauty is often only skin deep.

"You're late," the man says as if he knows me, a friendly smile touching his lips, his green eyes crinkling at the edges, mischief in their depths. I figure him to be about thirty-five. No. Thirty-three. I am good with ages and good at reading people. My kids at school often found that out when they were up to mischief.

I smile back at the man, feeling instantly comfortable with him when, aside from my students, I'm normally quite reserved with strangers. "And you forgot to pick up your tux, I see,"

I tease. In fact, I wonder how he pulled off getting in here dressed as he is.

He runs his hand over his sandy blond, one-day stubble that borders on two days. "At least I shaved."

My smile widens, and I intend to reply but a screech from a microphone fills the air. A man I recognize from photos as Ricco Alvarez claims the stage and stands next to the sheet covering a display, no doubt his newest masterpiece. Suave and James Bond–esque in his tuxedo, he is the polar opposite of the man next to me.

"Welcome one and all," he says in a voice richly accented with Hispanic heritage, as is his work. "I am Ricco Alvarez, and I thank you for sharing my love of art and children, on this grand evening. And so I give you what I call *Chiquitos*, or in English, Little Ones."

He tears away the sheet, and everyone gasps at the unexpected piece of art that is nothing like anything he's done before. Rather than a landscape, it is a portrait of three children, all of different nationalities, holding hands. It is a well-executed work appropriate for the occasion, though secretly, I had wished for a landscape where his brilliance shone.

The man next to me leans an elbow on his knee and lowers his voice. "What do you think?"

"It's perfect for the evening," I say cautiously.

"Oh, so diplomatic," he says with a low chuckle. "You wanted a landscape."

"He does beautiful landscapes," I say defensively.

He grins. "He should have done a landscape."

"And now," Ricco announces, "while the bidding begins,

I'll be circulating the room, answering questions about my many works displayed tonight and hoping to have the pleasure of meeting as many of you as possible. Please feel free to walk to the stage for a closer look at *Chiquitos*."

Almost instantly, the crowd is standing.

"Are you going for a close-up?" I ask the man next to me.

"Not much on crowds," he said. "Nor Ricco's attempt at portraiture." He winks at me. "Don't stroke his ego when you meet him. It's big enough as it is." He starts moving down the row toward the exit. I stare after him, feeling this odd flutter in my stomach at his departure, curious about who he is.

I frown as I repeat part of our conversation in my mind. Ricco. He'd called Ricco Alvarez Ricco and spoken of his ego as if he knew him. It's too late now to find out how he knows Ricco, and portrait or not, I am eager for an up-close look at the featured painting. I have not met Ricco yet and it is disappointing, but I am still thrilled at the opportunity to see his work.

Sometime later, I am enjoying a lingering walk through the gallery, exploring the full Alvarez collection on display, when I spot a display for Chris Merit, whose work I studied in college. He, too, had once been a local, but I seem to remember his moving to Paris. Excitedly, I head toward his work. His specialties are urban landscapes—mostly of San Francisco, both past and present—and portraits of real subjects with such depth and soul they steal my breath away.

I join an elderly couple inside the small room, where they debate over which of several landscapes to purchase. Unable to stop myself, I join in. "I think you should take them all."

The man scoffs. "Don't go giving her ideas or you'll both put me in the poorhouse. She gets one for above the fireplace."

"Stingy man," the gray-haired woman says, shoving his arm playfully and then eying me. "So tell me, honey." She motions between two pictures. "Which do you think is a better conversation piece, of these two?"

I study the two choices, both black-and-white, though Merit often uses color. One is a downtown shot of San Francisco in the midst of hurricane-like weather. The other is of the Golden Gate Bridge shrouded in clouds, the skyline of the city peeking out from behind it.

"A tough choice," I say thoughtfully. "Both have a bit of a dark edgy feel to them, and both have the 'wow' factor." I indicate the stormy downtown scene. "I happen to know that one depicts the impact Hurricane Nora had on the city back in 1997. To me, that makes for a conversation piece, and a little bit of history to boot, right there in your living room."

"You are so right, dear," the woman says, her eyes lighting up. "This is the one." She casts her husband an expectant look. "It's perfect. I have to have it."

"Then have it you shall," her husband declares.

I smile at the woman's joy, but not without a bit of art envy. I would love to be going home with the piece, as she will be, tonight.

"I understand you had a question for me," a male voice says, pulling my attention toward the display entryway where a man with neatly trimmed blond hair stands. He is tall and confident, an air of ownership about him. And his eyes—they are the most unique silvery gray I've ever seen.

"I'm Mark Compton," he says, "the gallery manager. And it looks like I owe you more than an answer to whatever your question is. It appears I need to thank you for assisting my customers." He glances at the couple. "I take it you've made a selection?"

"Indeed we have," the husband says, clearly pleased to have his wife make a decision. "We'd like to take it home with us tonight if possible."

"Excellent," he says. "If you'll give me a moment, I'll have it packaged for you."

He motions for me to walk with him, and I shake my head. "I'm in no rush. Help them with their purchase, and you can find me later."

He studies me a bit too intently, those silvery eyes of his rich with interest, and I am suddenly self-conscious. He is, without a doubt, classically handsome by anyone's standards, but there is also something raw and sexual about this man, something almost predatory about him.

"All right then," he says softly, "I'll find you soon." It isn't a statement that alludes to a double meaning, but yet, I feel one there. His gaze shifts to the couple. "Let's go ring you up."

The couple thanks me for my help and hurry after Mark. The minute they are gone, the minute Mark Compton is out of sight, I let out a breath I hadn't known I was holding and shake myself inwardly. And not just because of the way his eyes had assessed me so . . . so what? Intimately? Surely not. I still have this overactive-imagination thing going on from reading the journals. I do wonder if he is the he from the journals. He certainly has the animal magnetism Rebecca's words painted him with. But then, so does Ricco Alvarez. Good grief, I'm making myself crazy.

A staff member interrupts me before I can go on another "crazy" thinking spree, and removes the couple's purchase from the display. I force myself to stop overanalyzing and relax, basking in the solitude as I discover Chris Merit's newest work.

"You like Merit?" comes another male voice, this one familiar.

I turn to find the man who'd sat next to me during the presentation standing in the doorway. I give a quick, eager nod. "Very much. I wish they had some of his portraits, but his urban landscapes are magnificent. You?"

He leans against the wall. "I hear he doesn't have an over-inflated ego. That scores points with me."

I tilt my head and study him, relaxing into the easy conversation. "Why are you here if you don't like Ricco?"

Mark Compton appears in the doorway. "I see you didn't venture far," he says to me and then eyes the other man. "Don't tell me you're pimping your own work at Ricco's event?" He glances at me. "Was he pimping his own work?"

I gape. "Wait. His own work?" I shift my gaze to my nameless new friend, who looks nothing like the Chris Merit I've seen photos of. "Who are you exactly?"

His mouth quirks at the edges. "The man with one red shoe." And with that, he turns and walks away.

I shake my head. "What? What does that mean?" I turn to Mark. "What does that mean? The man with one red shoe?"

"Who knows," Mark says, his lips thinning in disapproval.

"Chris has a twisted sense of humor. Thankfully, it doesn't show up on the canvas."

My jaw goes slack. "Wait. Are you telling me that was Chris Merit?" I rack my brain over the pictures of him I've seen and I remember him differently. Do I have his image confused with another?

"That's Chris," he confirms. "And as you can see, he has an odd way about him. He was standing in his own display room and didn't even tell you who he was." His hands settle on his hips. "Listen, Tesse tells me you . . . I'm sorry, I didn't get your name?"

"Sara," I supply. "Sara McMillan."

"Sara," he repeats, his tone low, as if he was trying it out on his tongue, trying me out on his tongue. Seconds pass, and the small display area seems to get smaller before he adds, "Tesse was right. Rebecca is on a leave of absence."

His tone shifts back to all business now, and I wonder if I imagine the raspier tone. I am, after all, excelling at making myself crazy. "I see," I say. "Is there a way to reach her?"

"If you figure out a way, let me know," he says. "She took a two-week cruise with some rich guy she was dating and that turned into the entire summer. I agreed because she's good at her job and the clients love her. But depending on interns who don't know what they're doing is killing me. I'm going to have to get someone in here to cover for her who actually knows what she is doing."

"The entire summer," I repeat uncomfortably, focusing on the oddity that represents. All summer is a long time for a working girl to leave her job behind. And Mark's comment about the "rich guy" hit me just as wrong for some reason, though it could have been merely his frustration over Rebecca's extended leave. Or maybe ... could he be jealous over this rich man? My brows dip. "Leaving you high and dry like this—that doesn't sound like the responsible Rebecca my sister described."

"People aren't always what they seem," he says and motions toward Chris Merit's displayed art. "The art does not always mimic the artist. You never know the real person until you slide beneath their surface."

Or look in their dresser drawer, I think guiltily. But Rebecca didn't seem like someone to run out on her job to me. She loved her job. Then again, I might be wrong. As seduced as Rebecca had been by this world she'd created, she'd been scared, too. And I want to know why more than ever. What created such obsession, such fear?

A sudden burn for answers, a need to leave here tonight with something more than I came with overcomes me, and before I can stop myself, I blurt, "I can cover Rebecca for the rest of the summer. I'm a teacher, so I'm on break. I have a masters of arts from the Art Institute and a bachelors in business. I interned for three years at the Museum of Modern Art, and I know art. All art. Test me if you like."

His eyes narrow a fraction, the silence crackling between us for several long seconds. "You're hired, Sara McMillan. You can start on Monday. I'll let you enjoy the rest of your evening." He lowers his voice. "Then you'll be all mine." He turns and walks away.

I blink, stunned. He'd just hired me, but he hadn't even

asked me one single question. I hadn't asked about hours or pay. I inhale a sharp breath. I'd come here to find Rebecca, to make sure she is alive and well. Instead, I am about to be Rebecca, or rather, be the marketing director for the gallery. So I can find Rebecca, I tell myself. Something has happened to Rebecca, and I have to prove it. That's why I'm here. No other reason.

Four

I am still standing in the middle of Chris Merit's display, in stunned disbelief, when something snaps inside me. I am hot and confused and feeling like the world is spinning around me. I've spent money I don't have on the ticket for the night, but I can't get out of this gallery fast enough. I run for the door, not literally, but I might as well be. This heat I feel is unexplainable, considering the gallery is chilly, and I need air desperately. I need to think. I need to figure out what is going on inside me, because it is nothing I know as familiar.

Exiting to the street, I welcome the cool night air washing over me. I turn quickly to my left and intend to head for my car, when the strap of my purse catches and snags on the brick of the building and somehow it snaps open. The contents spill to the ground. With exasperation, I squat, trying to retrieve my items. This is so my life, and there is a tiny part of me comforted by my familiar clumsiness, by something that feels like me.

I mean, who else can manage to catch their purse on a wall of all things?

"Need some help?"

My gaze shoots upward to find Chris Merit at eye level, and for a rare moment in time, I can't find the words to ramble with my nerves. While I'd felt comfortable with him inside the gallery, I am dumbstruck now that I know who he is. He is brilliant. He is also incredibly good-looking and squatting down on the ground with me, which somehow feels wrong. This night has me feeling as if I am in the twilight zone. There is no other explanation for how bizarre it is.

"I . . . ah . . . no," I manage. "Thank you. I got it. It's a little purse. Doesn't hold much." I scoop up my lipstick and a tiny wallet, and slide them back inside the bag before pushing to my feet.

He grabs my keys and stands, towering over my five feet four inches by a good foot. I hadn't realized how tall he is when he'd been sitting beside me at the Ricco event, or how earthy and deliciously male he smells, but the wind lifts and the scent tickles my nose. He is different from Mark, not so sophisticated and debonair, more raw, and yes, like his scent, earthy.

He gives me another one of those devastating smiles he'd used on me in the gallery and dangles my keys in the air. "You might need these to go wherever you're going so fast."

"Thank you," I say, and accept them. His fingers brush mine, and electricity charges up my arm, across my chest, and steals my breath. My eyes meet his, and I see awareness in the deep green depths of his stare. Only I'm not sure if it's the same kind of awareness I feel. Maybe it's simply that I hide my feelings horribly and he now knows I'm reacting to him, and it amuses him.

"You're leaving early," he comments, his hands going to his hips, which pushes back his blazer enough for me to see the stretch of his black T-shirt across his impressive chest. I approve, as I'm sure the rest of the female population does.

"Yes," I say, and jerk my attention to his face, to a full mouth that has me a bit breathless, but then everything has me breathless tonight, it seems. "I need to get home."

"Why don't I walk you to your car?"

He wants to walk me to my car. I'm not sure why he would want to do that. He doesn't even know me. Is it possible that he felt that same electricity I did, or do I amuse him and he wants to continue the entertainment? Mark did say he has a strange sense of humor. "Why didn't you tell me who you are?" I blurt, not liking the idea of being a joke.

His lips quirk. "Because then you would have told me you loved my work even if you hated it."

My brows dip. I'm not sure how I feel about that. "That's sneaky."

"It spared you the awkwardness of pretending to like my work."

"There wouldn't have been any awkwardness. I like your work."

"And I like that you like my work," he approves, a warm glow in his eyes. "So . . . shall I walk you to your car?"

My escape has been further waylaid, but I'm not sure that is a bad thing anymore. "Okay," I squeak, appalled at my lack of voice. There is a reason I don't date much: I'm horrible at it. I get shy and I pick the wrong men, who use both of those very things against me. Dominant, controlling men, who seem to turn me on in the bedroom and off in real life. It's genetic. I'm quite certain that had I a sister, she would have been just as foolish about men as myself and as my mother had been. And while Chris, at first impression, doesn't strike me as arrogant or controlling, his failure to tell me who he was earlier in the evening was in fact a way of controlling my reaction. Not that I think he is interested in me. I'm overanalyzing and I know it. Chris Merit could have his choice of women and, in fact, probably has. He doesn't need to add little ol' me to the list.

"You know my name," he says, pulling me from my reverie. "It's only fair I know yours."

"Sara. Sara McMillan."

"Nice to meet you, Sara."

"I should be the one saying that to you," I say. "I wasn't joking when I said I love your art. I studied your work in college."

"Now you're making me feel old."

"Hardly," I say. "You started painting when you were a teen."

He cast me a sideways look. "You weren't joking when you said you studied my work."

"Art major."

"And what do you do now?"

I feel a little punch to my gut. "Schoolteacher."

"Art?"

"No," I say. "High school English."

"So why study art?"

"Because I love art."

"Yet you're an English teacher?"

"What's wrong with being an English teacher?" I ask, unable to curb the defensiveness in my tone.

He stops walking and turns to me. "Nothing is wrong with it at all, except that I don't think that's what you want to do."

"You don't know me enough to say that. You don't know me at all."

"I know the excitement I saw in your eyes when you were in the gallery."

"I don't deny that." A gust of wind rushes over us and goose bumps lift on my skin. I don't want to be scrutinized. This man sees too much. "We should walk."

He shrugs out of his jacket, and before I know what's happening, it's wrapped around my shoulders and that earthy raw scent of his is surrounding me. I'm wearing Chris Merit's coat and I am dumbstruck all over again. His hands are on the lapels and he is staring down at me. My gaze catches on the brilliant colorful tattoo that covers every inch of his right arm. I've never been with a man with tattoos and never thought I liked them, but I find myself wondering where else he might have them.

"I saw you talking to Mark," he says. "Did you buy something tonight?"

"I wish," I say with a snort, and my embarrassment at the unladylike sound that comes too naturally only drives home reality to me. We are from two different worlds, this man and I. His is one of dreams fulfilled, and mine is one of impossible dreams. "I doubt I could afford one of your brushes, let alone a completed piece."

His eyes narrow. "You shouldn't walk away from something

that intrigues you." His voice is a soft rasp of sandpaper that still manages to be velvet on my nerve endings.

Suddenly, I'm not sure we are talking about art, and my throat is dry. I swallow hard and though I hadn't decided I was really going through with it, I blurt, "I'm taking a summer job at the gallery."

His light blond brow arches. "Are you now?"

"Yes." I know it is the truth as I say the word. I know I've already decided I am going to take the job. "I'm filling in for Rebecca until her return." I search his face for a reaction, but I see none. He is unreadable—or am I just too affected by his nearness to see one?

His hands are still on the lapels and he doesn't move for a long moment. I don't want him to move. I want him to . . . I don't know . . . but then again, yes I do. I want him to kiss me. It's a silly, fantastical moment—no doubt brought on by the journals—that has me blushing. I cut my gaze, feeling as if the heat in his will scorch me inside out. I motion to my car, shocked to realize it's only one parking meter down. "That's me."

Slowly, his hands loosen on my—or rather his—jacket. I immediately walk to my car, willing myself not to dump my purse again. I click the locks open and I stop by the curb before opening my door. I turn to find him close, so very wonderfully close. And that scent of his is driving me wild, pooling heat low in my belly.

"Thanks for the walk and the jacket." I shrug out of it.

He reaches for the jacket and takes it, and I hope he will touch me and fear that he will, at the same moment. I am so out of control and confused.

His green eyes burn hot like fire before he softly says, "It's been my pleasure . . . Sara." And then he just turns and starts walking, without another word.

Hours later, I sit on my bed in a pair of boxers and a tank, legs crossed, with that box and a screwdriver in front of me. I have no idea why the idea of taking the job at the gallery makes opening it seem imperative, but it does, and it is. Rubies trim the lid and an etched, abstract design is in the center. The latch holding it closed looks old and easy to break and just as beautifully designed as the rest of the box.

"How very artsy," I murmur, tracing the design with my fingers. The idea of destroying the box doesn't sit well with me, nor does invading Rebecca's privacy. So why, why, why do I know I am going to open this box? Why do I have to know what is inside? "Curiosity killed the cat, Sara."

It doesn't seem to matter. Of their own will, my hands go to work. I slide the flat end of the screwdriver between the lips of the lid and base and apply pressure. The latch pops easily.

My adrenaline surges, and my heart thunders in my chest. I have no idea why I am hanging on a thread, why I feel like this box is so important, why I feel any of this is important. Slowly, I lift the lid, and luxurious red velvet is the first thing I see. I suck in a breath at what is cradled by that velvet, and my heart thunders all over again.

Five

I blink at the unexpected contents of the box. A paintbrush and a picture that has been torn into two pieces so that only a woman is left. This is Rebecca. I don't know why it didn't seem odd to me that I hadn't seen any pictures of her in the many personal effects I studied in the storage unit. There hadn't been a picture of her on the gallery website, either. Perhaps I didn't notice these things before now because I didn't want to know what she looked like.

Reaching for the photo, I hold it between my fingers and study it, study her. She is beautiful and petite with long, sandy brown hair, and a brilliant smile that tells me that at the moment this picture was taken, she was immensely happy. I can't make out her eye color, green I think, where mine are brown. Her image mesmerizes me, and I wonder why she tore the picture. I wonder who was in it with her and who took the photo. Even more so, I wonder why she kept the picture after she tore it up.

My brow furrows as my attention shifts to the paintbrush. It's such an odd thing to save, but then, so is half of a picture. I pick up the brush and run my fingers over the bristles that have a hint of a yellow paint at the tips. The wood bears no marks or logo. It's clearly a sentimental item, which isn't so unexpected really, considering she worked at the gallery. So was the man in the journal an artist? The prospects of who he might be are far reaching. My stomach knots as I think of Chris. I keep thinking about Chris and those greener than green eyes.

I seal the picture and the paintbrush back inside the box and set it on my nightstand. My laptop is also on the bed with me and I power it up before typing "Chris Merit" into the search bar and clicking on images. Almost immediately I get photos of two different people and realize that one is an older version of Chris. His father had been a famous classical pianist who'd lived in Paris. I don't know how I forgot such a thing, or how I tied the image of father with son, though the resemblance is uncanny.

I google Chris and he comes up in Wikipedia. He is thirty-five, not thirty-three, and he's dated a couple of models and an actress. Right. Way, way out of my league, so I have no idea why I read into anything tonight with the man. My lips thin as I note that he has never been married. My mother's words come back to me. Any man who isn't married by thirty-five is either gay or he's got skeletons in his closet. A knot forms in my throat. God, how I miss her, how I wish she was still here so I could call her now. Okay, so maybe I wouldn't call her now and explain my obsession with another woman's sex life. I bite my lip. Am I obsessed with another woman's sex life? No, I tell myself immediately, rejecting the idea. If I'm obsessed, it's with her safety.

And if Chris has skeletons, could Rebecca have discovered them and become a liability? It sounds so much like a novel that laughter bubbles from my lips. Besides, with further reading, I realize Chris lives in Paris. Chris must be here for a visit. He is probably gone already.

Unbidden, disappointment fills me. Chris is the first man to interest me in well over two years, since Michael Knight, the CEO of a large computer company, whom I'd met at a charity event. I'd soon realized he was the kind of man I found alluring for all the wrong reasons. The kind that dominates and controls and makes you feel all feminine and protected. That is, until he shreds everything you know of yourself to pieces. I'm still not sure I understand why he appealed to me, or why men like Mark, who ooze that kind of power, still appeal to me. I only know that dating men who initially appear to be sensitive and caring, like I had in the past, doesn't seem to be working for me. Chris, well, he doesn't seem to be one of those power-control freaks like Mark, but then I doubt I'll ever see him again.

I reach for one of the journals and begin to read.

I told him I wouldn't see him again. He told me he'd decide when I see him and when I don't. I should have known I couldn't simply walk away. I should have known he'd come for me and that I, weak as I am, would not be able to resist him. Before I knew what was happening, I was in the storeroom in the middle of the day, with others nearby.

He shoved me against the wall and then tore down my panties. His lips pressed close to my ear, his breath hot on my neck as he said, "You know the rules; you know I have to punish you." I squeezed my eyes shut because I do know. I know and not only do I know but I also want him, too. That's what I've become, what he's made me. I was wet and aching and all but ready to beg for the very thing I craved . . . punishment.

The first smack of his hand on my ass was pure pain, but I didn't scream. I couldn't scream. Not when I could be heard. But somehow, as it always does, the pain turned to pleasure. The need for him was intense, complete. He entered me and I barely contained my cry, my need. He couldn't fuck me hard enough to suit me. I was powerless to the pleasure that is him.

When it was over, he turned me around, tugged my dress and bra down and clamped my nipples, ordering me to endure the pain for fifteen minutes. Assuring me he will know if I take them off sooner. And then he was gone, and I stare after him, my sex spasming from the orgasm he shouldn't have been able to give me. Every nerve ending I own is aware of the sting of my bottom and ache of the clamps biting down on my nipples. I am unable to stop the pain, unable to fight my desire for him. I am helpless. I am frighteningly aroused.

Monday morning, I stand in my bathroom, with my second cup of coffee on the counter next to me, brushing my long brown hair to a silken mass. It is eight in the morning, and I will soon leave for the gallery. "You can start Monday" should have been a lead into my asking "What time?" Since I had not had enough sense to do so, I'd decided before bed to wake early enough to arrive thirty minutes before opening.

With a brush of powder, I finish my makeup and step into the emerald-green sheath dress, a black jacket, and black heels, which is my go-to special-occasion outfit. The same outfit that I'd worn to my teaching interview years before when, like today, looking professional was the goal. I am, after all, attending to adult needs rather than those of high school kids wearing jeans and T-shirts. I never opted for jeans myself, though some of the faculty did. My youthful appearance needed the intimidating effect of high heels and skirts. With high school students, respect can go a long way. I inspect my appearance in the full-length mirror behind the door with approval. It's not Chanel or Dior, like many of the gallery customers will favor, but on my budget, it will have to do.

After finishing my coffee, I make my way to the car, and I'm officially as nervous as my students normally are on their first day of school. I can't believe I'm really taking this job, and I feel both terrified and excited. "Right," I say to myself. "Like there was any doubt you would?"

Guilt twists in my stomach at the idea of Rebecca's potential misfortune being my good fortune. I am not sure I can live with that idea. No one has met with misfortune, I promise myself. I'm going to find out that Rebecca is perfectly fine and happy, and be able to embrace this world I love, if only for a while.

By the time I arrive at the gallery fifteen minutes later, I am having doubts about Rebecca's safety again. I wonder why, if Rebecca is perfectly fine and happy, and I am to believe she has been whisked off to some exotic haven in a way permanent enough to let her things go, would the gallery say she is returning?

I have forever longed to spend my days surrounded by fine art, and I know that the day I leave this world behind for mine, it will be painful. But I am on this path now, and in my gut, it feels as if I am doing what I am meant to do. Even as I park in the back of the gallery and get out of my car, my heart feels like it might explode from my chest.

I cross the small employee parking lot, and after trying the door and, finding it locked, I knock.

The young girl I'd wanted to hug the night before appears and smiles a warm welcome before opening the glass door. "You must be Sara."

"That's me," I say, and return her smile. "I guess you heard I was coming?"

"Yes, and I'm so glad you're here." She is wearing a pale pink dress with a pin clip in her dark hair that makes her look even younger than when I'd first met her. "We really are short staffed, so this is a blessing."

I enter and let the door shut behind me. The woman—or girl, rather—doesn't seem worried about relocking it, which concerns me. This might be a small gallery, but it is considered one of the most prestigious, with highly sought-after art and plenty of money moving through the place.

"I'm Amanda," she declares. "I'm an intern for the next year, working as the receptionist."

"Nice to meet you, Amanda," I say.

"Mark's having breakfast with Ricco this morning to discuss the show last week." She motions with her head. "I'll show you your new office."

I hesitate before following, and at the risk of offending Amanda, turn and lock the door. I give her an apologetic smile. "Sorry. I'm an art fanatic and the idea of someone busting in here and stealing some of the art is enough to make me downright nauseous."

She pales visibly. "Thank you. Mark would have been furious to find it unlocked."

The discomfort and true fear that rolls off her is disconcerting. I know right then that the protectiveness I had felt for her last night was going to become a common theme.

I fall into step with Amanda, and we head down the narrow hallway, behind the art displays. "Mark's a tough boss, I take it?"

She gives me a quick glance. "He's rich, good-looking, and pretty much perfect. That's what he expects here, too. I'm not always so good at being perfect."

"Other people's perfection is a facade we create when we are second-guessing ourselves," I tell her, but deep down, even in the short meeting I had with Mark, I agree with her assessment of him. Well, except the rich part. I have no idea if he has money, but if he does, it's not from simply managing an art gallery.

"Hmmm," Amanda murmurs skeptically, "I guess I do second-guess myself around him, but only because he's so intimidating. When the man looks at me, I feel like I'm going to come unglued."

I picture those intense gray eyes of his, and just the idea of seeing Mark again has my adrenaline racing and I am not quite in touch with myself enough right now to know why. Since I have no intention of sharing this with Amanda, I smile with encouragement instead. "I bet we can make him a little less intimidating if we stick together."

She gives me a bright smile. "I like that idea."

I warm at her response, and the schoolteacher and nurturer in me is certain I am so going to be her mama bear.

We enter another hallway that is lined with various works of art that I barely refrain from inspecting. There will be time for that later.

"I'll introduce you to the staff when they arrive," Amanda informs me. "There are seven of us total, aside from you, two of whom are part-time interns. They're all coming in late after working an event we had last night."

"How'd you get so lucky, to come in early?" I ask as we stop at a doorway I assume leads to the offices.

She cut me another sideways look. "I spilled a glass of wine on a very important client last night at our small tasting. It's my punishment."

My brows dip, and a chill slides down my spine. "Punishment?"

She keys in a password on an entry panel before turning her attention back to me. The smile of moments before has disappeared. "Mark's big on punishment." She starts walking and forces me to follow, and I have the distinct impression she doesn't want to give me the chance to ask for more specifics.

We pass several dark offices before she pauses at a door and flips on the light. "You'll be working in Rebecca's office."

I don't move. I stand there, feeling icy cold, as I remember the journal entry from the night before. You know the rules; you know I have to punish you.

Six

I walk into Rebecca's office and the scent of roses flares in my nostrils. Searching the room, I find a small candle on the shiny cherrywood desk that, while not burning, seems the logical source of the sweet floral perfume. The little personal touch I assume to be Rebecca's reminds me that I am here to find her and punches me in the gut when it should be encouraging, a sign of her return. Searching for more of that encouragement I should be feeling, I glance at the two bookshelves to my right, where various art books are displayed on stands and a dozen or so others are shelved, and find nothing to cling to.

"If you hit the red button on your phone, you'll reach the intercom to my desk," Amanda murmurs.

"Great," I say, stepping behind the desk and stuffing my purse into a drawer. I can't seem to get myself to sit down in the red leather chair. In her chair. "What's my extension?" I ask because I'm trying to buy time to snap out of the uneasy feeling tingling through my nerve endings.

"Four," Amanda replies.

My gaze lifts and my breath hitches at the sight of the painting on the wall directly in front of me. I think Amanda says something else but I don't know what. I am riveted by the fine strokes of brilliance done by none other than the famous American painter Georgia O'Nay. I know now why there had been a keypad for a password to enter the back offices, and the candle suddenly has more significance because this glorious oil on canvas features red and white roses. It must be worth a cool thirty thousand, and I can't imagine it's not real to be here in the gallery. It is spectacular, and it is on the wall I will be staring at every day. The same wall that Rebecca had stared at each day she'd been here.

"From Mark's personal collection," Amanda informs me, clearly noting the way I'm gaping. "He has a piece in every office."

I jerk my attention in her direction to find her leaning on the doorframe. "His personal collection?"

She gives a nod. "His family owns a number of art galleries and an auction house in New York called Riptide," she explains. "He changes out the pieces every few months from what I understand. We actually have customers who schedule appointments to see what he brings next." Stunned at this news, I am again in a rare state of speechlessness at the mention of one of the most elite auction houses in existence, selling everything from celebrity property to fine art.

She laughs without humor, a hint of unease in its depths. "Everyone wants a piece of that man."

I tilt my head to study her, noting the emphasis on every-one. "You included, Amanda?"

With a wave of her hand, she dismisses that idea. "I am so beneath him and most of the customers who come in here."

Her insecurity washes over me, stirring old feelings I don't like but I can identify with. "That's not true. You are not be-neath him, or anyone, for that matter."

"I appreciate that, but after this summer, I've decided that geology and dig sites are where I belong. A little dust and sun will do me better than champagne and fine art."

"Don't make that decision because you feel beneath Mark."

Her expression turns solemn. "I'm not. I . . ." She seems to consider her words and decides against them, instead motion-ing over her shoulder. "Why don't I show you the break room. I need to get some coffee started, and there's some paperwork for you to fill out. I can explain while I make it."

A few minutes later, Amanda has shown me the exact mea-sure of coffee that Mark wants used if I'm ever the first one to arrive, and I'm sitting at a small wooden table across from her as she fills two ceramic cups. No Styrofoam like in the teachers' lounge for this place.

"How long has Rebecca been gone?" I ask.

Amanda sits down across from me. "Well," she ponders thoughtfully, pouring sugar into her coffee as I opt for straight powder creamer. "I started two months ago and she was already gone, so at least that long."

"She must have something pretty serious going on."

"No one has ever said, at least not to me, and I'm just glad Mark looked at the summer schedule and decided to hire." She slides a piece of paper in my direction. "That's the summer schedule."

I glance over a calendar with growing excitement as I note weekly wine tastings, several exciting artists who will be visiting, and a number of private parties. This is the world I have longed to live in for, well, ever.

"It's a busy schedule, right?" Amanda asked, seeking my agreement.

"Very, but that's a good thing."

"Not when Rebecca was at the helm of most of it, and even knowing this, Mark has interviewed at least fifteen people and hired no one until you. Thank goodness you did whatever you did to win him over because I've been helping and I'm in way over my head."

Whatever I did to win him over, I repeat in my mind. I did nothing, and he hired me without so much as a question. Why? Because I asked about Rebecca? Because I pretended to know her. Oh crap. I told Mark that I had a sister. This is why I hate lies. They always come back to haunt you. My heart begins to thunder in my chest at the idea of being cornered and busted in this one. I'm still contemplating how to best make this right, what my story will be, when Amanda slides a folder across the table.

"This is the new-hire paperwork and some test Mark said you need to take."

"Test?"

"Yes. Test. Do you have a problem with that Ms. McMillan?"

Mark's voice, dark and commanding, draws my gaze, and I barely stop myself from sucking in a breath at just how striking my new boss really is. He is wearing a light gray suit that enhances the unique silvery quality of his eyes, which are more pale blue in this lighting, instead of gray as I had first thought. His features are finely carved, his bottom lip full, his jaw strong. He is tall, and athletic, his blond hair neatly styled. He is . . . beautiful.

"I'm a schoolteacher, Mr. Compton," I finally manage to say. "I love a good test. I'm simply curious as to what kind of testing."

"We'll start with basics, and I'll decide where we go from there," he says, cutting a quick look at Amanda. "I'll finish up the paperwork with Ms. McMillan, Amanda." He is curt, authoritative. Intimidating. Intimidatingly sexy.

"Oh yes," she says, popping to her feet like a jack-in-the-box who's just had its handle cranked. She wasn't kidding about being intimidated by the man, and with him present, I am not without understanding of how she feels.

"Coffee is ready, by the way," she announces to him, and I can feel her angst, her plea for his approval that she doesn't get. She grabs her cup and heads toward him, and he steps aside to allow her to exit, but his eyes are locked on me, impassive, unreadable. That insecure part of me that Michael played on flares its ugly head inside me, that part of me so like Amanda. Heat lashes through my veins and I will it away. I could so easily want to please this man, and it terrifies me that I still have that in me.

You are not the same person you were with Michael, I tell

myself. I'm not naive. I'm not inexperienced. I will not be captivated by this man's power, his presence, even if I am not blind to his appeal. I am in control. Besides, he is my boss, not my lover.

He saunters to the coffeepot and fills a cup and, without asking, refills my cup. His eyes meet mine before he moves away, and I see the steel there, I see the dominance in the otherwise polite act. He didn't ask if I wanted more coffee. He simply decided I did and thus I do. I need to establish parameters with this man and do so now. I am not going to touch that cup.

In an instant, he's claimed the seat across from me, and the entire room along with it, and I am staring into those silvery gray eyes and I do not dare look away. I tell myself it's my show of strength, but deep down, I know I am captivated, commanded, to hold his stare.

"I wasn't sure you'd show up today," he finally says.

"Why wouldn't I?"

Several seconds tick by before his lips quirk slightly and he reaches into the folder and passes me a piece of paper and a pencil. "I hired you without so much as a reference check, on pure instinct. My instincts, Ms. McMillan, are very good. I'd like you to prove that an accurate statement." He reaches for the powdered creamer.

I glance down at the paper and see ten questions, quickly determining they are all related to medieval art.

"Begin," he orders softly.

I glance up at him to find him settling back into his seat, clearly intending to watch me write the test. He wants to intimidate me, and I do not want to let him. My jaw sets, and I reach for the pencil. I can feel him watching me, and I am flustered to realize my hand shakes ever so slightly. Men like him do not miss such details. He knows it's shaking. He knows he's affecting me.

I forcefully clear the haze from my mind and focus on the questions, which are quite advanced but well within my expertise. I finish them quickly and flip the paper around for his review.

He's still leaning back in his chair, deceptively casual, watching me, his gaze hooded, his expression once again impassive. He doesn't reach for the test, but instead, his attention flicks to my cup.

"You aren't drinking your coffee, Ms. McMillan."

"I'm over my limit for the day."

"Limits are meant to be pushed."

"Too much caffeine makes me shaky." The words—the lie—is out before I can stop it. Where are all these lies coming from?

He leans forward, and I can smell his clean, spicy male scent. "Sharing a cup of coffee," he says, "is a bit like celebrating a new partnership, don't you think?"

The challenge he has just issued crackles in the air, along with some other, unnamed electricity that had my throat thick and my heart racing. It's just a cup of coffee, but yet I sense that this is about so much more, that this is another test that has nothing to do with skill but rather with him. Me. And I don't know why I want to comply, to please him. Of course I do,

I tell myself. He's the kind of man who expects those around him to follow his lead. I cannot fight his will and be here. I tell myself that is why I comply, why I do as I wish. I tell myself I am not weak, and he is in control of the job, not me. I reach for the coffee.

Seven

I sip from the nearly cold beverage, peeking at my new boss from under my lashes as he reviews my test. He is powerful, this man, controlling, arrogant, everything I swear each day I do not want in my life, and yet I am drinking the coffee to please him. This would be acceptable if it were simply because he is my new boss. But it's not. Deep in my core, I know I am seduced by this place and by him. He is interesting to me in ways I don't want him to be, in ways I know spell trouble.

I tip the cup back again and try to savor the bitterness as a reminder of what this kind of man does to me. It strokes my tongue with acid and it's too much to take. I down the rest of the cup.

Immediately, his gaze lifts to mine, and I barely contain a grimace. His strong mouth hints at a curve, his eyes glint with something I can't quite identify, and I wish I don't want to as badly as I do. "Congratulations, Ms. McMillan. You passed your first test."

I have the distinct impression that he isn't talking about the one on paper but rather something completely different. My compliance with his "request" I drink my coffee despite my discomfort, I am almost certain.

"You doubted that I would?" I challenge, telling myself that I am talking about the questionnaire, not the coffee.

"I hired you without an interview."

"Yes," I say, and my fear he'd done so because I'd been asking about Rebecca, that he sees me as the next her—and I'm not sure that is a good thing; in fact, I'm fairly certain that it is not—twists me in knots. I press forward with a facade of courage. "Why exactly is that? You don't seem like a man who makes rash decisions."

"Why did you take the job without asking how much you will be paid or even what time to arrive, Ms. McMillan?"

My heart skips a beat, but I refuse to cower to this man, or any other again. I've lived that experience too many times in my life. "Because I love art and I have the summer off. And since I know far more about the gallery than you do about me, it wasn't an uneducated decision. That puts the ball back in your court, Mr. Compton. Why hire me without an interview?"

He does not appear amused by my counter. In fact, I'm not sure he isn't a bit irritated. He studies me for an eternal moment, those silvery eyes so intense they turn me to ice and fire at the same time. He is unnerving. I do not want this man to have the ability to rattle me.

"You want to know why I hired you?"

"It wasn't what I expected."

"Why offer your services if you don't expect them to be accepted?"

"A moment of passion," I admit. "And a summer of freedom."

He gives me a tiny incline of his chin, as if accepting that answer. "I could feel your passion. It spoke to me."

My throat goes instantly dry as the words drop between us, heavy with implication, the air thick with a rich, creamy awareness that I tell myself I am imagining, that I reject. He is not for me. This place is not even for me. It's Rebecca's.

"You impressed me, Ms. McMillan," he adds softly, "and that doesn't happen easily."

My breath nearly hitches at his words, and I am shocked to realize, despite my thoughts moments before, just how much I want this man's approval, how much I need confirmation it's real. I don't want to want it. I don't want to need it. Yet . . . I do. I wait three beats to calm my racing heart and then ask what I must know. "How exactly did I do that in such a short time?" My voice is not as steady as it was before, and he must notice. He is too keen not to.

"As I'm sure you know, there are cameras in most galleries, including this one. I was watching when you bewitched the couple that was shopping the Merit display with an absolute passion for art. If not for your guidance, they may have gone home to think about the purchase."

Even the idea of him watching me on camera, as disconcerting as it is, doesn't stop the warmth that spreads through me at his compliment. He is everything Amanda said he was, but he is even more. He is successful, and he belongs in a world I have only borrowed but long to own. Oh yes. I so want his approval, and I hate myself for needing it. Hate. It's a strong word, but I have a history that makes it so damn right for this occasion.

"Knowledge and competence are far easier to find than true passion," he adds, each word drawing me further into his spell. "I believe you have it, which is why I can't quite figure you out."

"Figure me out?" I ask, straightening a bit, uneasy that this might be headed toward my claim of knowing Rebecca. Toward the sister I don't have and haven't thought of a way around.

He sinks back into his chair, studying me intently, his elbows on the arms, his fingers steepled in front of him. "Why is someone so clearly enthralled with this world teaching school?"

"What's wrong with teaching school?" I ask, just as I had when Chris Merit had thrown the same ball at me.

"Absolutely nothing."

I wait for him to continue, but he doesn't. He just stares at me with keen observation that makes me want to shift in my chair.

"I love teaching," I state.

He arches a skeptical brow at me in reply.

"I do," I insist, but quickly, reluctantly add, "but no, it's not my true passion."

His reply isn't instant. He lets me squirm a bit under his scrutiny. "So I ask you again," he finally repeats. "Why are you teaching school?"

For a moment, I consider some fluffy answer designed for avoidance and decide he won't let that slide. My chest tightens as I admit something that I keep bottled up where I don't have to deal with it. Something I have told no one, but I am about to tell him. Maybe it's liberating. Maybe I need to say it out loud once and for all. I feel so damn guilty that teaching isn't fulfilling. It should be fulfilling. "Because," I say in a voice that to my dismay cracks slightly, "a love of art doesn't pay the bills."

If he notices my discomfort, he doesn't show it. Again, his expression is impassive, unreadable. "Which brings my curiosity back to what we've already covered. Why not ask what wage you will be paid?"

"I have enough of an idea of the going rate to know why this has to be a summer job that I don't do this full-time." A pinch of irritation and defensiveness sneaks up on me. "And you walked away before I could get the opportunity."

He laughs and it surprises me more than anything else he has done thus far. "I suppose I did." He turns somber quickly and considers me for so long and so intently that I feel like I'm going to lose my mind. What is he thinking? What is he about to say? I am being judged and I know it. I tell myself that I don't know him well enough for his opinion to matter, but like his approval, it does. He is of the world where I so yearn to belong.

"Perhaps," he says, "I didn't want to give you the chance to decline."

"I can certainly see you as a man who prefers to do the declining yourself," I say before I can stifle my reply.

He laughs again and sits up, scrubbing his clean-shaven jaw. "You don't pull any punches, do you?"

I shake my head. "Not today."

His smile widens and it is a gorgeous, handsome smile that could melt chocolate. "Let's see how true that is. Your top three Italian artists are whom?"

I sit up straighter, my blood pumping, immediately alert. My answer is instant. "Present day: artist and sculptor Marco Perego. Pino Daeni for his soft, romantic characters. Contemporary Italian master artist Francesco Clemente who is one of the most illustrious European trans–avant garde artists today."

He arches a brow. "No Da Vinci?"

"He's in a class by himself and is the expected answer that tells you nothing about my personal tastes."

His eyes light, and I think he might be pleased with my answer.

"Damien Hirst," he says, throwing out the name of a famous artist.

I am in my element, and I reply easily. "He's in his forties and already one of the most acclaimed contemporary artists alive. He's worth an estimated one billion dollars. In 2008, he sold, through Riptide—which your family owns—the full exhibition Beautiful Inside My Head Forever, with 223 works for $198 million, breaking the record of the most expensive auction by a single artist."

A smile lingers on his mouth, the same mouth that I keep looking at with ridiculous obsession, and this time, I know I see the glow of approval in his eyes. I am warm again, energized anew. Comfortable in a way I hadn't been before this moment with this man.

"Impressive, Ms. McMillan."

I smile, not even trying to suppress my pride at his words. "I aim to please."

"I must say, I'm getting that idea, and I like it." His voice is low, laden with silk. "I like it immensely."

Without warning, the air crackles with a charge that steals my breath. His eyes have darkened with something akin to a predatory gleam. My body responds without my permission, tingling with awareness that I don't want to feel yet I do. I am frustrated with myself for being affected by a man I will not dare cross a line with. A man who is dangerous to me, who might well have been dangerous to Rebecca.

"Excuse me, Mr. Compton," Amanda says from the doorway. "But you have a call."

"Take a message," he replies, never taking his eyes off me. And despite my vow, I am transfixed by their color, by the intensity of his stare.

Amanda delicately clears her throat. "It's Mrs. Compton about the auction that begins in an hour at Riptide."

Mrs. Compton? The spell is broken, and I gape. I know I do. I can't stop myself.

He sighs and flicks Amanda a look. "I'll call her back in five minutes."

"She's pretty clear she wants to talk now."

His tone grows sharper. "I'll call her back."

"Yes," Amanda says, looking flustered. "I'll tell her."

My new boss returns his attention to me as Amanda disappears. "Mrs. Compton would be my mother," he explains, definite amusement in his eyes now. "And just to be clear, the only woman I let boss me around. Unfortunately, as the manager of Riptide, she excels at it."

"Oh," I say, surprised, and suddenly he is not nearly as intimidating as before. "Your mother." I smile yet again. He's a control freak. I know this already, but I think he might not be as bad as I'd feared. I didn't miss the hint of affection to his tone that tells me he loves his mother. I've always thought that says something about a man. "Her skill at bossing you around has nothing to do with that maternal bond, then?" I am teasing him, and it just happens. I can't stop myself.

"Perhaps it just might," he admits, and I am pleasantly surprised at the very human admission, the tiny bit of vulnerability he allows me to see with it.

He taps the folder. "There's plenty of reading for you to do in the folder. Amanda will get you set up on the computer and then there will be online testing. Pass them and we'll talk about just what your role will be here. If you can play with the big dogs, and interact with Riptide quality transactions, I can assure you that money won't be an issue."

My heart races with this news. Could this really be happening? Could I really have the chance to make art my life? "I'll get right on the tests."

He leans in closer. "I see something special in you, Ms. McMillan. I'm hoping you're going to prove me right." Without another word, he pushes to his feet and leaves the room. I stare after him, my teeth worrying my bottom lip, my heart in my throat. I didn't manage to get an answer about my salary, but I tell myself he's alluded to a sizable package. Most importantly, though, I am frustrated at myself because I haven't asked about Rebecca. You will, I promise myself. When the time is right, you will.

Eight

Thirty minutes later, I have managed to claim my new office, on loan from Rebecca, of course, which I refuse to let myself forget. Amanda has already logged me into the computer and headed back to her desk. I am now alone, with the door shut, ready to start to work.

I pull up my new e-mail and I have a message waiting from Mark, or rather, Mr. Compton. I wonder if he intends to stay that formal with me, when I've heard him call Amanda by her first name. I click on the e-mail.

Welcome, Ms. McMillan:

You will find a link to a number of tests below. Each is a timed evaluation to ensure you cannot use the Internet for help, though I'm sure you would never consider doing such a thing.

May the odds be ever in your favor, and mine as well.

Mark Compton

I laugh at the reference to *The Hunger Games*, and I am shocked but pleased that my new boss has a sense of humor. I feel silly now to have been so intimidated and affected as I was by him during our meeting. Logically, I know I was responding to this fascination I have with this world, this deep desire to belong here, that wasn't about him at all. It was, and is, about me, about my past, about ghosts and skeletons I'm being forced to face just by sitting at this desk. And the journals, I remind myself as the soft scent of roses I now associate with Rebecca teases my nostrils.

I pull open the drawer to my right and find a lighter and set the flame burning on the candle. The flame flickers with life, and my gaze falls on the brilliant rose colors on the wall. I picture Rebecca sitting here and somehow I feel as if she is over my shoulder, but it is not frightening. In fact, I feel almost comforted, as if the dancing fire from the wick is a sign she is alive and well. I feel hope that she will return, and perhaps I will have a place in this world as well. Do I dare believe I can chase this dream and really make a living at it? Excitement and hope expand within me. I want this so badly it hurts and it frightens me. I know why I have never tried, and one of those reasons, money, seems to be resolved with the inference I will be paid commission on my sales. The other reason, though, is dauntingly big. If I fail, if I must go back to my old life, it will destroy me.

"You have to try," I whisper to the empty room. "You have to."

New resolve forms, and I shake off my fears. If I am to stay here, if I can prove I'm worth keeping around, then I need to get busy. I quickly dig into my testing, and though the questions are challenging, I am pleased at the ease at which I complete the first few exams. I'm just finishing up a fourth, and stretching, considering seeking out a caffeine escape—this time one that is supposed to be cold—when I hear a knock on my door.

"Come in," I call, not sure why my stomach flutters in anticipation of my visitor, but the feeling isn't completely unwelcome. It's been a long time since every piece of my day has felt like an adventure.

An Asian man in his late twenties appears in my entryway. "I'm Ralph, the accounting dude."

"Ralph," I say, with a nod, and I barely contain a smile at both his dude reference and his red bow tie and crisp white shirt. There is something friendly about this man that I like instantly.

"Yeah, yeah, I know," he says, clearly reading the meaning in my smile. "I don't look like a Ralph. My folks wanted me to fit into the American mold, but they weren't American enough to know Ralph isn't exactly a cool name. But I like that it's unexpected. It disarms people right off the bat and, like you, it makes them smile."

"I like that," I say, smiling even bigger now. "I think you should be in sales. You could make that work for you."

He snorts. "And deal with all the arrogant rich people who

come into this place? No, thanks." He softens his voice. "Mark is all I can handle."

Laughter bubbles from my lips. "You'll have to share your secrets to that little trick."

"I'll buy you coffee sometime soon and tell you all his secrets."

"I'll take you up on that."

He waves and departs, pulling the door shut behind him, and I return to my testing. An hour later, the material has turned daunting, and my mood has shifted from energized to frazzled. I can see why I might be tested on random collectible items if I am to work with Riptide, but wine, opera, and classical music? I know absolutely nothing about these nonart subjects, and I decide now might be a good time to find out how lunch works around this place.

I head to the lobby and find Amanda behind her desk with a tall, pretty young African American girl about her age standing with her. "Hello, Sara," this newcomer greets. "I'm Lynn, and I'm interning here this summer."

Lynn is dressed in a cream-colored suit, and her hair and makeup are impeccable, but her personality is casual and warm. I chat with her, and Tesse, also an intern—and the girl who had been at the hostess stand last night—joins us. I'm pleased that I like everyone I've met. I feel good with these people. Unfortunately, Mary, a pretty and rather robust blond salesperson closer to my age, is so busy she can only wave and give me a quick greeting.

"So, Amanda," I say when I am finally alone with her again.

"Is it common to be given testing on wines and music to work here?"

She nods. "We have so many events that Mark uses the testing to determine where we can best service the clientele. In fact, we have a wine tasting next Friday night."

My stomach knots. Could wine really be my undoing?

"Excuse me," a woman in dark-rimmed glasses says, appearing at the desk. "Can someone help me with a Chris Merit piece, please?"

An image of Chris standing in front of me, holding his jacket around me, makes my belly do a flutter. "I would be happy to help you," I offer, suddenly very eager to visit his display again.

Amanda looks shocked, and I assume that means I'm not allowed to be on the floor yet. I pretend not to notice and head to the sales floor.

An hour later, the woman has left with a six-figure purchase that has me glowing with excitement and the rush of having made a sale.

Ralph winks at me as I pass his office, which I've now discovered is next to mine, ah, Rebecca's. My stomach growls, and I realize I haven't eaten anything and a glance at the ridiculously expensive, absolutely fabulous antique clock in the hallway says it's two o'clock. Jeez, how did that happen?

I turn back to the reception area to ask Amanda if I can run out and find myself toe-to-toe with Mark. He is taller than I remembered, and I crane my neck to meet his stare. "Ms. McMillan," he says tightly, and I am immediately aware of his displeasure. Why is he displeased? I just brought in six figures to the gallery.

"Mr. Compton," I say.

"Why have you not completed your testing?"

"I was, ah, helping customers."

"Did I tell you to help customers?"

I wet my lips nervously, and his gaze flicks over my mouth. It's unnerving. He's unnerving me again. "I just thought—"

"Don't think, Ms. McMillan," he says tightly. "Do as I say."

Old, familiar feelings spiral down my spine, feelings of inadequacy, of needing to please—a moth to a flame that is sure to burn me alive—surface. I reject them and straighten. "I took every test I'm capable of taking. I don't know wine or opera or classical music. I'm sure you'll find the job-related ones to be exemplary."

"All the tests are job related," he corrects, "if you wish to operate at a higher level, which I understood you to say you did. Did I get that wrong, Ms. McMillan?"

There is a crispness to my name that was not there before, and I am remotely aware that I am in front of Ralph's open office, that he can hear and see everything.

"No," I reply softly, firmly. "You are not wrong, Mr. Compton," and I am shocked to realize I have emphasized his name as he did mine. There is a rebel inside me that refuses to sink into my old habits, and I am suddenly proud of myself. "But I cannot test on what I do not know."

"Testing allows me to decide where to start teaching you," he says in rebuttal.

"At the beginning," I reply. "Since the only thing I know

about wine, for instance, is what color it is when it's in my glass."

He arches a light blond brow. "Really? That much?"

"That much," I confirm.

He considers me a moment. He's good at doing that, considering me, putting me on edge, no doubt on purpose. "Do you have a laptop?" he asks finally.

I frown, not sure where this is going. "Yes."

"Do you have it with you?"

"Yes."

"So you know how to use it?"

I am so not pleased with the snarky question. I lower my voice, unable to stop my reply. "That's a little like asking a rich, arrogant gallery owner if he knows he's a rich, arrogant gallery owner."

His eyes light up with amusement. "I am rich and arrogant, Ms. McMillan. I like being rich and arrogant. I thought you, too, wanted to be rich yourself. Or was I mistaken?"

My throat goes dry. Rich? Is he joking? "I don't recall any such opportunity."

"And you won't until you learn what I need you to learn. Since I can't trust you to stay off the floor, take your laptop to the coffee shop next door. Amanda will give you a study manual so you can remedy your . . . deficiencies."

I narrow my gaze at him, aware he is trying to bait me. I'm not going to bite. I give a nod. "Of course, Mr. Compton. I'll get right on that."

His lips twitch. "Check in before you leave for the night. I'll want to quiz you."

• • •

Fifteen minutes later, I walk into Cup O' Café next door to the gallery, and the rich scent of brewing coffee, and something distinctly chocolate, touches my nostrils. If the coffee tastes as good as this place smells, I am going to love it here. Not to mention the decor, all warm browns and leather, with a hardwood floor, is soothing in a way that contrasts the caffeinated high people come here for. I can use soothing right now.

I gaze around me and see any number of cute round wooden tables available, and I can tell the seating wraps around to the other side of the encased pastry display. I like to watch people, so I choose a seat in the middle of the café so I can see what's going on around me. Not that I should be watching people. It seems I have studying to do. How very ironic for the schoolteacher, I think with a tiny snort, that has me reprimanding myself for poor manners I can no longer afford.

It's not long before the college-age boy behind the counter rings up my white-chocolate mocha, and since it's past two o'clock and I haven't eaten, I justify a chocolate muffin the size of Texas, and lamely promise to eat low-fat popcorn—my go-to diet solution—for dinner. Finally, I'm sitting at my table, waiting for my coffee to be made and nibbling on my chocolate delight. Regretfully, I break out my netbook, wishing it was the other, not to be named brand computer, but feeling hopeful I can afford one soon.

Once I've powered up, I set a wine taster's guidebook on my table. Flipping through the book, I find it is written with an assumption I know something about wine. I find Amazon on my search bar and type in "Wine for Dummies" and get several choices. By the time I've picked one and I'm ready to read, my coffee has arrived and I sip the piping hot sweet concoction. It's heavenly, and I mentally roll up my sleeves and start reading.

I have no idea how long I have been reading, but I'm half-way through the Dummies book and I still feel like a dummy, when I hear, "You must be Sara."

I look up to find a beautiful Hispanic woman in her midthirties with big striking brown eyes. She is wearing an apron, so I assume she works here.

"Yes," I respond. "I'm Sara."

"I'm Ava, the owner here." She sets a cup in front of me. "White mocha. My guy Corey at the register told me what you ordered. Mark called over here and said to get you whatever you've been having on the house as a reward for perfect scores." She laughs and rolls her tongue, making a sexy sound. "Sounds sexy."

I roll my eyes rather than my tongue. "If being tested on everything from art to opera is sexy, please shoot me now."

She laughs. "I should have guessed. I know the crew next door well enough to know he's put them all through the wringer."

"How long have you known them?" I ask, thinking of Rebecca.

"I've been open five years and I've known Mark that entire time." She wiggles a brow. "Why? You want gossip?"

I perk up at that. "You have gossip?"

"Honey, I always have gossip." The phone rings, and she glances over her shoulder. "Corey's on break. I'll be back."

She rushes away, and a sudden tingling sensation dances

along my neckline and draws my attention to the edge of the pastry bar to my left. My lips part in surprise at the incredibly sexy man sitting a few feet away, and not just any incredibly sexy man, but the same man whose been haunting my thoughts almost as much as Rebecca these past twenty-four hours. Chris Merit is here. I can't believe it. My stomach does a crazy but-terfly flutter as my eyes meet his, and I see amusement in his expression. Not only is he here, but I know he's also been watching me, and I have no idea how long he's been here.

Why didn't he come over? Why isn't he coming over now? Should I go to him?

"I'm back," Ava declares before I can decide what to do next, but I can barely pull my eyes from Chris. When I finally do, he's still watching me. I can feel it in every inch of my body. I am so hypersensitive to this man I cannot focus on what Ava is saying. There is only Chris.

Nine

The bells on the coffee shop door chime, but I barely hear them. I'm still looking at Chris, and he's still looking at me. His eyes are warm, and I am warmer. I've known plenty of good-looking men, but this one affects me beyond good looks, he sets every nerve I own to tingling.

"He comes here almost every day," Ava whispers, and my gaze jerks to hers. I glance beyond her and see her employee has returned.

"You mean Chris Merit?" I ask, hungry for what insights into the artist she might share with me.

She nods. "There's something about him, aye?"

"Aye," I agree wholeheartedly.

"It's the mystery, I think. No matter how I try, I can't draw him into a conversation of any substance. Well, that, and let's just face it, the man makes denim and leather look as edible as chocolate."

The bells ding again, and a group enters the building. Ava sighs. "Regretfully, I must attend the counter. We'll have to chat later."

I muster a smile, still feeling Chris's stare, still tingling all over. "I suppose that steals my excuse to put off my homework."

"Homework," she repeats, and rolls her eyes. "Mark really is the proverbial principal with a ruler in his hand. I feel sorry for his employees. How about lunch one day this week? We can set it up before you leave."

"Yes, great," I agree without hesitation. Ava seems quite nice and surely she knew Rebecca. Knows, I correct silently. There is no past tense. Rebecca is fine. "I'd like that."

My cell phone rings, and Ava scurries off to help her customer who has now morphed into several more. I dig my phone from my purse and forget everything but the call when I see Ella's number. "Ella?" I answer excitedly.

The line crackles with electricity. "Sara!"

"Ella?!"

More crackling.

"I'm okay. Travel . . ." *crackle* ". . . am . . . road trip . . . beautiful . . ." More crackling and then nothing. The line is dead.

I sigh and set the phone down next to my computer, glaring at the device where it rests. Why has hearing Ella's voice, confirming she is safe, not brought the comfort it should? I'm worried about her beyond reason. Everything just feels so . . . off.

"Is everything okay?"

I look up and blink in surprise to find Chris standing in front of my table, and the worries of moments before are temporarily banked. His light blond hair is mussed up, like he's been running his hands through it, and he's wearing a dark blue snug-fitting T-shirt and dark blue jeans. Unlike Mark, he is not classically good-looking but more raw male hotness. He looks scrumptious and add to that how sexy his talent is to me, and I am suddenly more self-conscious than ever. I try to reassure myself I've done nothing ridiculous and foolish that he might have bore witness to. Though I'm fairly certain I inhaled the volcanic muffin in a rather unladylike fashion.

"Okay?" I ask, my voice raspy, affected. I am so incapable of playing it cool with this man, or really any, for that matter, but this one more than most.

"You looked like the call upset you."

"Oh no," I assure him quickly, and it hits me that not only was he watching me, but he also isn't shy about admitting it. "My friend was calling from Paris, and we had a bad connection. I really wanted to hear how she was doing." I seize the opportunity to find out how long Chris is in town. "Didn't I read that you live in Paris?"

He motions to the seat. "Can I sit?"

"Yes. Of course. I should have offered."

"And yes," he says, settling into the chair across from me. "I own a place in Paris, but I split my time between here and there. San Francisco stirs my creativity. I can't stay away long."

I'm thrilled to discover he lives here, and intrigued by his creative process. I yearn to ask questions about his work but I hesitate, after Ava's reference to his being a private person. Besides, the table is small, and I can smell the same earthy male scent from last night, and the effect is drugging. I'm not sure I can ask intelligent questions, so I settle on easy small talk. "I had no idea you were local, but then, I've been pretty removed from the art scene for the past few years."

"But you're back now."

"For the rest of summer," I agree, watching him closely as I add, "or until Rebecca returns."

His brow furrows. "She's coming back?"

"You don't think so?"

He shrugs. "Not a clue. I barely know her, but she's been gone so long that I assumed she'd found a new job."

"Mark says she's on a leave of absence. From my understanding, some rich guy whisked her away to travel the world."

"And you have no idea how long until she returns?"

"You summed up the general gist of the situation. I'm here until she's here." Or until I prove I'm worthy of staying around when she returns, I remind myself.

"Hmmm," he murmurs. "That open-ended vacation is rather . . . odd."

"She must be an exceptional employee."

"Right. Must be."

I don't miss the hint of sardonicism tingeing his tone, and I am quite certain he doesn't like Mark any more than Mark seems to like him.

"Wine?" he asks, indicating the book on the table with a lift of his chin.

"Apparently, it's not enough to know art to sell art. I must acquire a knack for talking about fine wine, opera, and classical music, about all of which I am clueless. I'm being tested, and since I do like a glass of wine here or there, it seems the least intimidating."

His lips thin with disapproval. "You don't need to know anything but art to sell art."

"As much as I agree, I'm a slave to Mark's demands." Rebecca's writing replays in my head, catching me off guard. You know I have to punish you. I am immediately uncomfortable, and my nervous rambling tendency proves it is alive and well. "My knowledge of opera or classical music amounts to absolutely nothing, and frankly I don't enjoy either." My misspeak washes over me immediately, and I can feel blood drain from my cheeks. His father had been a famous classical pianist. "Oh God. I'm sorry. Your father—"

"Was brilliant," he says, and his expression is unreadable, his tone even. "But as with all things, music can be an acquired taste. How 'clueless' are you about wines?"

I blink at the abrupt change of subject, and I'm so off-kilter, I don't seem to possess the ability to filter my comments. "I know how to point to the name on the menu, and the waiter brings it."

Amusement dances in Chris's green eyes, and his mood is instantly transformed from intense to relaxed. "And you pick the wine you point to how?"

"It's a highly complex method," I explain. "First, there is my mood. Do I want red or white? Once that choice is made, I move to the choice of chilled or not chilled. Finally, step three, comes down to—what is the cheapest glass of wine that meets my decided upon criteria." He is smiling but not laughing at me, and I am both charmed and pleased.

"You do know you live in wine country, right?" he teases. There is a sultry flirtation to his voice that I hope I am not imagining.

"Neither my apartment nor the school where I teach sport vineyards in the backyards. I suppose I'm highly uncultured."

His mood turns somber. "You're not uncultured, far from it, but I assume your feeling that way is the whole idea in all of this. Mark looks for a weakness and uses it to disarm people. Not that a lack of knowledge in those areas is a weakness—unless you allow it to be."

I tilt my head, studying him. "You don't like Mark, do you?"

"Liking him is irrelevant. He gets the job done."

In other words, he doesn't like Mark. "Has he tried to find your weakness?"

"He tries to find everyone's weakness."

He's avoiding a direct answer, and I can't think of a way to ask again. "I fear he's found my weakness or, rather, weaknesses, rather easily."

"You're better off letting your customers be experts in everything else, while you ask questions and feed their egos. You stick with art and you'll be golden."

"A brilliant plan if I ever heard one."

His lips quirk. "Brilliant? I like your choice of words."

I purse my lips. "Like you don't hear brilliant about your art all the time."

"I don't listen to my own hype. Besides, for every brilliant there's a critic."

I study him a moment, his strong jaw, his intelligent green eyes, and I realize I've stopped being all nerves and fear. I'm remarkably at ease right now, considering Chris has managed to wake every hormone I own and some I didn't know I had. "I sold two more of your paintings today."

His eyes soften and warm at the same time. "And you did it without any knowledge of wine and opera. How is that possible?"

I find myself laughing easily and it feels good. Until this moment, I didn't realize just how tense I am, how on edge, and it amazes me that this man I barely know has disarmed me. Our laughter dissolves into a crackling current that steals my breath away. Our eyes lock, and heat pools low in my belly. I want this man but I am so out of my league. I know this, but my body doesn't seem to care. I am but a ship passing by, a teacher headed back to class, and he is talented beyond belief, a man who's worth millions, who has seen things I have only read about.

"Are you one of those wine snobs?" I ask, hungry for details about what makes a talent such as his tick.

His mood shift is instant, the shutters over his eyes dropping, the tension in the air almost palpable. I regret the question, though I don't know what was wrong with it.

"I know wines very well," he says, his tone flat as he glances at the thick leather watch he's wearing—that is far more biker than the millionaire he is—and then back at me. "I'm booked for a meeting with your boss that I need to get to." He studies me for an intent moment and his eyes warm again, and I can almost see the ice melting before me. "Don't play his games, Sara, and he can't beat you at them." He pushes to his feet. "Until next time."

"Next time," I repeat softly, wondering if there will be a next time. He saunters to his table and grabs a leather backpack and leather coat. He is wearing biker boots, black leather, with silver buckles. I've always favored men in suits, men who were refined, and well, like Mark. Chris isn't those things, and yet he intrigues me in every possible way.

I expect him to pass my table, and I hold my breath, waiting, trying to think of some witty, cool something to say to him, wondering what he will say to me. Instead, he disappears down a back hallway I assume must be an exit. He is gone, and I am left wondering if it's for good, if I will ever see him again.

An hour after my encounter with Chris, my cell rings, and Mark orders me back to the gallery. Like a good little soldier, I pack up my things and prepare to do as told.

"Okay," Ava declares, appearing by my side, "we have to do lunch. I've never seen Chris Merit talk to anyone as long as he did you. I want the scoop."

I blink at her. The scoop? I do not have a scoop to give, but if I did, my little encounter with Chris feels private and personal. I wouldn't want to share it. "There's nothing to tell. I sold several of his paintings, and he was thanking me."

She wiggles a dark brow. "You made him richer than he already is. Now there's a way to get a man's attention. And boy did you grab his attention. He looked like he wanted to gobble you up. I'll call you tomorrow so we can set up lunch, unless I see you here first." She rushes away and I stare after her.

Gobble me up? Chris looked like he wanted to gobble me up? I replay my encounter with Chris in my mind and try to think of a steamy moment she might have witnessed. There were times when I thought I'd felt a spark between us but didn't dare believe it was more than my wishful thinking.

My phone buzzes with a text from Mark. Still waiting. I grimace. He is such a control freak that I have no problem seeing him as the dominating man in the journal. It is an idea I find both erotic and scary at the same time because I do not know where Rebecca is. Deep in my core, I am certain she is lost forever, damaged in an irrevocable way.

I shake off the grimness of my thoughts and head back to the gallery to find Amanda behind the counter, packing up her things for the day.

"Mark's waiting for you in his office," she says.

"Which would be where?"

She smirks. "Door at the end of your hall. Good luck, and I really do hope I see you tomorrow."

I blanch. "Hope?"

She holds up her hands. "Oh no, you took that so wrong. I didn't mean you were going to get fired. I meant that I hope you come back. I know you don't care for all the testing."

I relax a fraction. "I'll be back."

She smiles and slips her purse over her shoulder. "Good. Excellent. And, you know, I'm happy to quiz you if it would help any."

"You're versed in wines, opera, and classical music?"

"Nope," she says, "and I don't want to be. But that doesn't mean I can't help you study. I happen to think you'll be great to have around. It's just a feeling I have."

A smile touches my lips. "Thank you, Amanda. I appreciate your offer and I might just take you up on it."

"I hope you do," she assures me. "I'll see you in the morning." She lowers her voice. "Good luck with the beast. That's what we call him. It's so very appropriate."

With a much needed laugh at the nickname, I reluctantly head through the door to the right of the desk that leads to the offices. The sense of balancing uneasily on a tightrope about to tumble off consumes me. I knock on the corner door and hear Mark's deep voice tell me to enter. That one word is more of a command than most can muster in a full sentence. The man really is one big ball of bossiness.

Hoisting my briefcase and purse fully onto my shoulder, I shove open the door, wishing I'd dropped off my things by my office. The minute I bring Mark's office into view, I forget the dull throb of the load I'm carrying for the spectacular sight of the oval-shaped room, with a massive glass desk in the center. I am overwhelmed with the magnificent art on the walls to my right and left. On some level, I am certain Mark wanted me to see this place, to see him looking powerful, more king than man, in the center of it all.

But it is the spectacular mural covering the entire half-moon wall hugging "the king" that I find utterly spellbinding. My eyes travel the exquisitely painted design of the Eiffel Tower, and I instantly know the technique and the artist. This is Chris's mastery. These two men were once friends. They had to have been, and yet now they barely tolerate each other.

"How was your coffee, Ms. McMillan?"

I snap my attention from the painting to Mark, wondering how he manages to make a question sound like a demand. Don't play his games, Sara, and he can't beat you at them. Chris's words repeat in my head and they resonate within me, but I feel trapped. I cannot be fired before I find out what happened to Rebecca.

"My coffee was excellent, and thank you for the second cup. It certainly helped clear the fog of too many wines and not enough time."

"Sit and tell me what you studied and what you learned." He motions to the brown leather chairs in front of his desk, indicating he wants me to sit in the one to his right. My urge is to claim the one to his left, all too aware this action would displease him. I am clearly conflicted over this man. I want to please him. I do not want to please him. But experience with overbearing men such as Mark prevails, and I choose to do neither. How high I jump now will determine how high he expects me to jump later.

When I don't move, he arches a brow. "Am I so intimidating, Ms. McMillan, that you do not want to sit?"

My chin lifts, and I meet his steely gray eyes. "As much as you try to be, Mr. Compton, no, you are not. Your tests, however, are. I'd prefer to wait to be drilled on my knowledge until I can adequately impress you. I do not, however, want to wait to work the sales floor until such time."

"We do not always get what we want, Ms. McMillan." His expression is inscrutable, but his voice is lower, velvety, and not for the first time today, I'm not sure we are talking about my job. "Everything I do is calculated and with purpose. You'll learn that sooner than later. There's a wine tasting here on Friday night. The attendees are not high school students. They're wealthy, refined customers, with refined tastes. I need you ready for them. I need you focused on preparing for that event."

Refined. The word bites with insult; be it real or imagined, it has the same effect on me. A sense of inadequacy fills me, a long-lost enemy, threatening to bring me to my knees. Anger flares its ugly, unexpected head, and it's far easier to embrace. "Then I guess I'd better get home and study." Somehow, my voice is steady.

His eyes narrow and darken, and I'm pretty sure he knows he's hit a hot spot with me. I've got to learn to control my reactions and put on a game face.

"Are you aware that Riptide hosts a variety of wine tasting events in conjunction with some of the top wine producers in the world?"

I blink. "No. I am not."

"Are you aware that we hold an annual charity event in conjunction with the Trans-Siberian Orchestra?"

My stomach falls to my feet. Why didn't I do my research? "No. No, I am not."

"Then I'm sure you've now realized that I am only trying to help you, Sara," he says. "I see something bigger than a summer on my local showroom floor for you. If that's not what you want, then by all means, I'll set you free in the gallery tomorrow to sell to your heart's content."

My anger transforms into near panic. "No. I don't want that. I want to do more. I can do more."

"Then trust me."

I swallow hard, taken aback by his words. "Yes. I . . . okay. I'll learn what you need me to."

His eyes light with approval. "Good. I'll give you a reprieve tonight. Go home and study. First thing tomorrow morning I'll test you to see just how far we are from where we need to be."

. It is a dismissal confirmed by his reaching for his phone.

"Thank you," I murmur, and head for the hallway in a blur of confusion. It baffles me how I've let a summer job become a plea for a new life but it has, and there is no looking back. To work for Riptide, even through this gallery, would be a dream come true. I want this as I have not wanted anything in my life.

I pass my door and smell the roses from the hallway. Back stepping, I realize I've left the candle burning for all these hours. I'm eager to escape this place, to get home and try to analyze what has happened to me today, what has happened to me since the day I began reading Rebecca's journal.

Quickly, I blow out the flame and note a letter-size envelope on my chair with my name scribbled on it. I recognize the handwriting. I've studied his signature, his script. Rounding the desk, I snatch the envelope and rush for the door. I do not want to stay here and open it. I want to be alone before I dare a peek.

Finally, when I am locked inside my car with the engine running, I stare at my name on the yellow paper, not sure what I am waiting for. In a frenzied rush of movement, I unseal the flap and pull out a piece of drafting paper and gape.

Inside is a drawing of me sitting at the coffee shop table in deep concentration, and it's signed by the artist. I have become a Chris Merit original.

Ten

You can't keep thinking of everything as being Rebecca's or you will make yourself crazy, I tell myself as I settle into my office chair on day two at the gallery. It's a hard-earned conclusion I'd come to while lying in bed the night before, staring into the darkness. Thus why I am exhausted today, but at least I've resolved to claim this place as mine. I have to, otherwise how will I rise to the challenge my new boss has put before me? How will I truly reach for the dream of a successful career in art, after all of these years of convincing myself I could not?

With a vow to form my own identity at the gallery, I sink deeper into my leather chair, behind my desk. Before me sits my impulsive purchase of a new, beautifully jeweled, red leather journal that I'd picked up at Ava's coffee shop a few minutes earlier. My hope is that writing down my own thoughts will help me stop thinking obsessively about her thoughts, or at a minimum, help me to understand why confusion rules my every waking moment.

I pick up the red ink pen I'd also purchased and open to the first blank page, where I write "August 21, day two at the gallery." Guilt twists in my chest, and I set the pen down again. You are not forgetting about Rebecca. You're simply clearing a path to finding her.

Inhaling, I pick up the pen again and stare down at the journal, seeing only a mental image of the drawing of me that Chris had left the night before. Or rather, of a woman who looks like me but different. I am not the girl that a famous artist is inspired by, but yet, I am, or I was yesterday.

A buzz from the phone on my desk jolts me from my thoughts, and I answer automatically. "This is Sara McMillan."

"Good morning, Ms. McMillan." There is an unexpected smile in my new boss's tone, and I relax, if only marginally.

"Good morning, Mr. Compton."

"I've been called away to New York on Riptide business until Thursday."

The tension in my gut uncurls, and my spine relaxes. Breathing room. Yes. Yes. Yes.

"That doesn't mean you can sneak onto the sales floor," he chides, as if he's plucked the idea from my brain before I ever had it. Which I hadn't, but, well, I would have. "Friday, Ms. McMillan. Your goal is to be as ready to impress me then as you possibly can be. I trust you studied well last night?"

"I certainly did." I want this opportunity. I will not allow a knowledge barrier to defeat me.

"Excellent. Then you can log into your e-mail and click on

the link I've sent you to begin testing. I won't grade the test, at least not for now. It's simply a tool for you to use to see how you're progressing."

The good news keeps coming, and I know my smile can be heard in my voice. "That sounds perfect."

"Ms. McMillan," he says sharply, prompting a reply that I dutifully offer.

"Yes, Mr. Compton?"

"Have a good day."

The line clicks and goes dead.

Two hours later, it's nearly noon, and I'm making myself crazy. The names and regions of wines, and wine manufacturers, are running together and I decide to turn to my old faithful solution to all that is wrong in life. Coffee. It is my one real vice, so I figure why not indulge with an Olympic-style commitment? Besides, Ava mentioned having lunch together. She hadn't been at the coffee shop when I'd bought the journal, and I haven't heard from her, either. I figure it can't hurt to try and catch up with her now. My curiosity over what she might share about this strange new world I inhabit is killing me. And despite my grand declaration of owning my new office and job, on some level I know I will never fully feel that I do, not until I uncover the mysteries of Rebecca's whereabouts.

After heading to the front desk and making idle chitchat with Amanda and a few of the other staff members, I barely contain the urge to help a customer. Amanda warns me off the action with a promise of Mark's wrath, and I quickly head to the coffee shop again. I scan the empty tables, and there is no denying my disappointment to find Chris nowhere in sight.

Choosing the same table I'd worked at yesterday is an easy decision. Habits, things that feel normal—these are things I crave, just as I do the coffee I am about to order.

By two o'clock, neither Ava nor Chris has appeared in the shop. I've thirstily downed two white mochas and switched to black coffee. There is no denying I am shaky and need food. Waiting to eat in hopes of sharing lunch with Ava has not paid off. The good news, though, in the hazy tunnel that is my caffeinated high, is that my knowledge of the featured wines for the tasting Friday night is rapidly expanding.

The kid from behind the counter approaches my table and refills my coffee without me asking and grins. "Mr. Compton says to keep your cup full."

Right. Mr. Compton says. I manage a tight-lipped smile and a "thank you," but I am uneasy with my new boss having my drinks monitored. It is as if he is trying to ... hmm, what? The answer comes to me immediately. Control me. A variety of emotions flash inside me and slowly expand. There is something very sexy about a man like Mark Compton in control, but sexy or not, it's also quite uncomfortable for all kinds of reasons I've found better left under the rug.

Comfortable is overrated, a voice in the back of my head screams, and I know that inner voice is my subconscious demanding to finally be heard. The truth of the matter is, I've spent every day since college graduation wallowing in boring predictability. Except when you were with Michael. I grind my teeth. Predictable is far better than what I was with him.

I remind myself there are ways out of predictable ruts that do not include men like Michael ... or Mark. Right. Other ways. It had taken me reading someone else's words, stepping into her life, to find excitement. How sad am I? I squeeze my eyes shut and reprimand myself. This is not her life. It's yours.

Resolve forms. I am determined to get to work, to make today count toward a new career. I force my eyes open and reach for my book, effectively knocking the coffee from the table. Fabulous. Just fabulous. Coffee is on my table, the floor, and, yes, my only pair of good black heels that match my staple black skirt. My cheeks are, no doubt, as rosy as my silk blouse.

I snatch up the few napkins I have beside me and wipe the table to salvage my computer before it becomes a victim of my shaky hands. Task complete, I squat to attend my dripping wet shoe and the floor.

"Looks like you need these."

The familiar voice tingles along my nerve endings, and blood rushes to my cheeks. No. Please. Do not let this be happening. He squats in front of me, and my gaze locks on his powerful thighs where his hands rest. Strong, artistic hands that are holding napkins for my spill. Slowly, my gaze lifts to find a set of alluringly green eyes belonging to Chris Merit, staring into mine. Once again, this famous, gorgeous man is squatting on the ground in an effort to help me recover from a mishap.

"You have the most amazing knack for showing up to witness my acts of clumsiness," I accuse.

His lips curve, and his green eyes twinkle with specks of yellow. No. More like light flecks of gold shimmer. "I prefer to think of it as a knack for coming to your rescue," he declares huskily, and winks before he proceeds to wipe up my mess. Oh good God. I've made Chris Merit my janitor. And he winked at me. I can barely breathe.

He stands up and heads to the trash, moving with a confident male grace that is momentarily spellbinding. I'm frozen in place. I can only stare at him in wonder. Which, I realize, snapping to my senses, is not a good thing when I am in a skirt and squatting on the ground.

I pop to my feet and then have to lift my foot and swipe a remaining wet spot off my shoe. I've just dropped the used napkins inside the empty cup when he returns and stands by my table. Close to me. Really close. An earthy, wonderful scent teases my nostrils and stirs longing inside me. I love how this man smells and I have a newfound liking for faded jeans and biker boots I doubt I will ever lose. And try as I might, I cannot help but remember him holding the leather jacket he's wearing today around me the other night.

"Ah, thanks," I manage to say, sounding as frazzled as I feel. "I'm embarrassed."

"Don't be." His eyes are warm and remind me of summer green grass, his voice rich with sincerity. "I think you're adorable."

"Adorable," I repeat, my tone deadpan. "Not what a girl wants to be." It's what a man calls a kid sister or the girl he doesn't want to date. Not that I thought he wanted to date me. I don't know what I thought, what I think now.

"Then what does a girl want to be?" There is a teasing tone to his words that matches his expression.

Beautiful. Sexy. I want to be either or both to this man, but I wouldn't dare to say such things so I settle on, "Not clumsy."

"You're interesting."

"Interesting?" I query. What is it with him and Mr. Compton and the whole interesting thing? It has to be an artsy thing I'm out of touch with. "I . . . well. I guess that's better than clumsy." I'm not sure it's better than adorable. I just don't know.

"You still don't like that choice of word."

"It's . . . fine."

"You inspired me to draw you."

"The adorably interesting and clumsy inspiration," I say, feeling self-conscious but then quickly feeling bad about the remark. I soften my voice and add, "But thank you. I'm flattered you drew me, and I was absolutely breathless when I opened the envelope." I can't contain my silly smile. "Now I own a Chris Merit original." My brows dip. "Unless you want it back."

He laughs. "Of course I don't want it back." He hesitates. "You like it?"

Is there a hint of uncertainty in his voice, deep in those gorgeous eyes? Surely not. He's made millions off his work. He can't have an uncertain bone in his spectacular body.

I press my hand to my racing heart and pat it. "I love it." Unfortunately, my heart isn't the only thing in high gear. My stomach growls and not softly. In fact, it's loud. Very loud. I squeeze my eyes shut and feel my cheeks, once again, flush red.

A soft, sexy laugh slides from his lips. "Hungry?"

I dare to look at him and feign ignorance. "What gives you that idea?"

"Just a guess," he teases. "But since I'm starving, I was hoping you might be, too."

He gives me a hopeful smile that I feel clear to my toes. He's smiling at me but not laughing at me. I like this about him, the way he makes me ultra-aware of him, but somehow comfortable, too.

My stomach growls again, and I laugh. "Oh my gosh, I do believe I am hungry." I shake my head. "You have a way of finding all my weaknesses."

"If food's a weakness, then I have it, too. Do you like Mexican? Diego Maria's is a few blocks down the road. It's a hole-in-the-wall Mexican place, but it's good eating. I hang out on their patio and sketch some afternoons."

"Do they serve wine?" I ask.

"They're more of a beer and tequila kind of joint."

"Good, because I don't even want to see wine on a menu for the next hour."

"I take it Mark is still trying to force the wine thing down your throat?"

"If you mean, Mr. Compton, then yes."

He rolls his eyes. "Mr. Compton, my ass." He lifts his chin at me. "You in for Diego Maria's?"

I nod and smile, and he looks pleased, even relieved? No. That's silly. I shake off the ridiculous notion and try not to grin like a schoolgirl. I'm going to lunch with Chris Merit, and I'll have the chance to talk to him about his work. He heads to the table he'd been sitting at yesterday and hikes a backpack he's yet to unpack onto his shoulder. Relief washes over me. I did not want to find out he'd been watching me again and I hadn't been self-aware enough to know.

I quickly pack my red leather bag and am about to slide it onto my shoulder when he reaches for it. "I'll carry it for you."

My lips twitch. "I really think you should let me carry it. I fear the cute girly bag will blow your cool-artist-in-leather image. Besides, it's light. I'm good, but thank you."

With obvious reluctance, he drops his hand. "If you change your mind, I'll happily risk my cool-artist-in-leather image that I didn't know I had."

A smile slides easily to my lips. "And I'll have my phone camera ready if I do."

He chuckles, and the sound of that rough, masculine laughter does funny things to my chest and, well, pretty much my entire body.

We step outside, and the cool wind off the ocean screams a welcome and has me grateful my blouse is long-sleeved. I suppress a shiver for fear Chris will offer me his coat again, though the idea isn't an unpleasant one. I simply don't understand the dynamic between us and I'm not sure I can be clearheaded with anything that has been on this man's body touching mine.

We begin the short stroll to the restaurant, and I am intensely aware of how close he is, how big he is. I am so confused with this man. He makes every nerve ending I own buzz, and yet I am oddly comfortable with him. There is something beneath the surface I can't put my finger on, something that defies his easygoing exterior, and I burn to understand what it might be.

He cuts me a sideways look. "How's the gallery stack up to your schoolteaching so far?"

"I've become student instead of teacher, which was really the last thing I expected when I dove into this new adventure."

"That confident you know your art, are you?"

"Yes. I am. I know my art. I know my artists. Well, I thought I did. I had you pictured as your dad for some reason."

A smirk plays on his lips, and I get the feeling he's enjoying some secret joke. "Did you now?" he asks, and motions to the opening in the black steel-encased patio of the restaurant. "We can just grab a table out here, and they'll send someone to take our order."

Since it's midafternoon, there's no crowd, and we have a choice of all of the six tables inside the black steel. I head for the one against the railing so we can lean against it and view the Golden Gate Bridge along with miles and miles of beautiful blue water. It's a view I never get tired of enjoying, and as hard as it is in the compact city, I manage to avoid it far too often.

I settle into my seat, and the wind rushes over me, pulling a shiver from me before I can contain my reaction. I look up to find Chris standing above me. No. More like towering over me.

"You're cold." It's not a question.

"No," I assure him. "I love this view. I'm—" A gust of hard wind overtakes me, and there is simply no escaping the impact or the chattering of my teeth. "Okay." I hold my hands up in surrender. "I'm cold."

Surprising me, his hand gently wraps around one of my wrists and he pulls me to my feet. We are close, toe-to-toe, and

I cannot seem to breathe. In defiance of the chill of my skin, heat forms beneath his touch and begins to climb a path up my arm and over my chest. He stares down at me, and though his expression is impassable, I can feel the tension curling between us.

Hair blows into my eyes, and he releases my arm and tenderly brushes the hair from my eyes, his fingers lingering on my cheek. "Let's go in where it's warm." His voice is as gentle as his fingers sliding from my face.

He opens the door for me, and I enter, nervously avoiding eye contact, trying to will my heart to stop beating at an impossible pace. Soft Mexican music touches my ears, and I see no more than ten tables, only one of which is occupied.

He lifts his chin at the small, two-seater table inside a bay window. It is both out of the reach of the wind and, by my standards, intimate. "Looks like the best seat in the house to me. How about to you?"

I nod my approval. "As long as it comes with a few hot peppers to warm me up, I think it's perfect."

"A daring eater, are you?" he asks, as we head to our seat.

"Eating is the one thing I can say with certainty I do without a single inhibition."

He pulls out my chair for me and his eyes twinkle with evident mischief. "Eating is one of many things I do without inhibition."

My eyes go wide before I can stop them, and he laughs before adding, "Don't worry. I won't share the other things unless you ask nicely."

I sit before I dare to ask what things he's talking about,

surprised by how close I am to taking the bait. "Sounds like a question to ask over tequila, which would never work anyway. I'd be too tipsy to remember your answers."

He settles my briefcase, with my purse slipped inside, on the back of the chair and his fingers brush my arm. The silk is no barrier to the sweet friction of this man's touch. I suck in a breath at the impact, and my gaze is captured by his for several intense seconds.

"No tequila allowed then," he comments softly, before he moves to his seat and grabs a plastic menu from beside the napkin holder and hands it to me.

I eagerly accept it, looking over my options, my head spinning with this man's wild ride.

"If you're as daring an eater as you claim to be," he comments, "I highly recommended the chicken fajita tacos with fire sauce."

"I'll take that dare," I agree readily.

A fifty-something robust Hispanic waitress rushes to our table and greets Chris in Spanish, and even if I didn't have a basic handle on the language—as in barely even basic—the way her face lights up as she speaks to him tells me she is quite fond of Chris. It's also clear that Chris is not only equally as fond of her as she is him, but also that his Spanish reaches well beyond entry level.

The two of them chat a moment, and Chris shrugs out of his jacket. My gaze goes to his tattoo, and I cannot make it out completely because of his sleeve. I'm intrigued by the design and the rich colors. Is it . . . could it be . . . ? Yes. I think it's a dragon.

"Sara," Chris says, switching back to English and pulling my attention from the intricate design as he adds, "this is Maria of the restaurant name. Her son is Diego, the main chef."

Maria laughs, and it's a friendly, infectious laugh. I like her, and I like this place. "Chef?" she demands. "Ha. He's the cook. We don't need him getting fancy ideas. He'll let them go to his head and have us expanding across the country when I like it right here at home." She gives me a half bow. "And it's very nice to meet you, Sara."

"Nice to meet you as well, Maria."

Chris holds up the menu that matches the one I haven't looked at. "You in for the taco recommendation?"

I nod eagerly. "Sí, dame el fuego." Or "Yes, give me the fire." They both laugh.

"You speak Spanish, señora?" Maria asks hopefully.

"Badly," I assure her, and she grins.

"Come in often and we will change that."

"I'd like that," I say, and I mean it. I really do like this woman and I know it's because she's everyone's mother, just the way my mother had been.

"Corona for me, Maria," Chris orders, and glances at me. "You want one?"

"Oh no," I say quickly. "I'm a lightweight. I have to work." I glance at Maria. "Tea. No. Wait. I'm on a caffeine high I need to come down from. Make it water."

"The Corona will bring you right down," Chris suggests.

"From spilling things to falling over," I say. "You really don't know what a lightweight I am. I better not go there."

Maria rushes off to fill our order, and another man sets chips and salsa in front of us before filling our water glasses.

I'm eager to learn more about Chris, both as a man and an artist, and the instant we are alone I take advantage of the opportunity. "So you're trilingual? I assume you must speak French, to live part of the year in Paris."

"Je parle espagnol, français, italien, et j'aimerait beaucoup dessinez-vous à nouveau. Modele pour moi, Sara."

The French rolls off his tongue with such sexiness my throat goes dry and I feel tingly all over. "I have no idea what you just said."

"I said that I speak Spanish, French, and Italian." He leans closer, and his eyes find mine. "And then I said that I would very much like to paint you. Pose for me, Sara."

Eleven

Chris wants to sketch me again? No. Not sketch. He wants to paint me, and I think he means in his studio. I am stunned speechless. My throat is dry and my mouth will not form words. This silent reaction to stress I'm developing is new to me, but then, I'm always an extremist. Mute silence or ramblings at the speed of lightning, there really seems to be no in-between. Still without words, I blink at Chris, who is watching me intently, and I cannot read anything but expectation in his expression. He is waiting for a reply. Say something, I silently order myself. Say anything. No. Not anything. Something witty and charming.

Thankfully, I am saved from my mental scramble for the perfect reply when Chris's beer appears in front of him. A soft flow of air escapes my lips, as Chris launches into a conversation in Spanish with the man who now stands by our table. I grapple for what to say when we return to our topic of Chris painting me, but I am pulled into the conversation before I resolve my thoughts.

"Sara, meet Diego," Chris says, "the other half of Diego Maria's."

I try to focus on the conversation with Diego, who is about Chris's age and has a sleek goatee and warm brown eyes, but I am intensely aware of Chris's long fingers as he squeezes his lime into the beer. It's crazy to be so drawn to someone's hands, but of course, I remind myself, his hands are gifted in ways most could never be. I'm light-headed with his impact on me, not to mention a very real need to eat, so as the two men talk, I am content to mostly listen while I nibble on several yummy, warm salted chips with some salsa. Diego, it seems, is planning a trip to Paris and is seeking advice about where to stay and what to do, which Chris is graciously offering. I am taken aback by the way Chris, a famous millionaire artist, acts as if he isn't those things at all.

Our waiter, the real one, not Diego, appears with our food, and Diego excuses himself to allow us to be served. "Sorry about that," Chris says. "He's been off every time I've been by since I got back from Paris three weeks ago." He motions to my plate. "How's it look?"

I inhale the spicy aroma and my stomach cheers with joy. "It looks and smells absolutely divine."

He picks up his lime and motions to one on the side of my plate. "They aren't the same if you don't use this." He squeezes the juice onto his food.

"I've never put lime on my tacos, but I'm game to try."

I quickly follow his example, relieved we've turned our attention to food, not my posing for him.

"Before you dig in, I should warn you that hot means hot. Really hot. So if you aren't sure you can take it, then—"

I'm too hungry for caution. I pick up my taco and open my mouth, with my stomach cheering me on and welcoming substance.

"Wait—" he says, but it's too late for me to stop, even if I consider it an option, which I don't.

Fire shoots through my mouth and bites a path down my throat. I gasp and almost choke. Oh my God, I said bring the fire, but I didn't mean literally. I drop the taco and curl the fingers of one hand around the cloth napkin in my lap, while my other hand goes to my throat.

Chris shoves his beer at me, and I don't even hesitate. I grab it and gulp several long, cold swallows and still I can barely breathe. When the heat finally eases, I am breathing hard. "I should never have said bring the fire." I take another drink of his beer, the bitterness of the liquid somehow easing the burn. Sanity returns and I stare at the half-empty bottle and then at Chris. I drank his beer, right after I made a fool of myself, and all but choked. I shove the beer toward him. "Sorry. I forgot myself." Why do I keep embarrassing myself with this man?

He grins and slugs back a drink of the beer. My lips part and my fingers curl on both sides of the table as I watch the muscles of his throat bob. I am acutely aware of the intimacy of sharing his drink, of my mouth having been where his is now. He sets the nearly empty bottle down, his eyes locking with mine, the steam in his stare telling me I'm not alone in my thoughts.

"You really do have quite the knack for witnessing me embarrass myself," I manage in a voice raspy from the heat of the food, or maybe, simply because this man exists on planet Earth.

"I told you, I'd prefer it to be called a knack for rescuing you."

Rescuing me. Though this is the second time he's said this; it radiates through my body, deep into my soul, and something long suppressed within me stirs, then raises its ugly head. I don't need to be rescued. Do I? In that deep down spot the word rescue has touched, an old part of myself screams, Yes, yes, yes. You need to be rescued. You want to be rescued. You want to be taken care of. I straighten and twist my fingers together in my lap. Silently, I battle my inner self. No. No. No. I do not want to be rescued. I do not need to be rescued. Not anymore. Not for a long time now. Not ever again.

Chris lifts a hand toward the kitchen. "Diego," he calls out. "Can we get Sara an order minus the fire sauce?" They exchange comments in Spanish before Chris refocuses his attention on me. He studies me intently, and I can tell he's trying to read whatever emotion is stamped on my face. Good luck, I think, because I can't even read what I'm feeling myself.

"How's your mouth feeling?"

I wet my burning lips and his gaze follows, his expression darkening, and every nerve ending I own tingles in reply. "Fine," I comment, "but no thanks to you. You should have warned me how hot it was."

"I distinctly remember warning you."

"You should have tried harder. You knew I was starving."

"You say that past tense. Are you saying you're not any-more?"

"My tongue is raw and may never be the same, but actually, yes, I'm still starving."

"Me too," he says softly. "Ravenous, in fact."

My throat goes dry. Really dry. More dry than the other ten or so times he's caused such a reaction in me. There is a charge in the air, crackling all around us, to the point I almost think sparks must be evident. I can feel this man in every part of my body and he has not even touched me. I don't remember ever feeling this aware of a man in my life. I don't want this to be my imagination, but I'm not sure I am confident enough in myself to be with this man. I thought I was past all my self-doubt, but I'm not sure I am.

Desperate for a reprieve from whatever this thing between us is that threatens to consume me, I reach for a distraction. "You should eat before your food gets cold."

"Señora." Diego appears by my side and takes my plate. "Are you okay? Our fire is real fire." He casts Chris a disapprov-ing look. "I thought señor would have warned you."

Chris holds up his hands. "Hey, hey. I did warn her."

"After I took a bite," I counter, enjoying my opportunity to join in with Diego and give him a hard time. In some small way, it takes just a bit of the edge from my embarrassment.

"Before you took the bite," he corrects.

Diego says something in Spanish that sounds like frustration directed at Chris and then looks at me. "He should have told you before you took a bite. I am sorry, señora."

"Don't worry about me or keep apologizing," I plead. "Really. I'm more than fine, or I will be when you two men stop watching me like I'm about to go up in flames."

A waiter appears and sets a new plate in front of me before taking my old plate from Diego and disappearing with it.

"I had them include two sauces on the side for you to try," Diego explains. "The green is mild. The red is medium. Neither will burn your mouth."

I give him an appreciative nod. "Gracias, Diego. I should have tested the sauce before I took a big bite, but the food just looked and smelled so good I couldn't resist digging in."

His face colors with the compliment, but it doesn't stop him from mercilessly worrying over me a full extra minute before he rushes off. I am now left under the amused scrutiny of this brilliant, too sexy artist who hasn't eaten a bite because of me.

"Please eat," I urge him softly. "Your food is even colder now than before."

"Try your food first and make sure it's okay."

"Oh no," I scoff. "I'm not going to try it while you watch me do something else ridiculously clumsy."

Mischief dances across his features. "I like watching you. You spark my creative side."

My stomach flip-flops at the reference to the sketch. "You can't watch me and eat."

"I could argue that, but in the interest of getting you to eat, let's dig in together." The final word rasps with an underlying meaning, or maybe, I simply want it to.

"Fine," I agree. "Together."

His lips quirk and so do mine. Without breaking eye contact, we both reach for a taco and only look away when we each take a bite. This time, spicy, delicious flavors explode in my mouth, and I moan with pleasure. Either this is great food or I am too hungry to know better.

Chris swallows his mouthful of fire without so much as a blink and stares at me with a look that I can only call hungry. "I take it that's a sound of satisfaction?"

I find my own fire again, but this time it's in the form of blood flooding various inappropriate parts of my body considering our public location. "What can I say?" I manage. "The end of starvation is quite delicious." I use the spoon by my plate to taste the green sauce. "And so is that. I like it."

He holds out his beer to offer me another swallow, and I am all but certain he is purposely reminding me of our intimate act of sharing. I stare at the beer, remembering his mouth, where my mouth had been, before I force my gaze to his. "No. Thank you."

He considers me a moment, his expression unreadable, and then slowly lifts the bottle to his mouth and takes a deep swallow. Again, I watch the powerful muscles in his throat bob, feeling my muscles, the ones low in my belly, tighten. What is this man doing to me?

He lowers the beer, and I quickly, guiltily, reach for my taco and dig in. Chris does the same, and I begin thinking about all the questions I yearn to ask him. When does he paint? Where does he paint? What's his inspiration? His favorite brush? Questions I know he has heard a million times and probably doesn't want to answer, so I hold back.

"This is the perfect corner for watching people," he comments.

I follow his lead, searching beyond the glass to the activity on the street, thinking about how black-and-white I've let life become when I want to live it in color. We fall into a surprisingly comfortable silence, both of us watching the people scurry by on the street. A man and woman arm in arm. A woman struggling to get a little boy to put on his coat. Another woman who pulls her coat close to her and seems to be crying.

Chris turns a thoughtful inspection on me. "Everyone has a story. What's yours, Sara McMillan?"

The question takes me off guard, and I fight the answer that comes insistently to my mind. I have no story, not one I wish to claim. "I'm just a simple girl living out a summer dream of being around the art that I love."

"Tell me something I don't already know about you."

"I have not one single artistic bone in my body, so I have to live vicariously through you."

"Let me paint you and you can."

I scrape my teeth fretfully over my bottom lip. "I don't know."

"What's not to know?"

"It's intimidating to be painted by someone like you, Chris. Surely, you have to know that."

"I'm just a man with a paintbrush, Sara. Nothing more."

"You are not just a man with a paintbrush." And my gaze lowers, caressing a three-inch scar along his jawline I haven't noticed until now, and I wonder how it came to be. I wonder

122

who the man beneath the art really is. My eyes find his, search the green depths of the stare that has already seduced me ten times over. "What's your story, Chris?"

"My story is on the canvas, where I'd like you to be."

Why is he so insistent? "Can I . . . think about it?"

"As long as I can continue to try and talk you into it while you do."

I take the opportunity to ask a question I've been burning to know the answer to. "How long are you in town?"

"Until it doesn't feel right anymore."

"So you don't have set times of the year you're here and set times you're in Paris?"

"I go wherever I feel right at the time with one exception. Every October I'm in Paris to participate in the annual celebrity charity event at the Louvre."

"Where the Mona Lisa is on display." There is a wistful quality to my voice I don't even try to hide. I would die to see the Mona Lisa.

"Yes. Have you ever seen it?"

"I've never been out of the States, let alone a famous Paris museum. Actually, aside from my childhood home in Nevada, this is it for me."

"That's unacceptable. Life is too short and the world is too large and too full of the art you love not to see everything you can."

"Well, the nice thing about the art I love is its ability to allow the viewer to experience a piece of the world, or a story that can never be theirs, through someone else's eyes. I've certainly seen Paris through yours." I briefly think of the mural behind Mark's desk but shove aside the thought. I don't want to change the tone of the light conversation.

"Sounds like you're convincing yourself you don't need to travel when you want to travel."

Ouch. I almost flinch. Talk about hitting a nerve. First, about teaching instead of working in the art world, and now this. "Some of us are not rich and famous and able to soar around the world at will."

"Ouch," he says, repeating the word I'd only dared in my mind. "That hurt."

"Good, because pointing out that you can see the world and I cannot was insensitive, Mr. Rich and Famous Artist."

He wiggles a brow. "Who looks cool in leather."

"And that helps your case right now, how?"

"I can offer to show you around Paris."

I blink. Did he just suggest I go to Paris to see him? No. No. I'm reading too much into it. "Paris is a big order. I've decided to start my travel goals with New York City in the number one spot."

"For any specific reason?"

"Opportunity. Mark seems to think I'm Riptide material. That's why he's forcing me to learn wine, opera, and classical music."

His expression doesn't change but the charge in the air does, snapping tight with tension. "Mark told you that he's going to get you a job at Riptide?"

"Well, I guess he more alluded to it."

"Alluded how?"

"The general gist was that he sees bigger things for me than a summer on the gallery floor, but to achieve those things I need to be ready to interact with the type of clientele Riptide events attract." I frown to realize his finger is tapping on the table. "What? What is it?" My cell rings with horrible timing, and without taking my eyes off Chris, I dig it from my purse. I glance down and cringe at the sight of Mark's number before I look at Chris again. "It's . . ." My voice trails off. I don't think Mark's name will go over well right now. "I have to take it." I punch the ANSWER button and immediately hear Mark's voice.

"Have you quit your job without notice, Ms. McMillan?"

I cut my eyes to my plate, trying to hide from Chris my stress over the agitation crackling in my boss's question and willing my heart to stop racing. "I'm grabbing a late lunch. It was after two and I hadn't eaten all day."

"It's after three."

I bite my lips. Crap. How did I let time get away from me? "I'm headed back now."

"Now would be good, Ms. McMillan. Amanda needs to review details with you for Friday night's event. Call me when you get to the gallery."

"Yes. Of course, I—" The line goes dead. I glance up at Chris.

"That was Mark," he supplies.

I give an awkward nod. "I'm late back to work."

He grabs his wallet from his pocket and tosses a hundred-dollar bill on the table for what I estimate to be a forty-dollar ticket. He's sliding on his jacket, clearly ready to go, and I quickly reach for my purse to pay my half of the tab.

"Don't even think about it," he says, and his easygoing manner is nowhere in sight. My hand freezes on my wallet, and I open my mouth to argue but decide against it. He is edgy and . . . mad? Surely not. Why on earth would he be mad?

"Thank you." I slip my purse over my shoulder.

He pushes to his feet and motions to the door. I stand up and fit my briefcase strap over my shoulder with my purse. "You don't have to walk me back."

His eyes glint with a hardness that matches the set of his jaw. "I'm walking you back, Sara."

His tone is steely and almost as sharp as Mark's had been. Uncomfortably, I head to the exit, unsteady on my heels as he holds the door and I step outside. What's wrong with him? Why has he gone from fire to ice?

We begin our walk, faster this time, and the cold wind has nothing on the chill between us. Conversation is nonexistent, and I have no clue how to break the silence or if I should even try. I dare a peek at his profile several times, fighting the wind blowing hair over my eyes, but he doesn't acknowledge me. Why won't he look at me? Several times, I open my mouth to speak, but words simply won't leave my lips.

We are almost to the gallery, and a knot has formed in my stomach at the prospect of an awkward good-bye, when he suddenly grabs me and pulls me into a small enclave of a deserted office rental. Before I can fully grasp what is happening, I am against the wall, hidden from the street, and he is in front of me, enclosing me in the tiny space. I blink up into his burning stare, and I think I might combust. His scent, his warmth, his hard body, is all around me, but he is not touching me. I want him to touch me.

He presses his hand to the concrete wall above my head when I want it on my body. "You don't belong here, Sara."

The words are unexpected, a hard punch in the chest. "What? I don't understand."

"This job is wrong for you."

I shake my head. I don't belong? Coming from Chris, an established artist, I feel inferior, rejected. "You asked me why I wasn't following my heart. Why I wasn't pursuing what I love. I am. That's what I'm doing."

"I didn't think you'd do it in this place."

This place. I don't know what he's telling me. Does he mean this gallery? This city? Has he judged me not worthy of his inner circle?

"Look, Sara." He hesitates and lifts his head to the sky, seeming to struggle for words before fixing me with a turbulent look. "I'm trying to protect you here. This world you've strayed into is filled with dark, messed-up, arrogant assholes who will play with your mind and use you until there is nothing else left for you to recognize in yourself."

"Are you one of those dark, messed-up, arrogant assholes?"

He stares down at me, and I barely recognize the hard lines of his face, the glint in his eyes, as belonging to the man I've just had lunch with. His gaze sweeps my lips, lingers, and the swell of response and longing in me is instant, overwhelming. He reaches up and strokes his thumb over my bottom lip. Every nerve ending in my body responds and it's all I can do not to touch him, to grab his hand, but something holds me back. I am lost in this man, in his stare, in some spellbinding, dark whirlwind of . . . what? Lust, desire, torment? Seconds tick eternally and so does the silence. I want to hold him, to stop whatever I sense is coming, but I cannot.

"I'm worse." He pushes off the wall and is gone. He is gone. I am alone against the wall, aching with a fire that has nothing to do with the meal we shared. My lashes flutter, my fingers touch my lip where he touched me. He has warned me away from Mark, from the gallery, from him, and he has failed. I cannot turn away. I am here and I am going nowhere.

Twelve

～

Thursday, January 12, 2012

There are roses everywhere in my room, and I feel like a princess who's found her Prince Charming. Okay, so maybe he's not exactly my childhood version of Prince Charming, but life changes how you look at things. I just finished counting the vases again because I can't help myself. There are twelve of them, each holding a dozen beautiful, sweet-smelling buds. New buds soon to blossom. And the card. Imagine me sighing right now. The card is so perfect. I can't stop staring at the words. They are delicate and ready to bloom like you are, little one. Like me. I do feel the roses are like me. I do feel ready to bloom, ready to go wherever he leads me. He's hard sometimes, demanding, but he makes me feel protected. He makes me feel special. I think I'm ready to put aside my fear of the things he wants me to do with him and to take the next step. The idea of him being my "master" is incredibly arousing. He is so . . . powerful.

I know I've let fear hold me back. I'm not really sure what I'm afraid of. Unfamiliar feelings? What he will do to me if I grant him full control? He has kinky desires, and it's scary to think about taking part in those things. What if he binds me and does something to me I don't like? And why does the idea of being that submissive to him turn me on? That I could want that is a part of me I don't understand, but I know I can no longer run from me, any more than I can run from him. I need him. I need him so badly that the pain of potentially losing him is far worse than the pain he might inflict during our games. I can—

"I take it you're ready for our event tonight, Ms. McMillan?"

My heart lurches, and my gaze jerks from one of the first journal entries Rebecca ever penned—at least, that I have in my possession, to the doorway where Mark stands. Dressed in a pinstriped black suit, his sculpted body and broad shoulders consume the archway, just as he consumes the air around me. It's Friday evening and the first time I've seen him since he'd left town. I suspect my reaction to seeing him is vastly more potent for a variety of reasons. Chris's silence. Ella's continued lack of communication. Even Ava from the coffee shop, who teased me with gallery gossip, has been MIA. I'm swimming with sharks alone, which brings me back to my reaction to Mark's sudden appearance, the ultimate shark.

I'm more certain than ever that Mark is the man in the journals. The evidence is overwhelming. The roses and their connection to Mark's art collection. His dominant personality and the money Rebecca infers her lover possesses in many of her writings. "Master" has to be Mark, and it is all I can do not to blush as I remember the intimate acts I've read with him as her master.

No. It's not knowing this man is Master that rattles me. It's how well I relate to what Rebecca responded to in him. Her need to hand over everything to someone else, including her pleasure and, yes, her pain. To trust that much.

"Your silence is making me nervous, Ms. McMillan," Mark chides, and his voice deepens with demand. "Are you ready for tonight?"

Heat floods my cheeks as I realize I've simply been gaping at him. "Yes is the right answer, correct?" I inquire, unable to keep the apprehension from my voice, so no doubt, it shows on my face. I am beyond nervous about the tasting and fearful I will look foolish to the experts I will be interacting with.

"Yes is the right answer, Ms. McMillan, especially since the tasting begins in one hour."

I wet my lips, and his gaze follows the action, and unlike when Chris had done so, when I'd felt warm all over, Mark's attention is unsettling. "Yes then."

"You aren't convincing me."

Flattening my hands on my desk, I will myself to stand up for what I believe in, to claim control of me and not give it to him. I am not Rebecca. "Mark," I begin, and his brow quirks with irritation and forces me to quickly amend my choice of address. "Sorry. Mr. Compton. I have to be honest with you. I don't like to pretend to be an expert when I'm not. And I'm not." He has to recognize this. The man has haunted me with e-mails, phone calls, and computer testing for days on end, but he says nothing in reply. "I worry I could lose credibility when it comes to what I do know, which is art."

He studies me with an inscrutable mask on his too-handsome face, his jaw set in a hard line. I cannot read him, and time stretches eternally until finally he speaks. "Do you want me to let you in on a little secret, Ms. McMillan?"

The word secret conjures many things where Mark is concerned, but at this particular moment I cannot escape the thought of him spanking Rebecca in the storage room and clamping her nipples. Of him punishing her, of him wanting to punish me. I see myself in Rebecca's role, pressed against the wall, him against me, and it's not the first time. It's illogical because I don't want Mark, but I am spinning out of control, spiraling into some deep, dark cavern of something I don't understand.

"What secret?" I finally manage.

The sharpening of his gaze tells me he hasn't missed the far too drawn out pause before my question or the telling rasp to my voice. He is pleased with my reaction, and realization slaps me in the face. The journal is lying open on the desk. How did I not think of the possibility he might recognize it as Rebecca's, that he might know I'm reading about her, with him? I think ... I think he does know. I think he wants me to know.

"Ready for the secret, Sara?"

Sara. He called me Sara. Instinctively, I know this indicates no shift in our relationship. This is his way of telling me he can call me whatever he likes, while I must call him by his formal surname. He is reminding me he is the boss and I am subservient to him.

I swallow against the dryness in my throat, and nod. "Yes," I manage, and despite the one-word reply, I feel empowered with my voice. At least he has not rendered me mute. I am not this man's to control. But your dreams of working in this industry are, my subconscious reminds me, and resentment burns in me at the truth inside the unwelcome thought.

"I never expected you to be ready to talk to experts tonight like you are one yourself," Mark announces.

I blink in confusion. "I don't understand. You said I had to study and be ready for tonight."

"I challenged you to see what you are made of. If you hadn't given me a valiant effort to rise to said challenge, why should I consider you for more than a mere sales rep?"

Chris's reaction to Mark's dangling carrot, aka opportunity at Riptide, slides into my mind. Is Mark really planning to help me do more than local sales, or is he simply manipulating me? Is he . . . playing with my dreams? Or has Chris simply planted the idea in my head, and I'm making myself crazy because of him?

"You've done well this week," he continues. "Tonight you have my permission to confess your lack of knowledge to my customers. Simply allow them to teach you. They'll be eating out of your pretty little palm, and you'll, without question, please me with your stellar sales."

I can barely believe he's telling me to do exactly what Chris suggested days before. My emotions twist in knots. I'm not sure how to react, and I respond on autopilot, a soldier trying to please her new captain. "I'll . . . do my very best."

Satisfaction slides over his features. "I cannot wait, Ms. McMillan, to see what you are truly capable of." His lips twitch. "I have a feeling we'll be discussing your reward for a night well done, tomorrow."

"And if I fail?" I ask. "Will I be punished?" I have no idea where my boldness has come from, but the question is out without me thinking.

His eyes narrow on me. "Do you want to be punished?" His tone is low, gravelly, and rather than his being angry at the question, I read a sexual undercurrent in his reply. Or maybe I'm suffering delusions born of a combination of Chris's warnings and my obsession with the journals.

"No," I answer, and this time there is no hesitation in my response. "I do not wish to be punished."

"Then continue to please me, Sara," he comments softly, and there is a hint of both satisfaction and reprimand in his tone. I can see this moment foreshadowing another, where he will say, "You were warned. You know I have to punish you."

He shoves off the doorjamb he's been leaning against. "In case you've not been informed, as a precaution, limo and cab service will be provided for my staff and guests this evening. You'll need to leave your car key in the front desk."

"But how will I get my car tomorrow?"

"You can expense a cab." His silver eyes darken to a deep gray. "It's a small price to pay for safety. I take care of those under my protection, Ms. McMillan."

He leaves without another word.

· · ·

Forty-five minutes later I am on the main floor of the gallery, worrying over the exact alignment of napkins and forks on one of several tables set up in front of a large oval window overlooking the courtyard. The lighting above my head is dim, the music nonexistent until the doors open, when a violinist will perform.

Nearby, Mary, the main salesperson for the gallery and the one person from the staff who hasn't been overly friendly to me, as well as several of the interns, are chatting among themselves. They don't appear nervous or to possess the same desire as I do to stay busy. My nerves are jangling louder than one of the San Francisco trolley bells. Even without the pressure of being a wine expert, at least tonight, I've read between the lines with Mark. I'm living one big test I can't afford to fail. I glance at the girls again, all in sparkly cocktail numbers that make my basic black skirt and light blue silk blouse look out of place.

"You look like you're about to jump off the Golden Gate Bridge."

Ralph appears by my side, and I finish placing a final fork and turn to find his black bow tie from earlier in the day has been replaced with a red one.

"Compliments always help soothe my nerves," I say sardonically, but then I love the man's wit and honesty. "I thought you stayed behind your desk?"

"If the bossman wants to fill me with expensive drink and pay for my ride home, who am I to argue? You'll learn to love these events. A little alcohol and people open their wallets and it puts the beast in a good mood." He studies me intently. "Now. Talk to me. What's got you so worked up?"

I straighten his bow tie purposely. "It appears I didn't get the memo on the spiffy evening dress code."

His gaze flicks several feet away to where Mary is in animated conversation with Mark, before returning his attention to me. "She's in charge of preparing the staff since Rebecca disappeared."

"Disappeared?" I ask, alarmed.

"Mary thought Rebecca's leaving was her chance to grab the bossman's attention, and it's been a big fail for her." He shrugs. "She's bitter and doesn't want competition." He points at me. "That's you, honey."

"Are you saying she has a crush on Mark or she wants the top spot at the gallery?"

"She has a crush on him, his money, and the job. Mark barely gives her the time of day, while Rebecca was a star who helped him with Riptide."

Disappointment tightens my chest. No matter how I frame my duties, I am simply a fill-in for the summer. "Why Rebecca and not Mary for Riptide?" Why me and not Mary? "I get the impression Mary does well on the sales floor."

"Salespeople are a dime-a-dozen, easily replaced by a herd of interns dying to be in this business and willing to work for pennies. Mary fits that bill in Mark's eyes." He presses a finger to his chin and considers me. "You, though, are different. Mark sees something in you." His lips twist. "Mary knows it, too. I do believe she's ready to stomp on you like a cigarette."

My eyes go wide. "Stomp on me like a cigarette?" I ask, concerned for myself, but more so for Rebecca.

He rolls his eyes. "Has anyone ever told you you're melo-dramatic today?"

"No," I say, but then I've never been living someone else's life. "Has anyone ever told you you're melodramatic?"

He winks. "All the time. And to put your mind at ease, the harshest thing Mary has in her is messing with your un-derstanding of the evening's dress code. At heart, she's nothing more than a submissive little pet."

"And what am I?" I ask, thinking a pet seems right up Mark's alley. A submissive pet, at that.

"A daring, gorgeous butterfly," he comments, fluttering his fingers in the air.

"I'm no butterfly," I say, laughing at his silly imitation. "And since when are butterflies daring?"

A waiter walks by with a tray of wine on a direct path to a line of servers who are waiting by the door in preparation for opening, and Ralph grabs two glasses from him. "Since you," he replies, and thrusts a drink into my hand. "Gulp that down. You're wound too tight tonight. You need to ease up."

My skin prickles with awareness and my gaze shoots to Mark, and I am instantly far more deer-in-headlights than daring but-terfly. He eyes the glass I'm holding with an arched brow before his mouth quirks at the corners, and he nods his approval. His approval. I have pleased him. I will not be punished. I am appalled this is the direction my thoughts have gone and at the certainty I feel that he knows my reaction, and enjoys this control over me.

Ralph whistles low. "You have that man by the balls like very few do, honey."

I blanch. "That's crazy. I do not have him by his . . . no. I—"

"Doors are opening!" Amanda calls out to the room from the hostess desk. I down my wine and shove my empty glass at Ralph.

An hour later, I am standing with a sixty-something gentleman whose résumé includes being the ex-CEO of a rather large bank, and chatting with him about the Ricco Alvarez show, which he'd also attended. The room is swimming with at least fifty people, among them waiters who are wading through the pool of fancy dresses, expensive suits, and big pocketbooks, with selections of wine. I've sold two pricy paintings, neither of which were Chris's, most likely because I'm avoiding his display for reasons I'm trying not to think about.

I'm also buzzing from several wine samples I've consumed, which has made me form a new respect for Mark's insistence everyone leave their keys in the desk up front.

"So, dear," Mr. Rider, the ex-CEO continues, "I'm interested in an Alvarez painting, but I'm not certain I see the exact piece I want here on the showroom floor. Is there a way to arrange a private viewing of his more precious pieces?"

"I most certainly will see what I can arrange," I assure him, though I have no clue what I can, or cannot, do. "I'm sure you know the gallery's resources are many."

"And you, Ms. McMillan, certainly are their newest asset." He retrieves a business card from his pocket. "Call me Monday, my dear."

I beam at his departing form and with the prospect of viewing Alvarez's private collection along with him.

"I take it your smile means that went well?"

The familiar male voice radiates through me, and I can almost feel my body quiver from inside out. I whirl around to find Chris standing behind me, a rebel in denim and leather among black ties, and his surprise appearance does far more to impact me than Mark's had. Every muscle I own tightens deliciously at the sight of him, and I'm not the only one to react to his ruggedly handsome good looks. Two women walk by, their eyes raking over Chris with admiration, their heads tilting together to exchange comments.

"What are you doing here?" I ask, and, yes, there is accusation in my voice. I am illogically angry with Chris, and I cannot seem to figure out why. Oh, wait. He told me I didn't belong here and yet he still manages to make me hope he'd show up all week long.

His eyes meet mine and hold, and if he notices my temper, he doesn't show it. "I came to lend you moral support."

"Why would you want to support me?" I challenge, fighting the thrill inside me at the idea he came here for me. "You said—"

"I know what I said." He steps closer to me, his fingers curling on my elbow, his touch unexpected, electric. My body hums in reply, and I fight the seductive lethargy threatening to consume both my anger, and my capacity for logic. He told me to leave. He told me I don't belong.

My anger sparks all over again. "You said—"

"Believe me, I know what I said, and I was trying to protect you." His voice soft and rough at the same time, sandpaper with a silk caress I feel from head to toe.

My stomach knots, and I shove aside a blast of uncomfortable emotions his words evoke within me. I am too aware of his touch to fully process what I feel. My voice softens to a whisper. "You don't even know me."

His eyes darken, the dim light catching on the gold specks in their depths. "What if I said I want to change that?"

His words are everything I don't expect, and deep down, everything I had hoped for. I am shocked and pleased and in disbelief. More so, I am confused. The crowd, the swell of voices, and clinking glasses fall away with that question. I am staring up at him, and his eyes hold me captive. No, he holds me captive, this man, this artist, this stranger, who says he wants to know me. And I want to know him. I just plain want where he is concerned.

"You do know this is a black-tie event, correct?"

Mark's voice is a splash of ice water. I jerk around to find the sharp glint in his silvery gaze fixed on Chris and Chris alone. Power and supreme agitation radiate off my boss, while Chris appears completely unaffected or, perhaps, pleased at Mark's disdain,

Chris faces Mark, his hands out to his sides. "Artistic expression. Isn't that what you like about me?"

Mark's lips press into a thin line. "I prefer your expression to be contained on the canvas."

"Or in your bank account," Chris muses, and while his tone speaks of jest, there is a sharp undercurrent to his words that match Mark's steely stare.

"Excuse me." A forty-something female and her husband that I recognize from an earlier, rather unfriendly chat, interrupts us and their intense interest in Chris is evident. The woman is practically giddy with excitement. "Are you Chris

Merit?" she asks, and good Lord, she sounds breathless, when only fifteen minutes before she'd been pretentious and borderline rude to me.

Chris's eyes hold Mark's for several crackling seconds that the couple seems to be oblivious to, before Chris turns his attention to his admirers.

"I've been known to answer to that name," he replies, offering them one of the charming smiles that I've learned pack a real punch.

"Oh my God," the woman gushes, whisking a lock of red hair from her eyes and shoving her hand at Chris. "I love your work."

Avoiding Mark's gaze, feeling somehow as if I will be blamed for, well, something, I watch how Chris interacts with the couple. Eventually the husband wrangles Chris's hand from his wife's, to shake it himself, before he turns to do the same with Mark. "You really do know how to surprise your guests in all the right ways, don't you, Mr. Compton? You certainly have earned our business tonight."

Chris's eyes meet Mark's, and even in profile, I can tell Chris is barely containing a smile. "I was more than happy to attend," Chris comments, "but I did have one condition to being here." The couple hangs anxiously on Chris's words, and though Mark shows no reaction, I'm pretty sure he is, too. "I'm supposed to have a Corona beer waiting for me." He shrugs out of his leather jacket, a statement to Mark that he is staying, I believe, and a waiter quickly takes it. "Mark knows I like my beer."

The couple erupts into laughter I don't dare indulge in and turn expectant gazes on Mark. I wonder which is worse for

Mark—the use of his first name, or the request for a beer. "Oh, please," the woman pleads, "bring us a Corona, too. What fun to tell our friends we had a beer at a wine tasting with Chris Merit."

"Unfortunately," Mark replies, proving he can roll with the proverbial punches, "the beer didn't arrive as expected." He waves at a waiter who rushes over. "But I can certainly supply wine."

Chris doesn't push for the beer I doubt he really wanted, and soon we all lift our glasses in a toast. "To the painting I'm going to leave with by Chris Merit," the wife declares.

"I can't believe you asked for beer," I whisper when he takes my glass.

His eyes twinkle with mischief. "Believe it, baby. I'm a rebel with a cause." He hands off our glasses to a waiter.

"And what's the cause?" I ask, while Mark and the couple continue to chat.

"Right now," he replies. "You."

My lips part in surprise, but there is no time for a real re-action. The fuss has garnered attention, and suddenly we are surrounded by people who want to meet Chris. Graciously, he chats with the various customers, and I am both surprised and pleased as he introduces me to each.

A good hour passes, and Chris is as attentive to me as he is the visitors. At this point, he's doing all the selling, but the wine tastings have continued. The longer the event continues, the more I think I need to learn how to avoid drinking at events like this one. I am unsteady and in need of food.

Mark joins the small group we are talking with, and Chris hones in on him. "You got a minute?"

Mark inclines his head. "Anything for the artist of the night." And while the statement is true—Chris is the "artist of the night"—his tone drips saccharine.

Mark turns and walks away, and I expect Chris to follow. Instead, he slides his fingers through mine and pulls me with him.

Thirteen

I am all too aware of Chris's hand intimately twined with mine as we pursue Mark, or rather, as he drags me along for the ride. There is a possessiveness to his touch, and I have the sense I am a token in these two men's "whose dick is bigger?" contest, and now I am the one who is not pleased. In fact, I'm freaking out, and my heart is about to explode from my chest.

"What are you doing?" I demand, gently tugging on Chris's hand.

Still walking, he cuts me a sideways look. "What I came here to do. Protecting you."

I gape at this ridiculous notion. What is it with him and this "protection" hang-up? I contain the urge to jerk hard against him and demand he stop and explain himself, simply because we are in public. My mind races in search of a more discreet plan of escape before I end up trapped in one of the offices in the middle of their obvious war.

Mark surprises me and halts in the center of the gallery, away from the fifteen or so guests still mingling among themselves, where low voices mean discretion. Chris stops with him, and I don't have an option but to do the same since my fingers remain tightly tucked inside of his.

"I came here tonight to support Sara," Chris announces without preamble. "I expect her to get the commission off my sales."

What? I scream in my head. Oh my God. This can't be happening.

"Ms. McMillan and I will discuss her compensation between ourselves," Mark replies, and his tone is icy, his refusal to look at me damning. My heart sinks to my feet. I am as good as fired.

"That's fine," Chris states, "as long as the outcome of your conversation includes her getting twenty-five percent of my sales for tonight."

My stomach knots at both the ridiculously high figure and the demand Chris has made. Dread fills me as I realize what this must be about. Chris wanted me out of here. He told me to leave. I didn't listen, so he's forcing me out. Why? Why does this matter to him?

Mark's eyes flash with ice and settle on my face, and I am certain he is either going to fire me here and now, or he's planning my dismissal for the near future. Instead, he shocks me with a curt, "Twenty-five percent, Ms. McMillan. But be clear, future rewards will be negotiated between you and me or not at all. Understood?"

I blink at him, speechless, but still manage to calculate

twenty-five percent of the roughly three hundred grand Chris has sold tonight. Surely Mark has not just agreed to pay me fifty thousand dollars.

"Ms. McMillan," he snaps. "Are we clear?"

"Yes," I rasp. "Yes. I . . . of course. Understood."

Mark's gaze shifts back to Chris. "If there's nothing else, I have customers to attend and so does Ms. McMillan." He doesn't wait to find out if there is anything else. He turns on his heel and departs, leaving me reeling with the impact of what has happened. My adrenaline surges through me, anger curling in my stomach and chest.

Whirling on Chris, I barely muster the will to keep my voice low, and it's all I can do to remember the customers who might be watching. "What have you done?" The question comes out a hiss, and I jerk my hand back with as much discretion as I can muster, considering I'm shaking, but he holds it still.

"Made sure you're no one's captive."

"By getting me fired?" I tug on my hand again. "Let go, Chris."

"You aren't going to get fired, Sara."

"Let go of my hand," I ground out between my teeth.

He clamps his lips together, and with obvious reluctance, he releases me. "You aren't going to get—"

I walk away, cutting to my left, toward the hallway opposite the office leading to the fancy guest bathrooms, afraid I'm going to do the completely unacceptable and cry in public. I'm not a crier. I've never been a crier, but this is my dream Chris has destroyed. I thought I could be here, belong here. That a famous, gorgeous artist wanted me, when he was really just trying to destroy me. I am embarrassed and hurt. I hurt. This hurts. Chris hurt me.

Rounding the corner, I enter the hallway, and Chris is suddenly there in the narrow passage with me, pressing me against the wall, his powerful thighs framing mine.

My hand goes instinctively to his T-shirt–clad chest. I am immediately aware of the intimacy of the touch, of my body's reaction to the man who has betrayed me. "Don't shove me against another wall and try to intimidate me, Chris."

"I'm not trying to intimidate you. I was protecting you, Sara." His hands move to my waist, scorching me, and my reaction to the sizzling touch is instant. I cover his hands with mine, trying to control what he does next, but it doesn't help. Now, my hands are on his hands and his hands are on my body.

"Call it what you want," I ground out, "but you had no right to do what you did."

"He had to know he couldn't manipulate your dream. Money, and my many resources at your disposal, does that."

His words knock my anger and my breath away, and confusion consumes me. His actions and his words conflict at every turn. "Why would you help me? You said I don't belong in this world."

"Because I won't watch him gobble you up and destroy you."

I remember his words and understand now that he wanted me out of this gallery, not this profession. "Because he's a dark, messed-up, arrogant asshole who will play with my mind and use me until there is nothing else left of me I recognize."

"That's right."

"And yet you say you're worse."

He stiffens and cuts his gaze, seeming to struggle before fixing me in a turbulent stare. "I am, Sara, which is why you should run as far away from me as you can. And I should step back and let you."

"Then why aren't you?" I whisper.

His eyes hold mine, and what I see there, the depth of his desire, overwhelms me. He flattens his palm on my belly and I tremble beneath the touch, and he has to feel it, too. "Because"—his voice low, seductive, his hand traveling up the center of my body—"I can't stop thinking about you, and everything I want to do to you, everywhere I want to touch you."

His hand presses to the swell between my breasts, and my nipples ache with a wish he would touch them. His boldness ignites something sultry and dark inside me, a side of me that defies the good-girl schoolteacher who is appalled I haven't stopped this. I want him. I want him here and now, and any way I can have him.

And when his gaze lowers to my mouth and lingers, I know he is thinking about kissing me, and I have never wanted to be kissed so badly in my life.

"Do you taste as good as I think you do?" he asks, but he doesn't wait for my reply.

Suddenly, his fingers have tunneled into my hair and he's dragging my mouth to his. I am all soft submission, yielding to the moment, to the man. I melt into him, welcome the hardness of his body pressed to mine. And when his tongue presses past my lips, a long, wicked caress, I taste his hunger, his need. There is possessiveness to his kiss, to his hand on my back, molding me closer. I am lost in the ache that has become my need for this man, this stranger I cannot resist. He says he's protecting me; he says he's dangerous. I am conflicted, and sure I should be angry with him, but I am completely incapable and unable of processing why.

Remotely, I register voices sounding somewhere nearby, and some tiny part of my mind is aware we could be caught, but I am too lost to care. I do not want to stop kissing him and I am panting when Chris tears his mouth from mine and presses his lips to my ear. He gently strokes my hair, his breath warm on my neck. "Go the bathroom, baby, before someone sees us."

The endearment does funny things to my chest.

He turns me to the door, his hands on my waist, his body framing me from behind, and I can feel him hot and hard against my backside. It is all I can do not to lean into him. He kisses my neck. "I don't mind who knows what we are doing, but I don't want you embarrassed."

The voices grow louder, high heels clicking on the tiled floor. Reality blasts through me, and I dart for the bathroom door without looking back at Chris.

I rush into a bathroom stall, forced to hide until the ladies who have followed me inside the bathroom depart. Sitting on top of the toilet seat, I know I should be reprimanding myself over my wanton behavior, and worrying about my job. Instead, I squeeze my thighs together, all too aware of the dampness clinging to my panties, and replay every stroke of Chris's tongue against

mine. It is a testament to how affected I am by Chris. I am protecting you, he'd said. What he'd done was more like claiming.
His hand on mine with Mark, his demand I be taken care of.
His following me to the bathroom entrance and pushing me
against the wall. His mouth on my mouth.

A full five minutes passes, and the women chatter among
themselves and finally leave. I exit the stall and stare into the
mirror, barely recognizing the woman in the reflection. My hair
is a wild, dark brown mass and my lips are swollen. My eyes are
dark with unfulfilled desire.

High heels sounds outside the door, and my heart leaps
with the inevitable newcomer. I haven't had time to process
what to do about Chris, how to act when I exit the bathroom,
but I don't want unwanted scrutiny, either. I smooth my hair
and dart for the door, and I am shocked at who stands on the
other side.

"Ava." I blink.

"Sara!" she exclaims, and I join her in the hallway, only to
be pulled into a hug as she announces, "I was hoping I'd get
here in time to see you."

I scan over her shoulder, seeking out Chris, but he is nowhere visible. His absence gnaws at my gut, but I tell myself he's
still here. He's being discreet.

Ava releases me, and I step back, noting how her long, silky
black hair is styled with ringlets around her face, and she is
wearing a red siren dress. "You look terrific."

"Thank you. I love the excuse the gallery gives me to dress
up, but I barely made it. I flew in today."

"Oh? Where'd you go?"

Her lips curve with mischief. "A little last-minute romantic getaway. It was fabulous. Listen, I don't want to get Mark mad at you. I know you have to work the floor, but how about lunch on Monday?"

Mark. She'd called him Mark when no one else did. "I'd love that," I say, and remind myself she isn't an employee of the gallery, so why would she use his formal name?

A few minutes later, we've arranged a meeting spot, and I head to the gallery floor. Nervously, I look for Chris and don't see him. Mary is helping a customer, and Amanda and the rest of the crew seem to be hanging out at the front door, bidding customers good-night. I quickly check in with the few lingering guests and try not to let my mind go wild over Chris. But it is. He's gone. He used me to piss Mark off, kissed me, and then left. I am hurt, and, yes, I am angry all over again. My final customer is all about sampling wine, and this time, I dive right in. I'm going to be fired. I've been used and abused and turned on in a hallway I shouldn't have been doing naughty things in. I have a free ride home. I'm going to drink some damn wine.

By the time the final guests are gone, and I've gathered my jacket and purse, the staff is gathering for a cab line at the door. At this point, my head is buzzing and I feel a little queasy. I don't want to talk to anyone, and I sure as heck don't want to see Chris or Mark. Not that seeing Chris appears to be an option, but Mark is unavoidable since he's standing by the door, having what looks like a tense conversation with Ava—or the wine is distorting my impressions, which is quite possible— and the two of them are having a happy chat. Nah. Mark isn't the happy-chat kind of guy. More the whips-and-chains, and "pleasure me, baby," kind of guy. Oh boy, the wine has worked me over good and my mind is running a marathon of ridiculousness. Empowered by wine, and feeling quite the daring butterfly, I decide it's time to go home, and to do so with answers.

Unsteady, but with nothing to lose that I haven't already lost, I walk right up to Mark. He glances at Ava, a silent command in his look, and even she obeys him, waving to me as she departs. The world does what this man wants. Well, the world minus Chris.

"Am I fired?" I demand, fairly certain no one else is around, which on a nonwine night wouldn't be good enough. It works just fine for me now, though.

He crosses his arms over his broad chest and studies me with—what?—Interest? Irritation? The man is impossible to read. "Why would you be fired, Ms. McMillan?"

"Because of Chris."

"Chris made us both a lot of money tonight. Making money is not a terminating offense. Now, using Chris to manipulate me for money would be, but you wouldn't do that, now would you?"

"No," I say, and dare to go where I would normally never go, but then nothing is normal about the past few days. "And I don't want to be a part of the 'who's got the bigger sword?' contest you two have going on, either. I don't do cockfights. I just want to do my job and do it well."

He chuckles, and I think it's the first time I've heard him laugh. I'm not sure how I feel about my wine-induced braveness sparking amusement in a man so difficult to amuse.

"Smart decision, Ms. McMillan. Once you've slept off

the wine, I suggest you begin studying again. I'll test you on Monday."

I open my mouth to protest, and he arches his brow. It's a testament to his natural-born authority that I've already come to know that arched brow as a warning. "I'll be ready," I state, and with a little rebel left in me, I don't bother with "goodnight." I head for the door.

"Ms. McMillan."

I stop at Mark's command and glance over my shoulder, fearful my escape isn't as imminent as I'd hoped.

"Pain meds and a bottle of water before you sleep," he orders.

My boss is dictating my preventive hangover care, and I've just used the word swords in reference to his obvious cockfight with the man I just made out with in a public hallway. I am truly in an alternate universe.

"Yes, sir, Mr. Compton," I say, and continue on my way.

I step into a starlit, chilly night and find Ralph and several of the interns are loading up in a cab. I hold my breath, hoping I won't be noticed. Now that I'm staying at the gallery, my decision to drink too much jeopardizes the professional image I value. The door shuts behind Ralph, and I sigh in relief, but a sudden awareness turns my attention to my left.

My breath hitches as I find Chris, now wearing his leather jacket again, and leaning on a fancy black sports car I know is a Porsche 911. I know it's a 911 because, in an ironic twist, my father will drive nothing else. Chris makes the Porsche look sexy in a way I didn't think was possible. Not with my history with this car.

His lips curve, and his gaze burns a path up and down my body, and there is no question he's here for me. He'd come here tonight for me, he'd claimed, but he and Mark clearly have a power play going on, and I became a token in that game tonight.

I start walking toward him, trying my best to appear steady on my feet. Why I thought wine was a good idea, when I never drink, is beyond me. He is watching my every step, and his stare is a hot caress stroking my entire body. I remember his hands touching me, his mouth on my mouth, and sensation builds low in my belly and tingles down my thighs. I want him. He knows it, too, but I've been played with enough for one night. No, I amend. Enough for a lifetime.

"You left," I accuse as I stop in front of him, the wind blessing me with a rush of his clean, male scent and adding to my wobbling legs. I sway toward Chris, and his hand settles on my waist, my hip and leg pressing to his. Our eyes lock, and the instant charge between us all but sets sparks to the air. I am lost. So much for the bravado of being played with too much.

"I'm here now," he says softly, and there is a slight splay of his fingers on my waist.

I should push away from him, but I want to touch him instead. I curl my hand on top of my purse to control myself, the sting of him disappearing still present. "I thought you'd left."

"I didn't think you'd want to ride on the bike with your skirt on."

"We didn't talk about me riding with you. We didn't talk about anything."

"I planned to convince you, and I would have been back

long ago, but in my eagerness to return, I had a run-in with a police officer who didn't like my speed. He wasn't forgiving, but I'm hoping you will be."

My anger evaporates instantly. Not only did he go after a car for me, but he also managed to get a ticket in the process. A wave of dizziness washes over me, and I press my hand to my forehead. "Considering how I feel, I think I should thank you for trading in the bike." I drop my hand and it ends up on his chest, and his heart thunders beneath my touch. Because of my touch? Do I affect this man as he does me?

My gaze lifts, and the smoldering look on his face tells me I am right. I affect him as he does me. This cool, confident famous artist is reacting to me. "I'm guessing you now realize I drank a little extra wine after you left?"

"I kind of got that idea." He pushes off the car, his arm wrapping around my waist to steady me, and I am aware of every hard inch of him next to me. "Why don't we go get you some food? I know a great pizza joint, if you like pizza."

I'm relieved at the simplicity of pizza. "No fancy menu. No wine list. I'm sold."

"Then pizza it is," he agrees, and unlocks the door.

Once I'm folded into the soft leather of the passenger's seat of the car, Chris surprises me by squatting down beside me. His hand settles on top of my leg. "The belt can be tricky sometimes." He leans over me to pull it across my lap, his body intimately brushing mine, before he latches me into place. We stare at each other, the shadows dancing across our features. "We wouldn't want you to get hurt."

No, but I think he will hurt me, and I remember him

warning me away from him. I think he believes he will hurt me, too, but there is a current between us, an understanding of a line we've crossed, of it being too late to turn back.

His fingers brush my cheek as he pushes to his feet and shuts me inside the car, the darkness consuming me. I lean back into the plush leather, willing my head and stomach not to ruin this night.

Chris slides beside me into the car, and I glance at his profile and I wonder what he thinks of me and my wine fest. "This isn't like me. I never overindulge."

"Never say never, baby," Chris replies, and then turns the key, bringing the soft purr of an expensive engine to life.

I absorb those words, staring out of the window without really looking. Rebecca had done things she'd sworn she'd never do for her master. I wonder if I could talk to her now, would she agree with Chris? Would she say never say never?

Fourteen

Chris maneuvers the 911 into the drive of a fancy high-rise building not more than four blocks from the gallery. Before I can question the fancy location being home to a pizza joint, as he'd called it, a valet is already opening my door.

"I'll come around to get you," Chris says with a touch on my arm. He doesn't wait for a reply, climbing out of the vehicle and disappearing from full view.

I am both charmed and embarrassed at the prospect he believes the extra wine has made me a helpless lush. Worse, it wouldn't be an assumption completely without merit, and this night is exactly why I never let myself lose control. It always backfires.

I unsnap the seat belt about the same moment Chris appears at my door. Holding my skirt down, I slide my legs to the ground, all too aware of his scorching gaze on my legs.

His hand appears in front of me, and I hold my breath,

preparing for the impact of his touch, as I press my palm to his. He pulls me to my feet, onto the sidewalk beneath an awning, his hand settling possessively on my hip. The rich sensation of desire spreads through my limbs. I have never in my life reacted to a man this intensely.

Behind me, I hear the car door shut, and the engine rev, before the 911 pulls away. "This doesn't look like a place that serves pizza," I comment, but I am not looking at the building. It is Chris who has my full attention.

"Two blocks down," he explains. "We can walk there if you want, or we can go upstairs to my apartment."

Chris lives here, at least when he's in the States. The implications of our location are clear.

His long fingers curl around my neck, under my hair, and he lowers his mouth to my ear. "Be warned, Sara. I'm no saint. If I take you upstairs, I'm going to strip you naked and fuck you the way I've wanted to since the moment we first met."

The shockingly bold words ripple through me, and I am instantly aroused, squeezing my thighs together. He has wanted to fuck me since we first met. I want him to fuck me. I want to fuck him. Yes. Fuck. I want to give myself permission to forget good, proper behavior and fuck and be fucked. Wild, hot, uncontrollable passion, with no worries during and regrets in the aftermath. I've never let myself feel those things. When in my life have I ever experienced such a thing? When has any man ever made me think I could?

I press against his chest and lean back, my eyes seeking his. "If you're trying to scare me off, it's not working."

"Not yet," he says, dark certainty to his tone, to the lines etched in his handsome face. It is as if this is simply a seed already planted that cannot be stopped.

"Not at all," I counter.

He doesn't immediately respond, and his expression is a mask of hard lines, his jaw set, tense. Slowly, his fingers slide from my neck to caress a path down my arm until his fingers lace intimately with mine. "Never say never, Sara," he murmurs, and starts walking, pulling me with him.

Anticipation sizzles through me as we walk toward the automatic doors to be greeted by a man in a dark suit with an earpiece and buzz cut.

"Evening, Mr. Merit," he says, and glances at me. "Evening, miss."

"Evening, Jacob," Chris replies. "Pizza coming our way. Don't frisk the delivery guy."

"Not unless he's a delivery woman, sir," Jacob comments, and I get the sense these two are familiar beyond the casual exchange.

I lift a tentative hand at Jacob. "Hi."

"Ma'am," he replies, and there is a slight shift in his gaze I'm certain he doesn't intend for me to notice, but I do. I read it as surprise at my presence, and I can only assume I am far from Chris's normal choice in women. It isn't hard for me to imagine Chris being a blond bombshell kind of man, and where I hadn't felt insecure moments before, I suddenly do now. I am angry at myself for feeling such a thing when I've promised myself no more self-doubt. When I crave the escape, the freedom, I was so close to experiencing only moments before.

The elevator is right off the fancy lobby and past a security booth. Chris punches the button, and the doors open immediately. I follow him inside and watch as he keys in a code. The doors shut, and he pulls me hard against him.

My hands settle on his hard chest, inside the line of his jacket, and warmth spreads through me. "What just happened?" His hand brands my hip.

My breasts are heavy, my nipples aching. "I don't know what you mean,"

"Yes. You do. Second thoughts, Sara?"

I scold myself for being so transparent. "Do you want me to have second thoughts?"

"No. What I want is to take you to my apartment and make you come and then do it all over again."

Oh . . . yes, please. "Okay," I whisper, "but I think you should feed me first."

His lips curve into a smile, his eyes dancing with gold specks of pure fire. "Then you can feed me."

The bell dings, and the doors begin to open. Chris wastes no time pulling me to the edge of the elevator, and I watch in surprise as a gorgeous living room appears before me, rather than a hallway. Chris has a private elevator, and I am entering his private world, a world very unlike my own.

Chris releases my hand, our eyes lock, and I read the silent message in his. Enter by choice, without pressure. On some level I sense that once I enter his apartment, the decision to do so is going to change me. He is going to change me in some profound way I cannot begin to comprehend fully. I think he might know this, and I wonder why he would be so certain, what is etched with such clarity to him beneath the surface.

He has misplaced doubts of me in this moment, as he'd doubted me at the gallery. I can see it in his eyes, sense it in the air. I refuse to allow his lack of confidence in me, or anyone else's for that matter, to dictate what I can or cannot do ever again. I've been there, and I ended up on the sharp edge of a cliff, about to crash and burn. I'd recovered, and I am beginning to see that locking myself in a shell of an existence isn't healing. It's hiding. Regardless of what happens at the gallery, I'm done hiding.

My chin lifts, and I cut my gaze from Chris's and exit the elevator.

My heels touch the pale perfection of glossy hardwood floors, and I stop and stare at the breathtaking sight before me. Beyond the expensive leather furniture adorning a sunken living room with a massive fireplace in the left corner is a spectacular sight. There is a floor-to-ceiling window, a live pictorial of our city, spanning the entire length of the room.

Spellbound, I walk forward, enchanted by the twinkling night lights and the haze surrounding the distant Golden Gate Bridge. I barely remember going down the few steps to the living area, or what the furniture I pass looks like. I drop my purse on the coffee table and stop at the window, resting my hands on the cool surface.

We are above the city, untouchable, in a palace in the sky. How amazing it must be to live here and wake up to this view every day. Lights twinkling, almost as if they are talking to one another, laughing at me as they creep open a door to the hollow place inside me I've rejected only moments before in the elevator.

I swallow hard as the song "Broken" from the band Life-house fills the room, because Chris doesn't know how personal it is to me. I'm falling apart. I'm barely breathing. I'm barely holding on to you.

This song, this place with the words, and I am raw and exposed, as if cut and bleeding. Who was I kidding with the re-fusal to hide anymore? This is why I've hidden. The past begins to pulse to life within me, and I am seconds from remembering why I feel this way. I refuse to process the lyrics and shove them aside. I don't want to remember. I can't go there. I squeeze my eyes shut, trying to seal those old wounds, desperate to feel any-thing but their presence.

Suddenly, Chris is behind me, caressing my jacket from my shoulders. His touch is a welcome sensation, and when his arm slides around me, his body framing mine from behind, I am desperate to feel anything but what this song, no doubt aided by the wine, stirs inside me.

I lean into him and hard muscle absorbs me. There is a strength to Chris, a silent confidence I envy, and it calls to the woman in me.

His fingers, those talented, famous fingers, brush my hair away from my nape, and his lips press to the delicate area be-neath, creating goose bumps on my skin. And still, I barely block out the words to the song and their meaning to me.

As if he senses my need for more—more something, any-thing, just more—he turns me around to face him, and his fin-gers tangle almost roughly into my hair. The tight pull is sweet, dragging me from other feelings, giving me a new focus.

"I am not the guy you take home to Mom and Dad, Sara."

His mouth is next to mine, his clean male scent all around me. "You need to know that right now. You need to know that won't change."

But the song does change, and this time to another track on what must be a Lifehouse CD. "Nerve Damage" begins to play. I see through your clothes, your nerve damage shows. Trying not to feel . . . anything that's real.

I laugh bitterly at the words, and Chris pulls back to study me. And I am not blind to what I see in the depths of his green eyes, what I've missed until now but sensed. He is as damaged as I am. We have too many of the wrong things in common to be more than sex, and the realization is freedom to me.

I curve my fingers on the light stubble of his jaw, the rasp on my skin welcome, and I have no idea why I admit what I have never said out loud. "My mother is dead, and I hate my father, so don't worry. You're safe from family day and so am I. All I want is here and now, this piece of time. And please save the pillow talk for someone who wants it. Contrary to what you seem to think, I'm no delicate rose."

A stunned look flashes on his face an instant before I press my lips to his. The answering moan I am rewarded with is white-hot fire in my blood that he answers with a deep, sizzling stroke of his tongue. He slants his mouth over mine, deepening the connection, kissing me with a fierceness no other man ever has, but then, Chris is like no other man I've ever known.

His tongue plays wickedly with mine, and I meet him stroke for stroke, arching into him, telling him I am here and present and I'm going nowhere. In reply to my silent declaration, his hand cups my ass and he pulls me solidly against his erection. Arching into him, I welcome the intimate connection, burn for the moment he will be inside me. My hand presses between us and I stroke the hard line of his shaft.

Chris tears his mouth from mine, pressing me hard against the window, and I know I've threatened his control. Me. Little schoolteacher Sara McMillan. Our eyes lock, hot flames dancing between us and some unidentifiable challenge.

Some part of me realizes the window behind me is glass, and all things glass can break. He knows this, too, it's in the dark glint of his eyes, and he wants me to worry about it. He's pushing me, testing me, trying to get me to break. Because I slid beneath his composure? Because he really believes I am out of my league? And maybe I am, but not tonight. Tonight, as the song has said, I am broken, and for the first time perhaps ever, I am not denying the truth of all of my cracks. I am living them.

I lift my chin and let him see my answering rebellion. His fingers curl at the top of my silk blouse and in a sharp pull, material rips and the buttons all the way down pop and clamor in all directions. I gasp, in unfamiliar territory, and burning alive with the ache I have for this man.

He turns me to the window, and my hands flatten on the glass. Wasting no time, Chris unhooks my bra, and it and my blouse are off my shoulders in moments. He is behind me again, his thick erection fit snugly to my backside.

"Hands over your head," he orders, pressing my palms to the glass above me, his body shadowing mine. "Stay like that."

My pulse jumps wildly and adrenaline surges. I've been ordered around during sex, but in a clinical, bend over and give me what I want kind of way I tried to convince myself was hot.

It wasn't. I hated every second, every instance, and I'd endured it. This is different though, erotic in a way I've never experienced, enticingly full of promise. My body is sensitized, pulsing with arousal. I am hot where Chris is touching me and cold where he isn't.

When he seems satisfied I'll comply with his orders, Chris slowly caresses a path down my arms, and then up and down my sides, brushing the curves of my breasts. He's in no hurry, but I am. I am literally quivering by the time his hands cover my breasts, welcoming the way he squeezes them roughly, before tugging on my nipples. I gasp with the pinching sensation he repeats over and over, creating waves of pleasure verging on pain, and the music is fading away, and so is the past. There is pleasure in pain. The words come back to me, and this time they resonate.

His hands are suddenly gone, and I pant in desperation, trying to pull them back.

Chris captures my hands and forces them back to the glass above me, his breath warm by my ear, his hard body framing mine. "Move them again and I'll stop what I'm doing, no matter how good it might feel."

I quiver inside at the erotic command, surprised again by how enticed I am by this game we are playing. "Just remember," I warn, still panting, still burning for his touch. "Payback is hell."

His teeth scrape my shoulder. "Looking forward to it, baby," he rasps. "More than you can possibly know."

Fifteen

He unzips my skirt, sliding it down my hips. "Step," he orders, and my sex clenches with the command.

Obediently, I step out of the clothing, and I am now stretched out across the window for him to do with me what he will, wearing only my panties, black thigh-highs, and heels. The possibilities of exactly where this will lead are driving me wild. I have never been so turned on in my life, never so eager to be touched. It's illogical. I have a deep dislike for being ordered around, despite a past some might say indicates otherwise, except it seems, when it's by Chris. Deep down though, I know those journals call to me for reasons I prefer to ignore. Until this moment. Until Chris opened a door I'd left sealed.

"Beautiful," he murmurs, his voice gravelly, laden with evident desire. His hands curve around my hips, his palms exploring my backside, tracking the silk line of my panties down my cheeks. Trailing lower until he reaches between my thighs, he grabs the cloth and rips them away. My lips part in surprise, and I am panting. I arch forward and my nipples press to the cold glass, a bittersweet friction, part relief and part tease.

His palm flattens firmly onto my back, holding me in place, and oh God, the fingers of his other hand slide between my thighs, curving so that he cups my sex and strokes my clit at the same time.

"That's it, baby," he murmurs, widening my legs, teasing the sensitive, swollen flesh. "Hot and wet and ready for me. Just the way I want you." His hand on my back caresses over my ribs and he moves to palm my breast, flicking my nipple.

I am still lost in sensory overload when his mouth presses to my neck, his breath a warm tickle, and his hands, oh, his hands and fingers are doing such delicious things to my clit and nipples that I am on the edge of something intensely wonderful, and he's not even undressed yet.

His teeth scrape my lobe and I feel it in my sex, where I want him. Where I am almost desperate to have him. "I'm going to lick you all over before this night is over, Sara," he says in a seductive purr. "Suck your nipples until you are crazy with need, then spread you wide and lick you until you come and then I'm going to do it all over again. I'm going to make sure you are so thoroughly fucked that being fucked has a new meaning."

I moan with his words, with the boldness of this man, with the ease at which he can spin my world around and drive me wild. I am close to the sweet spot, moving against his hand, arching into his touch, when he shifts to my side and goes down on one knee.

He slides two fingers inside me, filling me, stretching me, as if he knew that is what I needed. A swell of need has me widening my legs, moving with the sweet rhythm of his strokes. I am panting and not quietly and I don't care. Tension curls inside me, and my orgasm comes in a hard spasm around his fingers that erupts into such pleasure my body jerks.

Chris wraps an arm around me, anchors me, and I am certain he is the only reason my knees do not give out. Time stands still as sensations ripple through my body, and Chris leads me to the other side of pleasure, his touch slowly turning more gentle. When finally my body relaxes, his tongue delicately strokes my hip bone, his cheek brushing against my skin with gentle, erotic friction that has my sex clenching all over again. I am breathless with his ability to be demanding and hard one moment, and tender the next.

"Don't move," he orders, and pushes to his feet, framing my body with his again, his hands traveling up my back, his lips pressing to my ear. "I'm going to fuck you now, Sara, hard and fast, with you exactly as you are now, and you're going to stay right where you are and let me do it."

"About damn time," I hiss through my teeth.

A low rumble of his laughter fills the air, tingling a path from my ears and stirring sensations low in my belly. But I am not pleased when he shoves away from me, no longer touching me, almost as if he is defying me, teasing me on purpose. I am ready to turn, to take over, to make my own demands, but I believe his promise to stop whatever he is doing if I drop my hands.

Relief washes over me when I hear the rustle of clothing

and the tear of paper—a condom I am certain. Soon. Soon he will be inside me. His hands come down on my hips, and his shaft presses between my thighs. Deft fingers stroke through the wet heat of my body, preparing me when I was ready long ago.

"Please, Chris," I moan, aching for fulfillment.

"Easy, baby," he replies, and oh yes, I feel him press between my legs, thick and hard, and exactly what I need.

Still though, he holds back, teases me, sliding his erection up and down in the wet heat of my swollen flesh. He can't want the way I do or he could not do this, and I silently vow to amend that, and soon.

"Payback—"

He thrusts into me, hard and deep, burying himself to the hilt and moaning with the impact. I moan with him and gasp when he lifts my hips, finding a deeper spot. There is no time to revel in the fullness of him inside me, the completeness my body needs. He thrusts again and the wild, wicked hard pump of our bodies together erupts into a frenzied dance. His hands are all over me, his cock is inside me, filling me, stretching me. Pleasing me. In a remote part of my mind, I think of the glass, of the two of us shoving against it. Of the possibility of it breaking, but I don't care. If I am going to die, I want it to be with this man inside me.

The bloom of orgasm begins to build and I try to fight it, unwilling to give up the sweet bliss of almost there. But he is grinding into me, touching me, pushing me, and I am weak. I stiffen, unable to move the seconds before I shatter, my body clamping down on the hard length of him and shooting darts of pure white-hot bliss to every inch of me.

A guttural sound escapes his lips, and he buries himself deep in the depths of my spasming sex, shaking with his own release. I want to push against him, participate in his pleasure as he has mine, but I am still trembling and weak with the final bittersweet ending to my orgasm.

For a few moments, the world spins and we are more animals than people, lost in a primal act, where nothing but satisfaction exists. When finally I blink the world back into view, twinkling city lights dot the inky canvas of the night. Chris is still inside me, draped over me, his hands on the window beside mine.

He nuzzles my neck. "How about that pizza?"

I smile. "You better make that two."

"If it means you have the energy to keep fucking me like you just did, I'll buy you a damn dozen." He slides out of me and a glow of satisfaction fills me with his words.

Now over my fear of falling out of the window, I turn around and lean on the glass and watch him pull off the condom, tossing it into a trash can by the couch. His jeans are unzipped, low on his hips but he is dressed all the way down to his boots. My glow fades. Suddenly, I am more than a little aware of my nakedness. "You never even got undressed."

He's back in front of me, wrapping his arm around me and stroking the hair from my eyes. "Because you stole my control, Sara, and that never happens."

My chest tightens at the tormented quality to his voice and I think . . . I think, for this tiny window of time, he needs me. Maybe I need him. I stroke his cheek with my fingers. "I was the one with my hands over my head, pressed against a glass that could crack. Actually, I still am."

"We are," he points out. "And it's hurricane reinforced. We're good."

My hand is resting on his chest, the steady thrum of his heartbeat beneath my palm, and it somehow makes me feel more alive. He makes me feel more alive. I want to do the same for him, to wash away his suddenly darker mood, as he has mine.

"You know, Chris," I say. "I do have a few boundaries."

He arches a brow, narrowing his gaze on mine. "What boundaries would you be referring to?"

"I'm not going home in a bra with my blouse gaping open. You ripped my shirt."

My reward is his sexy half smile, the same one he'd given me outside the gallery, by the Porsche. "I didn't hear you complain at the time."

"I'd lost my blouse. I darn sure deserved it to be for a pleasurable reason."

His eyes light with naughty mischief, and he nips my bottom lip. "I'll gladly buy you a new one so we can do it over again."

"I'll settle for borrowing one of yours right now. I'm not eating in high heels and panty hose."

He wiggles an eyebrow at me. "I would really like it if you would."

"Oh no," I say, and I smile and kick off my shoes for emphasis. "Not happening."

"Next time," he says with a wink, and the inference there will be a "next time" shouldn't please me for reasons I've already determined, aside from the fact that he's going back to

Paris. Without knowing why Chris is damaged; he is, and I am, and we are bad for each other. Next time isn't good for either of us unless . . . we need more than tonight.

Chris pushes off the window, away from me and surprises me by tugging his shirt over his head. And oh, oh yes, his abs are rippling perfection. I knew he was good-looking, I knew he was athletic, but every inch of him is rock-hard and sculpted in a way that only genetic and regular hours in the gym can do. The intricate tattoo covering his entire right shoulder down his arm, the one I'd hungered to see more clearly, has me spell-bound. The dragon is majestic, etched with such detail and skill, he could have drawn it himself.

"Do I pass inspection?" he asks softly.

I reach out to touch the design on his arm, only to have him capture my hand.

"If you touch me while you're looking at me like that, you won't get that pizza."

He steps closer and pulls his shirt over my head. I inhale his sexy scent clinging to it and me, and I hug it close, wishing it were him. "I'm not sure I care about the pizza."

"I'm not letting you pass out on me." His finger slides under my chin, lifting my gaze to his. "Now we're both half-dressed." He lowers his voice and adds, "On an equal playing field."

Equal. It is the last thing I expect from a man who'd completely dominated me minutes before. It doesn't compute. Power is taking, not giving. How can he do both? Who have I ever known who could?

"Equal would mean that I get to push you against the

window and forbid you to move, while I'm mercilessly teasing you."

His eyes darken, shadows swimming with gold flecks in the sea of his green eyes. "If I thought you were ready for where that will lead, I'd let you."

Let me? He'd let me? "What does that even mean, Chris?"

He reaches up and strokes my bottom lip, and the touch is gentle, but there is a barely contained edge beneath his surface I'm coming to know. "There is so much I could show you, Sara, but I'm not ready for you to run away." There is a sense of inevitable regret to his words.

I react to a sense of him pulling away from me without him actually moving—it claws at me inexplicably, I grab his arm and step closer. "Who says I'll run away?"

"You will," he says.

Does he think I can't handle more than tonight? Does he not see I need more than tonight? I need the escape. "You're wrong."

He shakes his head. "No, I'm not."

I open my mouth to argue, but his cell phone rings from inside his jeans pocket, I think. His ringtone is a concert pianist, and I'd be willing to bet my car that his father is the musician. I hate my father, I'd told him. What had gotten into me? And clearly, even with his father gone, he holds his in high regard.

Chris slides the phone from his low-hung jeans, and I'm fairly certain he chooses to answer the call to end our conversation.

"Right," he says. "My usual and hold tight just a sec." He glances at me. "What kind of pizza?"

The pizza place called him? I'm confused. "Cheese."

"Make my usual an extra large," he says into the phone. "Right. Thanks." He ends the call. "Pizza is on the way."

"That's what I call service."

"It's almost closing time, and Jacob went in to get a pizza for himself and asked if I'd called."

"Like I said, that's what I call service."

"I've known the owner a good ten years, and since he also owns the chopper shop I frequent, he likes me. I send him lots of business." He reaches for my hand and leads me to the couch. "Make yourself comfortable. I'll get us drinks and plates and we can eat right here." He smiles. "Unless you're tired of looking out of the window?"

I shake my head and sit down. The brown leather is soft and a bit chilly, and I shiver. "That was a very bad joke."

He picks up a remote and the gas fireplace to my right in the corner flickers to life. "I'm good at bad jokes."

"Yes," I agree, pulling a brown throw over me. "I know. *The Man with One Red Shoe?*"

"You don't like Tom Hanks?"

"That's an old movie."

"I'm a fan of classics." He sits down next to me and grabs another remote, punching a button. A massive flat-screen television lowers from the ceiling above the fireplace. He offers me the controller. "The key to my castle, at your disposal."

I am charmed and comfortable with this man in a way I don't remember being with anyone before him. I accept the remote. "And *The Man with One Red Shoe* is a classic?"

"Right along with *Austin Powers.*"

"*Austin Powers?*" I ask. "Tell me you aren't an *Austin Powers* fan."

"Have you watched *Austin Powers?*"

"Well, no," I concede, "but they look so silly."

"That's the point, sweetheart. It's an escape from reality." He pushes to his feet. "I'll grab us drinks and plates." His lips twitch. "Wine?"

"No," I say with emphasis. "I do not want wine."

"Corona?"

"No. Nothing with alcohol."

"That leaves you with bottled water or Gatorade."

"Water," I say. "I never drink calories I can eat. Leaves room for more pizza."

"I see," he replies, looking amused. "More pizza is always good. I'll be right back."

I sink down farther into the seat, and watch him walk toward the massive open kitchen overlooking the living area, and he is all long-legged male grace and flexing muscle. He's also one big contraction. Funny, charming, seemingly without the ego he has every right to possess. But there is more there. The man who'd faced off and won with the king of egos himself, Mark Compton. The man who'd pressed me against a window and took me with a dark passion I'd sensed came from a deep, troubled place. The man who'd told me he'd show me things but he wasn't ready for me to run. I burn to know what that means, what's beneath his surface. And for the second time tonight, I think we are two messed-up people destined to destroy each other, but I can't walk away. No. Can't isn't the issue. I simply don't want to.

Sixteen

Chris has just set plates and two bottles of water on the table when a strange buzzing sound fills the room. I frown. "What was that?"

"My version of a doorbell," he says with a boyish grin that is a complete contrast to the dark, edgy man who has just done wonderfully wicked things to me. "If a visitor manages to get past the elevator code, I still have to let them in from this side."

"That can't be the pizza, can it? They called about ten minutes ago." He glances at his watch and the thick silver and black leather design has become somehow erotic to me.

"Right at ten minutes," he confirms. "But I'm guessing they gambled and made my usual before they called me." He pushes to his feet, running strong hands down his legs.

"Where's the bathroom?" I ask, and stand up.

He motions to a door beside the fireplace and heads to the elevator. I watch him, trying to imagine how I'd react as a female delivery person if Chris answered the door, or elevator, with no shirt on. His tattoo. I never thought I was a tats kind of girl but his is hot, maybe the hottest thing I've ever seen. Or maybe Chris is simply the man who hits all my hot buttons.

He punches in a code in the panel by the elevator, and I can't see if there is a blushing female inside, but I do hear Jacob's voice and Chris's sexy rumble of laughter. The sound does funny things to my chest, the kind of funny feeling attached to unwelcome emotions. Oh boy. Don't go there, Sara. Don't start falling for Chris. This is an escape from reality.

He turns and heads back toward me, two pizza boxes in his hands, and all I can think of is being pressed against the window with him doing naughty things to me. I amend my prior thought. He absolutely hits all my hot buttons times ten. I refuse to clutter up a good thing with emotions and thoughts of tomorrow. When I was in this man's arms, he pushed my limits and left no room for anything but what he was making me feel. I am instantly hungry and pizza isn't what I crave. It's him and a desire to feel what he made me feel not so long ago.

He lifts the boxes in his hands. "They brought us two. If you're going to the bathroom, go now. Trust me. It's the best pizza on the planet when it's scorching hot."

I grin. "On the planet?"

"You bet, sweetheart, and I've done a lot of eating in Italy."

Laughing, I quickly scurry away and dart into a spare bathroom, where I flip on the light to reveal a room so luxurious it makes my master bath look like a porta potty. The darn thing even has a sunken tub. Out of the blue, my chest tightens and I lean against the door, forgetting my hunger and my urgency.

This life, Chris's life, the expensive everything around me, was my life when I was growing up, and I'm apparently having a rare flashback to the past. A part of me misses the girly things, like a fancy bathtub, soaps, and perfumes, but I quickly remind myself there'd been a price for those things. Chris is a different story. He earned this life, he owns it and deserves it, and I know my desire to do the same, to earn a tiny piece of this life is enticing me.

I shake off my thoughts and quickly use the bathroom and wash up, checking myself in the mirror in the process. My lips are bare and swollen, and my brown hair a wild mess. Not surprisingly, I look thoroughly fucked, but remarkably better than I remember looking in a long time. Fucked. Not made love to. I smile into the mirror. I like the freedom this new me is experiencing. It's sexy. He's sexy. I feel sexier than I have felt in my entire life.

"Hurry, woman!" Chris shouts out, and I laugh and exit the bathroom.

"Why do women do hurry so poorly?" he asks, as I join him on the couch.

"Why do men do impatient so well?" I counter, and my nostrils flare with the wonderful scent of baked bread, spices, and tomato sauce.

"Because you teach us impatience."

I snort. "Like you men are teachable? I don't think so."

He opens the lid of one of the boxes and the cheese is bubbly and yummy-looking.

"That looks and smells so good. I'm not even going to be embarrassed to let you see how much pizza I can put back."

He offers me a plate, and I happily fill it with a large slice. "You don't look like you can put down more than a slice or two."

"Obviously, you know the right things to say to a girl, especially after she's, ah, been naked." I smile, less embarrassed with this man than seems possible considering his hot, famous status. "But I assure you I can." I take a bite and moan. "Oh . . . hmm."

"Good, right?" he asks, and takes a bite of his own slice.

"So good," I agree, snatching a napkin from the roll he's set on the coffee table. "I'll be jogging a few extra miles this week, but it will be worth it."

"You're a runner?"

"It's my cardio of choice, and I can do it at home. I'm not much into group activities, and I hate the gym crowd."

"There's a private gym on the fourth floor. It's one of the reasons I picked the building."

"You have the whole floor. I'm shocked you don't have a gym here."

"I use the space for my studio, which I'll show you when we finish eating."

I'm going to see Chris Merit's studio, and I am reminded of what a superstar he is. "You don't act like a famous person."

"I don't think of myself as a famous person."

I finish my pizza and set the plate down, my hunger curbed enough to find him far more interesting. I pull one leg onto the couch. "But you are. You have to know you are."

He shrugs and grabs another slice of pizza for both of us. "I'm just me." He hands me my plate.

Absently, I accept the pizza. "You are one of the youngest,

most successful living painters in the world. You're brilliant, Chris."

"And because I know you truly admire my work, that matters to me. Believe me, there are plenty of people who want to be close to you for the wrong reasons when you're in the spotlight."

I take a bite of my pizza and consider him. He's already reaching for another slice. I'm still considering him when he takes a bite.

He arches a brow at my attentiveness. "What are you looking at me like that for?"

"You don't like people to know you're famous."

"I don't go around announcing it."

My brows knit as I start to piece together something. Or I think I do. "Wait. Do you intentionally use your father's photo for public forums?"

A slow smile slides onto his lips, and he disposes of his plate and motions to the box. "More?"

I set my plate on the table. "Not yet. You didn't answer my question."

He turns to face me, his leg on the couch as well, and scrubs his jaw, looking busted. "Yes. I've been known to slip in his photo here or there." He winks. "Fooled you, didn't I?"

"Your father looks like he's in his forties in the photo. I assumed you'd aged poorly."

"In other words, I fooled you."

I purse my lips and concede. "You fooled me."

We stare at each other, and our lighthearted mood shifts,

the air thickening with the mutual attraction our hot window encounter has done nothing to sate and everything to expand. Sitting here, studying him, I've officially confirmed in my mind what I'd thought earlier. While I don't doubt Chris really is lighthearted and fun, it's not effortless, either. He buries whatever he doesn't want me to know about. This man is far more than he appears to be on the surface and the glimpses beneath intrigue me.

My gaze drops to his arm, to the red, blue, and yellow of the dragon tattoo. I scoot closer to him, and my leg presses to his, sending an instant charge over my skin.

I swallow hard and I reach out, letting my fingers caress the dragon design. His muscles flex under my touch, and it is incredibly powerful to think I might be affecting him.

Slowly, my gaze lifts to his, and his is hot coals with simmering embers. "It's very . . . sexy." I'm surprised at how easily I say the words. I suck at flirting, but there is something different about me with this man.

"I'm glad you think so."

My palm glides down his forearm, and he catches my hand in his, as if he doesn't want to break the connection. "Why a dragon?"

"It represents power and wealth, two things as a very young man I knew I wanted."

"And you wanted money and power at such a young age?"

"Yes."

I want to ask why, but it feels too probing. "And now?"

"I have those things and with them comes security."

I think of how he'd used that power with Mark, about the

darker side I've seen of him tonight. He does like power, not in the abstract way Mark does, but he owns it in his own right.

"My first paintings were dragons. They're in my personal collection. I never sold any of them, or even tried."

"Here?" I ask eagerly. "I'd love to see them."

"Paris."

"Oh." Of course. Paris is his true home. I glance at his arm again. "The artist is quite talented."

"She is."

My chest tightens. A woman who he let create art on his body, who seems to have inspired him to create some of his own.

Gently, he brushes hair behind my ear, and I barely contain a shiver. "What do you want to know?" he asks.

About her. I want to know about her. "You'll tell me what you want me to know."

Surprise flickers in his eyes. "You are never quite what I expect, Sara McMillan."

"Neither are you."

His voice softens. "The tattoo artist was someone who got me through a hard time."

I'm holding my breath, and I don't know why.

"She's the past," he adds. "You're right now."

Air trickles slowly from my lips. I think he means this as a good thing but the words *right now* don't sit well. I have no clue why they bother me or why my stomach has knotted up. Right now is all that matters. I'm thinking too much. I don't want to think. I climb onto his lap and he shifts to sit with his back against the couch. Boldly, I straddle him, my hands on his shoulders.

"I'm here now. What are you going to do with me?"

For several seconds he sits there. He doesn't touch me. Tension radiates off him, seeps into me. He doesn't react, and I begin to feel self-conscious for the first time all night.

Suddenly, the fingers of one of his hands curl around my neck and he pulls my mouth near his. "Do you know what happens when you push a dragon? They burn you alive, baby. You're playing with fire."

My fingers curl on his cheek, and all self-consciousness is gone, forgotten. "I'm not afraid of whatever you're talking about. I think you keep warning me away because you're the one who's afraid."

His fingers knot in my hair and I gasp at the unexpected bite of his grip, holding me steady. "Is that all you got?" I demand, shocked at how much I want more. How much I want whatever is beneath his surface. I'm not scared. I'm aroused. I'm ready.

His eyes probe mine, his expression hard, intense. "I thought you were a good little schoolteacher."

"You're corrupting me," I declare, "and I seem to like it." I barely issue the challenge before he's pulling my mouth to his, and he is kissing me with unrestrained, burning passion. I taste the part of him I want to know, the part he's afraid of, and I burn to know more. Maybe he's right. Maybe I am playing with fire, but I cannot stop myself. Beyond reason, I will push him until he reveals everything.

Seventeen

I sink into his kiss, moaning at the wicked way his tongue is licking against mine, driving me wild. His palms skim my back and the shirt is lifted, I gladly raise my hands and let him pull it off me. He's filled his hands with my breasts before I can even lower my arms. And, Lord help me, his mouth is on my nipple, suckling and licking. My hands tunnel into his hair and his gaze lifts to mine. He watches me as he licks a circle around my nipple. I bite my lip from the pleasure, and he leans in to lick where my teeth have just worried, melding my naked breasts to his chest.

His hand slides behind my neck again. He likes holding me captive. I think he likes it a lot. I think I do, too. "You don't know what you're doing with me, Sara," he growls.

"But I want to," I whisper, and I haven't meant anything quite so much in a very long time. My hands slide down his sides, his skin hot, over hard, taut muscle.

His mouth claims mine again, full of demands, and . . . warning? Maybe. Probably. It makes me only hotter, hungrier. I fight the urge to pull his hair. His hands travel my body, possessing me, and oh yes, I want to be possessed by this man.

"Lean back," he orders, his hand on my waist, pressing me backward until my hands are flat on the table behind me.

My breasts are high, thrust into the air, and his eyes are ravenous as they take me in. I gasp as he slides his fingers between my thighs, stroking me.

"So wet." There is a rasp to his voice, a husky desire. "So hot." He's exploring me, teasing me, and his finger slides inside me and I can barely breathe. This isn't like before when I couldn't see him. He's staring at me, and I see the man, the passion, the glint of sexual prowess in his eyes that tells me I am out of my league, but I don't want to be.

He leans forward and scrapes my nipple with his teeth, and I realize this is more like before than I'd realized. I am once again captive. I cannot reach for him or I'll fall. He slides another finger inside me and suckles my nipples to the point of near pain, erotic, wonderful pain. "Chris," I pant, and I don't know what I am asking.

"Do you remember when I said I was going to lick you all over, Sara?" he asks, nibbling a path between my breasts, leaving my wet, aching nipples throbbing with the need for his mouth.

"Yes," I whisper. "Yes."

He flicks my clit with his thumb, spreads the wetness over my ultrasensitive flesh. "You want me to lick you here?" he asks, one hand sliding down to my stomach, the other working my body, pumping in and out of me.

My lashes flutter and I let my head fall back. "Look at me, Sara," he demands, and there is a sharpness to the words that snaps my head up.

"Do you want me to lick you here?"

I'm too close. The edge of orgasm is on me. "Yes, but ... I don't ... think I can take it. Not now." I gasp as his fingers are suddenly gone and he's lifting me. Before I can begin to clear the cobwebs I am on the couch and my legs are over his shoulders. His mouth closes down on me and warm pressure overtakes me. There is only sensation after sensation, and I am already lost, spinning into orgasm. I try to stop myself but it's impossible. This man, this glorious, sexy, dark, intense man has his mouth on me in the most intimate of ways after telling me he was going to lick me all over. I cannot breathe, and my entire body goes stiff before I jerk from the intensity of my body clenching. His fingers slide inside me, answering the need of my body, filling me.

A chill rushes over my body the instant I can catch my breath, cooling the fire on my skin. Chris follows it, enclosing me with his big body, and then he is kissing me. I can taste myself on him, salty and sweet, and I know this is his intent. And I know I'm not pushing him at all. I'm going only where he lets me. As if validating my thoughts, he moves, then is gone, leaving me wanting more. Controlling everything, controlling me.

He's standing above me, taking off his boots, and my heart thunders in my chest to realize he is undressing. I sit up straight, watching him, my mouth dry with anticipation. His jeans are gone in a flash, and his underwear with them, or else he was commando. I don't care. He is naked and hard and hot, his cock jutting forward, thick and heavily veined with arousal. For me. I want to touch him, but before I can move, he turns and snatches his jeans, searching in his pocket, and I hear the crinkle of paper, but it barely registers. I am spellbound by the man's backside, and I am still staring when he drops his pants and sits down next to me.

He hands me the condom, a silent challenge in his eyes. "Now I'm here. What are you going to do with me?"

Shifting to my knees, I wrap my fingers around the condom and blink at him. I am confused by the way he commands me when it comes to my pleasure, but he isn't commanding me to do anything to him. I have been commanded, ordered to my knees, ordered to do things I didn't want to do. I despised those moments in time and I wasn't turned on. But Chris could order me to do just about anything and I believe I'd melt with pleasure. I want to do many things to this man, and I am wet and ache with the fantasies I'm wickedly conjuring in my mind.

I feel empowered, sexy. I like this feeling. My gaze lowers to his cock and then lifts. "Do you want me to put this on you now or do you want me to lick you there first?"

His eyes darken. "Ah, my pretty little schoolteacher. I'm beginning to wonder, who's corrupting who?"

I am no more corrupting him than he is truly at my mercy, while I most definitely am at his. In fact, I'm not sure he ever could be at my mercy, and there's a part of me that feels I will never know this man until he is. The desire to show him I can handle whatever he throws at me is a seed taking root.

I let the condom drop to the couch, and one of my hands settles on his thigh, the springy hair there tickling my palm in a surprisingly erotic way, but then I am ultrasensitive, my body tingling all over. I wrap my free hand around the base of his erection, and his flesh is softness covering solid steel. I lean over him and lick the salty sweet drop of arousal there. It explodes on my taste buds and he moans. The sound of him turned on ignites my desire. I lick a circle around him, and suckle him between my lips.

I can feel his thigh tense beneath my palm, and I am enthralled with my ability to please him, but I want him to touch my head, to need this so badly he can't bear the idea of me stopping. Driven by this goal, I begin a slow glide up and down his length, and his hips lift with me. I can almost feel his need to hold me in place, but still he does not. I increase the pressure, and scoot closer, intentionally nestling my breast to his leg.

A low moan slips from his mouth. "Enough," he orders, reaching for me and pulling me to his lap.

No, I scream in my head, determined to take him all the way, but it's too late. He's too strong for me to fight. I am already flush against his chest, his hands in my hair, his mouth over mine. He was lethal, a drug . . . in some part of my lusty fog-laden mind, I remember the words of that first journal entry I'd read. Chris is quickly becoming my addiction, a drug I will never get enough of.

I can feel his erection press against my backside and I reach behind me to stroke him. He caresses my breasts, teases my nipple. "Get the condom, baby."

"We don't need it," I whisper, so ready for him I hurt with need. "I'm on the pill."

He stops kissing me and goes utterly still. My palms flatten on his chest and I'm not sure whose heart is beating faster, his or mine. Dread forms inside me with his reaction, and I instinctively know what he is thinking. I push back and stare at him.

Anger and hurt collide inside me. "You think I'm on the pill to sleep around. I don't believe you. Well, for your information I haven't slept with anyone in . . . a long time . . . and I won't be tonight again, either." I try to get off him and he holds me. "Let me go, Chris."

"Not a chance." He slides a hand up my back and neck, forcing me into submission, and this time I resent it. "I told you I wasn't ready to let you run away and I meant it."

"Let go," I demand. I'm hot and it's not all about anger, and that makes me furious with myself now, too.

"I'm not that complicated, Sara. I wear a condom and I protect myself. I fuck and I get fucked, Sara. That is who I am and what I am. I told you that."

His words are hard and they wash over me with icy clarity. I drop my gaze and I feel like I'm going to crack into pieces. He's right. I'm being emotional and no condom is stupid. How did I let myself drift into this territory? This is an escape; it's sex.

His fingers lace into my hair, palms framing my face, as he forces his gaze to mine. The stormy, hot turbulence in his eyes, a total contradiction to the ice of his words, steals my breath. "Damn it, woman," he hisses. "What are you doing to me?" He presses his forehead to mine, and his voice rasps with eternal struggle. "I didn't think about safe sex when you said you were on the pill. I wanted to know who the guy was who had you and lost you when I have no right to care. I don't want to care. I don't want to want to know."

But he does care, that's what he is telling me, and suddenly, I can breathe again. "He's the past," I answer, as he had told me about the tattoo artist.

"How past, Sara? How long since you were last with a man."

"Are you sure you really want to know?" My heart thunders in my chest. "Because if I tell you, I think you're going to—"

"How long?"

My throat restricts. "Five years. I stayed on the pill because . . . I just did."

He pulls back to study me. "No one for five years?"

I cut my gaze. "I don't want to talk about this." I repeat what I've already said. "That's my past and you're now."

His hand slides to my face, and he studies me, and seconds feel like hours. I fear he's going to think I can't handle this no-strings relationship. "That's right, baby," he finally whispers. "I'm now." He kisses me, his tongue sliding against mine, stroking me into a softer, needier place, where thinking thankfully isn't an option.

His hands are low on my back and his touch on my body affects me in a way I have never experienced. Every inch of my skin, is tingling and alive.

"I need to be inside you," he growls near my ear, his breath warm on my neck, before his lips brush the sensitive area.

My body clenches with the words. As impossible as it seems considering how hot this man has made me several times over, I have never been as aroused as I am in this moment. "Yes," I whisper. "Please."

He shifts my weight and presses into me. I gasp at the

sensation of him entering me, stretching me, pressing all the way to the deepest depths of me in ways beyond the physical. Chris affects me deeply, intensely, completely.

"Damn, you feel good, baby." His voice is rough, intoxicatingly aroused. Again I think, because of me. The idea is immensely pleasing.

One of his hands glides lower on my back, a possessiveness to his touch that brands me, as he presses me down against him. I arch into the movement, the stroke of his cock inside me a sultry play on my sensitive flesh.

He nips my bottom lip and licks the same spot. "You taste like honey and sunshine," he murmurs, and then surprises me in such an intense moment by smiling and adding, "and pizza."

I laugh and lick his bottom lip. "You taste like—"

"You," he finishes for me, and my stomach clenches in reaction as he softens his voice, "I taste like you, Sara."

The air seems to thicken around us, and the connection I've felt with Chris from the moment we met shifts and evolves into a living, breathing thing. It's controlling us now. It's claiming us. We are no longer ourselves, no longer the damaged, thinking creatures who can hold back and control what we say and do. We are simply two people who have lost the world around us and found this powerful, passionate moment.

Our mouths come together in unison, our tongues tangling in a wicked, emotionally charged kiss that is like nothing we've shared until now. I feel this kiss in every part of my body and beyond, and there is an unfamiliar emotion in my chest; on some level I know this is dangerous with this man. Falling for him is a mistake I don't intend to make and I don't want to make, but I can't fight the feelings overwhelming me. I can't es-cape the way he overwhelms me with sensations, though I have no real perception of really trying.

We are moving together, a sultry dance of passion, touching each other with hot, needy caresses, and I want to crawl under this man's skin. There is a desperateness growing inside me, in the way I touch him, the way I kiss him. The way I press against him. Sensations build within my sex, spread through my nerve endings. I crave the place they are taking me with bittersweet desire as I yearn to savor this experience, not end it.

Release comes over me too soon, and without warning, and I cling to Chris, burying my face in his neck. He moans as my body clamps down on his shaft and pushes me hard against his thrust. His arms are wrapped around me, holding me tightly when he shakes with his release.

When we both relaxed, wine and pleasure have collided with body-numbing effects, so much so that I am a wet noodle as Chris frets over cleaning us up and then lies down on the couch and takes me with him. His heart beats beneath my ear, and with the fireplace throwing warmth over us, my lashes grow heavier by the second.

Eighteen

Tonight I felt like I'd finally found him again. He was different. We were different. It was just he and I, alone in his playroom. I was so relieved, so tired of him sharing me. It hurts when he shares me, when he makes me feel I am not enough for him. He says that isn't the case. He says I fulfill his every fantasy. That I am a perfect sub.

I will remember tonight forever. Only my hands were bound and I stood in the middle of the room. He was naked and commanding, and it is in those moments that I would do anything to please that man. I was wet and aching with the burn for him to touch me, and finally, finally, his fingers brushed my cheeks, then trailed down my neck, over my breast and nipple. I shivered from the caress, and goose bumps had lifted on my skin. That's how much he commands my body.

His fingers returned to my face, trailing over my lips. "Suck," he ordered, and I drew his fingers into my mouth, ran my tongue around him. His eyes heated and . . .

My eyes snap open, a vague sense of awareness washing over me, and I blink into a beam of sunshine. Dreaming. I think . . . I've been dreaming about one of the journal entries again. I swallow against the dryness in my throat and the wet ache between my thighs. Realization comes to me in a cold blast of awareness. Oh God. I'm not home, I'm at Chris's, and I've managed to have an erotic dream that may or may not have included him as a witness to me talking or moaning or . . . I sit up quickly.

A blanket I don't remember pulling over me falls to my waist at the same moment as I bring Chris into focus, his back to me, and become instantly aware of his being fully dressed in distressed jeans and a brown tee of some sort, while I am completely naked. His hand is pressed to the living room window as he gazes out over the glorious new morning rainbow of red, yellow, and orange in the skyline I can't truly appreciate. Not when the dreaded morning after has arrived, glaring with its own colorful glory, complete with my wet dream that I'm hoping I haven't shared without my knowledge.

Chris seems to sense I'm awake and begins to turn. Reflexively, feeling exposed beyond my nakedness, I pull my knees to my chest and the blanket to my chin.

Discomfort does nothing to stop my reaction to this man. He is truly gorgeous. I drink him in like fine wine, savoring every detail. He's wearing the biker boots he'd been wearing at the coffee shop and his shirt has a Harley logo on it. His jaw is unshaven, shadowed with a sexy stubble, his longish light blond hair slightly damp, framing his handsome face. And his eyes, those intelligent eyes, glisten green and gold in the sunlight.

He's staring at me, too, his expression stark and unreadable. I will him to speak, to say one of his witty, light comments I find so soothing. He doesn't, and I am about a hair away from launching into the rambling habit I'm determined to leave behind in this new life of mine.

"Hi," I say when the silence drives me crazy, but hey, I've contained myself to one word. Progress is happening.

He leans against the window, clearly unworried about its breaking as I had been the night before. Well, for a short bit. I'd forgotten my fears pretty darn quickly when he'd started touching me. My body heats with the memory of him pressing me against that very same glass, and I remember the night before with feverish clarity—his hands, his fingers, his mouth. My breasts are suddenly heavy, my nipples aching. My cheeks burn with the impact of my thoughts.

Chris, on the other hand, remains more stone than man with tension banding around him. It whips and twists around the room, and begins to suffocate me, and old faithful becomes my only defense. I begin the dreaded rambling. "I, ah, it's morning, but you know that since it's daylight and well, it seems that . . . I . . . didn't go home."

Several heavy seconds pass, and I swear I can hear the hand on his watch tick, before he asks, "Did you want to go home, Sara?"

His question takes me off guard, and I have no idea how to answer. I am officially off-kilter. Had I? Well no. I'd been thoroughly pleasured and I'd all but passed out from pure female bliss. Would I have, had I woken up sooner? No. I wasn't in any rush to leave Chris, but I'm afraid Mr. "I'm Not the Guy You Take Home to Mom and Dad" will overreact to such a confession. "I . . . don't know."

"I didn't." His voice is soft, and he scrubs his face and looks upset by this declaration, before contradicting his own reaction by looking me in the eyes and clearly stating, "I didn't want you to go home, Sara."

I am confused and happy by this news, but . . . wait. I shouldn't be happy. Should I? This is a fling, an affair, and he will jet off to Paris and we will be history. I'm supposed to be living for the moment, enjoying what I can, keeping it light.

"You didn't want me to go?" I ask, unable to stop myself from seeking confirmation, from craving more from this man— the question is more what? Pleasure, I promise myself. This is about pleasure.

He studies me for such a long time; I fear I might ramble again, but thankfully, he saves us both from my undoing. "I don't bring women to my apartment, Sara," he informs me, his tone hard, gravelly, almost angry. "I don't have sex without condoms, and I don't ask about their pasts. And I sure as hell don't talk about mine."

Of all the things he's just said, I hone in on the one of the least consequence, considering I'm supposed to be trying to keep this about a sexy fling. Nevertheless, I do it anyway. My brows furrow. Is he really inferring he's talked to me about his past? Because if he is, and he considers what he's told me about, then I assume any real information I might garner would be downright criminal.

I study him and there is a fizzle of discomfort expanding and taking shape inside me. He seems really upset, as if . . . is he blaming me for making him do things he doesn't want to do? He is. I can see it in his face. Oh, good gosh. He's blaming me. A hot spot in the center of my chest begins to burn.

I drop my feet and clutch the blanket. "I should go."

"Please don't." His voice is soft, but it halts me with the raw vulnerability in its depths. There is true distress etched in his handsome face, as I imagine I must have on mine as well.

"You're confusing me, Chris."

"That makes two of us, baby," he says, and pushes off the window. "Give me just a minute." And just like that, he heads past me and up the sunken living room stairs, leaving me where I'm sitting.

What? Where is he going? I twist to watch him disappear down a hallway. Brows furrowed all over again, I face forward and search for my clothes without luck. His shirt isn't anywhere nearby, either. I'm captive. I can't leave. Do I want to leave? I think maybe I should. Or maybe I shouldn't. This man has me in a whirlwind of . . . feelings? Emotions? Passion. That's a safe word. Or is it?

Footsteps sound behind me, and Chris hurries down the steps and is in front of me in a snap. He is squatting in front of me, close, and he smells woodsy and fresh, and to my complete surprise, he is sliding a navy cotton robe about three sizes too big around my shoulders. There is a protective quality to his actions, and I am not sure I have ever felt more delicately female than in this moment. Never safer than with a man who is virtually a complete stranger, never with a man I'd almost called my husband. The rightness of this man and of walking away from my past, resonates through me. That decision brought me here.

I'm still clutching the blanket, and Chris glances down and back up, wordlessly urging me to let it fall. A low burn is expanding in my belly, sliding through my limbs. I want him. I want him in a way I barely recognize as within the realm of my capacity.

Our eyes lock and hold, and I see the shadows in the depths of his stare, and I think . . . I think he's letting me. My chest tightens with this realization, this certainty. I let the blanket slide into his hands, and I am naked, but I feel as if he is naked, too. I never bring women to my apartment. There is something happening between us, and I pray I was wrong last night. I pray it's not the beginning of two damaged people tearing each other apart. Some part of me needs Chris. Maybe we need each other.

Eternal seconds pass, and we don't move, don't speak. His gaze drops, sliding slowly, hotly over my breasts. "God, you're beautiful," he murmurs, a husky tormented quality to his voice that says more than the compliment.

I am shaken by the rush of emotion his words send through me. Yes. Oh yes. There is definitely something happening between us, something rich with promise and ripe with potential heartache, but I can't seem to care. My hand goes to his hair, stroking it, urging him to come to me, to be with me.

"Put your arms in, baby," he orders, and I sense his struggle, some internal battle that tells him not to touch me. I do as he commands and he pulls the robe shut and ties it.

He looks at me then, and he's found a place to bank whatever he was feeling. His eyes are lighter, his mood seemingly cooler. "I make a mean omelet. Are you hungry?"

His shift in mood flits through me without much resistance on my part. I've seen this in Chris several times before, and I'm coming to expect it. Being able to make him smile holds growing appeal.

I smile. "You're always feeding me."

"And yet we never seem to finish a meal." He rotates slightly to indicate the pizza boxes on the table behind him. "We didn't do the pizza justice."

"No, and you were right. It was really good."

His lips quirk. "In our defense, we had other things on our minds." He doesn't give me time to blush, and remarkably, considering what I've already done with this man, I would have. He pushes to his feet and pulls me with him, towering over me and reminding me how big he is, and why the sleeves of his robe swallow my hands.

"I'll cook if you make coffee," he bargains.

"I'll take that deal if I can find my hands." I hold them up and they are lost in navy cotton cloth.

He laughs and starts rolling up one of the sleeves. "You're melting away. Another reason to feed you. How's your head this morning?"

"If you mean from the wine, apparently I'm fine." I can't resist teasing him. "And I guess you weren't worried about taking advantage of me when I was intoxicated?"

He doesn't laugh as I'd hoped. His hand freezes on my sleeve and his gaze lifts. "I'm no saint, Sara. I've told you that."

"Yes," I agree tartly. "You have. Repeatedly."

"But you won't listen."

"I've heard every word you've said."

"Maybe I haven't said enough."

Exactly, I think. "You haven't said anything besides stay away and don't go."

His brows dip a moment before his lips curve into a smile. "You don't mince words, do you?"

"Not with you it seems. Or . . . hmmm . . . when I'm drinking." I cringe with the memory of the night before. "The wine got the best of me after you left last night. I marched up to Mark and told him that I didn't want to be involved in whatever your . . . well . . ." I press my fingers to my forehead. "I can't believe I said this."

His brows lift. "Now you've got me curious."

I drop my hand and dare to repeat the out-of-character words I'd spoken. "I told him I don't want to get in between whatever the cockfight is you two have with each other."

Chris barks out laugher. "I would have loved to have seen both of your faces when you blurted that one out." He motions toward the kitchen. "Come. I need to feed you, woman." He reaches for the pizza box, apparently without any plan to explain or deny the cockfight. Why? What is it with these two?

"Bathroom," I say, pointing the direction of the room I'd used the night before. "I'll meet you in the kitchen."

He grabs me and pulls me close, his breath trickling warmth on mine. "Just so we're clear, Sara. There is no in-between." The air crackles with electricity, and I am sure he will kiss me and

I burn for a taste of him. My body quakes inside and out. Please. Now. Kiss me.

I am hanging on a thread when he turns me to the bathroom before smacking me on the ass. I yelp with the unexpected swat and with a rush of heat at the memory of him doing the same thing the night before to my bare butt. His lips press near my ear. "Go now. It's never a good idea to keep a starving man waiting, Sara. You'd be good to remember that."

I suck in a breath and have no idea why, but I launch myself into action, as if I must follow his command, stopping only to grab my purse when I spot it on the ground. He is still behind me, watching me, tracking my every move. Every inch of me is tingling and warm with awareness, responding to his hot gaze, responding to his words, to his touch. Why is his hand on my backside so damn erotic? How can Chris redefine everything I know of myself in a matter of days? And what the heck did he mean when he said, "There is no in-between"?

Nineteen

Shutting myself inside the bathroom, I lean against the door and let out a breath, replaying Chris's whispered warning. It's never a good idea to keep a starving man waiting, Sara. Another one of his warnings lurks in the depths of the sensual promise of some kind of erotic punishment if I don't hurry up and . . . well, I don't know what, but I'm pretty sure I want to keep him waiting and find out. My lips tilt up. He really is doing a poor job of scaring me away. Mark's big on punishment. Unbidden, and with a sharp twist in my gut, Amanda's words come to my mind. For the first time since the wine had fed my boldness with my new boss, a cold blast of proverbial ice water douses the sizzling heat Chris has coursing through my veins. While Mark had agreed money was king and I was secure, I'm worried. Will I be punished? Have I ruined my chance at Riptide? My chance at a future when this fling with Chris ends?

Confusion twists inside me. Chris has guaranteed that I have a nest egg I can use to create a future in the field I love, but he's also potentially jeopardized the opportunity already before me. How do I thank him—and I need to—while I also ensure he doesn't cross the same line again? I'm clueless, truly clueless, and it seems an impossible balancing act, while I'm in Chris's apartment, in his robe, and wishing we were both naked again. I have only one real option. Enjoy having breakfast cooked for me by this sexy brilliant painter and look for the right opportunity to bring this all up. I have to find one because I have to thank him for the commission he's ensured I will receive.

I inhale and let it out, facing the truth deep inside me that I suppress all too frequently. While I've accepted life with limited resources, the chance to have some money, to chase my dream, is exciting. I'm almost afraid to believe it's true until I have the money. And Chris . . . Chris did this for me. I owe him more than a verbal thank-you, and I can think of all kinds of ways I'd like to say thank you. If he'll let me. For someone who comes off so friendly and warm, the true Chris is cautious and guarded.

Suddenly, I am eager to find my way back to my complicated artist—well, mine if only for a while—and I shove off the door and look at myself in the mirror. Oh, good gosh, I look like a creature from *Fright Night*. My hair is a wild mess, and my makeup is nonexistent except for mascara smudged under my eyes. Great. I'm with the hottest man I've ever known and raccoons have crawled through my hair and settled under my eyes. And I've spent so much time thinking, Chris is going to come looking for me.

Digging through my purse, I search for my brush and freeze

at the sight of one of Rebecca's journals. I swallow hard as I remember the exact entry inside that I'd awakened dreaming about this morning. No. More like reliving. I swallow hard at how vividly I'd conjured another woman's words into fantasy while Chris stood nearby, perhaps overhearing my sighs, moans, and who knew what else.

With a deep breath, I snatch the journal and set it on the counter, staring at it, barely containing the urge to read the entry in question. Every time I reread a page, the content becomes more meaningful, and pieces of the Rebecca puzzle fall into place. I ignore the idea, snatching my brush.

Quickly, I run it through my hair and consider applying makeup before settling for rinsing my face and applying some moisturizer. Makeup would look like I'm trying too hard. I think of the kiss I'd craved from Chris and been denied, and the urge to brush my teeth is intense. Out of desperation, I decide to use my finger and water on my teeth. Surprise, surprise. It's a wasted effort. I have no toothpaste. I grab some tissue and scrub my teeth before rinsing again.

Without much more ado, I give up and exit the bathroom. Stopping by the coffee table, I drop my purse and grab the plates and the drink cups we'd left there. Loaded up, I head toward the kitchen that thus far is producing no promising scent of cooking food.

I pass the archway between the living room and the kitchen and don't see Chris, but there is a massive rectangular island counter of gray-and-black marble with gorgeous gray wooden shelves above and below it. I follow the sound of movement toward a corner to the right, which appears to be a part of an

L-shaped room, but not without being distracted by the hollowed oval eating nook surrounded by floor-to-ceiling windows and more of the breathtaking view of the city. I love this kitchen. I love this entire apartment so far.

I turn into the bottom of the L and find a rectangular room with a counter and a stainless-steel sink on one side. Opposite is another counter with a stove, fridge, and the sexy owner of the apartment, who is busy gathering salt, pepper, plates, and various other items he needs, depositing them in a corner by the stove.

"This kitchen is a chef's dream," I declare, disposing of the dishes in the sink opposite him.

"It comes with the apartment, so don't start thinking I'm a master chef." He opens the fancy fridge with double doors and sets eggs and cheese on the counter. "There's a reason why I know all of the local restaurant crowd."

I move to the side of the counter on the opposite side of the stove from where he is working to watch him crack several eggs into a bowl. My gaze is drawn to his hands, and I cannot help but think of how expertly he'd touched my body, how expertly he handles a paintbrush. How expertly he'd known how to keep me on the edge and then take me over.

He glances at me, and I feel as if he's reading my thoughts. Part of me burns to boldly embrace what he's making me feel, but the old me—the real me?—rushes to cover up what I am thinking for no apparent reason. "I know how to shop in the frozen-food section of my grocery store and that's about it. My mom was . . . we . . . didn't cook."

He whisks eggs in a bowl and adds milk, salt, and pepper. "Was your mom too busy to cook or she didn't like to cook?"

How did I let this conversation start? "My father didn't like her cooking so she didn't cook."

He rests a hand on the counter. "He cooked?"

"Ah, no. My father doesn't do domestic tasks."

He fires up the burner and pours a little oil in the pan. "So who cooked? You or a sibling?"

"I'm an only child, and I don't cook." He glances at me, a curious expression on his face, and I know why. I'm making a simple question complicated because I always make things regarding my father complicated. "We had a private chef." The surprised look on his face makes me regret I've gone there and I motion to the coffeepot sitting in front of me. "I'm falling down on my job."

He hesitates a moment, and I think he wants to push me for more information, but thankfully, he seems to change his mind. "That was the deal. I cook. You brew."

"Aye, Captain," I say with a mock salute, and I reach for the canister, noting the glowing green time at the base of the fancy silver and black pot. It reads the early hour of seven thirty. Much too early for the knots in my stomach to form due to the family drama confessions I don't intend to make.

I set the lid aside and draw in the scent of the coffee and think of Ava for a moment. She'd smelled like coffee when I'd hugged her at the gallery. Or I was drunk and my nose was in overload like my big mouth that blurted out cockfight. "It smells like . . . Cup O' Café."

"Not even close," Chris says, joining me, his shoulder brushing mine, and I am blown away by the blast of awareness it creates, and thankful for how quickly it untwines the knot in my stomach. Our skin isn't touching, and still he does this to me.

He inhales the beans and then holds the canister to my nose for me to do the same. "That's the scent of a French blend by Malongo in Paris. I bring it with me when I come to the States. I love the stuff."

"I can't wait to try it," I say, and mean it. He loves the coffee, the pizza, and Tom Hanks. I love that he is passionate about so many things. About me? At least for now? I'll take it, I decide. His passion is contagious.

"Four scoops for a pot," he informs me.

I nod and get to work, two frying pans sizzling beside me. I'm pouring the water into the pot when I am struck by how utterly unexpected and comfortable this domestic experience with Chris is. His earlier confessions about never bringing a woman home lends to an assumption that he, too, is on unfamiliar territory. He never brings a woman home? Surely he means rarely. Doesn't he?

I glance at the perfectly formed omelets not yet filled and folded. "Looking pretty darn master chef to me."

He glances at me; his eyes alight with good humor. "Now you're giving me performance pressure."

I snort. "You and performance pressure don't compute."

His lips quirk but there's no denial to follow. He's confident. Whatever is beneath his skin, whatever the damage, it's not made him insecure.

He holds up some veggies before dumping them into the omelet. "Onions and peppers?"

"Why not? I'm already without a toothbrush. I'm lethal."

He laughs, a deep rumble of manly hotness that does funny things to my chest. I am hungry for him, not the omelet. "Call the front desk if you want," he suggests. "They pretty much operate like a hotel. You want it. They get it."

"Oh." I am surprised but pleased. "How do I call them?"

He motions to his left. "The phone on the wall behind the fridge goes directly to the front desk."

Elated with the idea of a toothbrush, I move to the phone and lean on another small counter, intending to pick up the receiver, but I hesitate. "Who should I tell them I am?"

Abandoning the food, Chris steps in front of me and his big, wonderful body is framing mine, his hips intimately pressed to my hips. I am instantly aroused, but then I'm fairly certain I'll stay that way with this man.

"Who do you want to tell them you are?" There is no mistaking the challenge beneath his words.

Oh, hell, he's having another mood swing, and we're walking on the dark side again. I'm going to get whiplash at this rate.

My fingers curl on the hard, warm wall of his chest. He's testing me, and I'm not playing his game. One thing I've learned since leaving behind my father, and, yes—Michael—is that I am me. I can be no one else, nor do I plan to try for Chris, no matter how hot the man is.

"I don't want to tell them anything," I say. "It's none of their business."

He studies me, his expression unreadable, but I have a sense of being in the eye of a hurricane. My read on his reaction to my reply is a big zero.

"When I said I don't bring women here, Sara, I meant ever. As in no one."

This is another out-of-the-blue remark; I assume it relates to the call downstairs in some random way yet to be explained. These are some choppy waters I'm wading in, and I'm wondering if I need to swim to shore, as in the one called my own apartment.

"Yes," I reply. "You've said that, and if you keep telling me that I'm going to decide it's your way of telling me to leave."

"I'm telling you because I want you to understand how much I want you here."

"Oh." He wants me here. On some level I know this, but having him say it surprises me and pleases me far too much for my own good.

"I want you to want to be here," he adds.

Surprised yet again, I sense rather than hear a hint of vulnerability in his voice. I tilt my head and study him. Yes. He's uncertain, and I get the idea that isn't something he's used to feeling.

"I do," I whisper. "I want to be here."

"Good." He strokes two fingers down my cheek, and slides my hair behind my ear, sending chills down my neck and spine. I am overwhelmed and my body quakes. I have never in my life responded like this to a man, and I'm trying to understand what it is about him that speaks so deeply to me. I've known good-looking men. I've known talented, gifted, and powerful men.

But none like this one. None so complicated, none so compelling beyond reason.

"You aren't going to like all that I am, Sara," he murmurs darkly.

"Another warning?" I admonish him. "You're above quota, at which point warnings become ineffective."

"Not a warning. I'm done warning you or you wouldn't be here."

"You've issued any number of warnings since we arrived last night."

"Yes," he concedes. "I suppose I have. So I might as well give you one more."

"The last one?"

"Not likely."

"The last one today?"

He ignores my hopeful question. "Nothing has changed, Sara. I'm still not the guy who'll give you a white picket fence."

"Thank goodness."

"I'm as far from white picket fences as you can get. Sooner more likely than later, you aren't going to like everything you find out about me."

My fingers uncurl on his chest, slowly splaying over the hard muscle. "Does that mean you're offering me an invitation to find that out for myself?"

He squeezes his eyes shut and seems to struggle for an answer before he looks me in the eye. "Against my better judgment, and because I'm seemingly powerless to stay away from you."

Chris Merit is powerless to stay away from me?

"What happens between us stays with us, Sara," he states, before I can formulate a reply. "I need to know you understand that. I'm an inherently private person, and I have my reasons for that and they aren't going to change. Don't let my casual friendships around the neighborhood and the high-rise building with room service, give you an impression otherwise. I choose who knows what about me and the staff here helps me keep it that way."

I wonder if he's been burned as I have by letting the wrong people into his life or is he smarter than I have been. Does he just never give them a chance? "I like that you're private. In fact, if you weren't, I wouldn't be here, Chris."

We stare at each other, and his scrutiny is so intense that I feel as if he's crawling inside me and searching my soul for confirmation that I've spoken the truth. Who or what made him this distrustful? Who or what damaged him? And does it really matter? I relate to him far more than I thought I could. I understand him beyond events and names and places.

I reach up and stroke his cheek. "Whatever happens between us stays with us." My voice is soft, hoarse. I am affected by this man on so many levels I can't begin to understand.

His eyes narrow and soften, and I watch the tension slide from his face, the flecks of gold fire flicker to life in his eyes. The air around us shifts, and I feel the now familiar swell of desire in my stomach, expanding and threatening to consume me. I feel an unexpected, intense rise of panic. I don't want breakfast, these few minutes of normalcy; I realize in their potential loss, I crave for some unnamed, unrecognized reason.

His hands settle on my waist, branding me through the thin

cotton, and his expression reflects he, too, is thinking of how close to naked I am.

His attention lowers to the opening of the robe and my nipples tighten and ache instantly. "Do you know how badly I want you right now?" he asks, his fingers sliding to the V of the robe and starting to tug it lower.

I want him—I want him as much as I want my next breath, but a voice in my head screams, Not yet. Not until after breakfast. I grab the robe and pull it closed before pressing my hand on his chest to hold him back. "Oh no. None of this or that or whatever we might do. Not until you caffeinate me, feed me, and let me brush my teeth." I grab the phone on the wall. "And aren't the eggs burning?"

"I turned the stove off," he says, laughing, a low and sultry sound that blends with the ringing of the phone line. He leans in and kisses my ear, his breath hot on my neck. "Because I was hoping to turn you on. I guess I'll have to try harder after we eat." He pushes away from me as a female attendant speaks into the receiver. "Can I help you, Mr. Merit?"

I stare at Chris's broad shoulders as he attends the food. He's left me breathless and aching and I wonder why the heck I thought breakfast was important.

"Mr. Merit?" the woman on the line queries, jolting me out of my reverie.

"Yes, hi. Mr. Merit would like a toothbrush and toothpaste, please."

"Of course," the woman replies. "I'll send them right up."

I replace the receiver and head for the coffeepot, removing two cups from the cabinet above it. I glance at Chris as he fills two plates with his creations and he smiles at me, his eyes brimming with mischief and fun. He's all too aware he's left me fanning myself, and he loves it.

"I like you in my robe." He wiggles an eyebrow. "I like you even better out of my robe."

Heat rushes over me and it's not from the stove. He's so charming and sexy. "I'd look better showered and dressed like you."

"I guess that's a matter of opinion."

I am glowing from his attention. How could any woman not glow from a compliment from Chris Merit? "How do you like your coffee?"

"Lots of cream. It's in the fridge."

I laugh at this announcement.

His brows dip. "What's funny about creamer in the fridge."

"I expected you to say you like it straight up. You know. The whole biker, cool artist persona. I thought you'd want your coffee so strong and black it grows extra hair on your chest."

"I have plenty of hair on my chest, as I'm sure you've noticed, and I like sugar with my poison."

It's an odd comment, and like so many others with Chris, I suspect it comes with a hidden meaning. I wonder if he will be around long enough for me to understand him, and I find I'm hoping he will be. Already, my vow to live in the moment with Chris is becoming a desire to live in the next one.

He was right. He's dangerous. Or maybe he didn't say dangerous. I'm not sure why he's warned me away so much, but I'll say it for him. He's dangerous and I've never wanted to live on the edge more in my life.

Twenty

A few minutes later, my toothbrush and toothpaste have been sent to us via a chute in the wall by the fridge that resembles the drive-through bank machines. I rushed off to brush my teeth before eating, which Chris had found amusing, and returned.

I am now sitting with Chris at his kitchen table, each of us with coffee sweetened with hazelnut creamer, which is apparently not easy to find in Paris and is a favorite of his.

"I've never tried hazelnut," I confess. "I'm kind of a straight vanilla girl." The silly statement is out before I can pull it back.

Chris's lips quirk. "Well then, I aspire to break your vanilla habit." He lifts his chin to my cup. "Try it."

Oh, good grief, he had to go there, but then I invited it. I wonder what he defines as vanilla. Me against that window? Was that vanilla? Not to me, but I've been so very vanilla for so very long. And I'm finally allowing myself to crave more from life.

"Or you can tell me what you're thinking instead," Chris suggests.

"Oh." I blink and realize I'm thinking a little too hard and obviously about the "vanilla" comment. "No. I don't think I'll share those thoughts."

He looks intrigued, but I ignore him and sip the coffee and the warm, nutty beverage as my reply. "It's good. Really good."

Approval etches his face, and his tone is all suggestion and sex. "I knew there was more than vanilla in your future."

My cheeks heat with the flirty remark.

"And she blushes like the good little schoolteacher," he comments. "You are one big contradiction, aren't you, Sara?"

He's right, of course. I feel like I'm swimming between two shorelines—one the bland simple life, the other dark and erotic—and I can't quite reach either. I shrug in reply. "I guess I am."

"I guess you are."

There is a sexy awareness between us as we dig into our food, and I'm hungrier than I realized, because the first bite awakens my stomach and taste buds. "I say you earn Top Chef markings. My omelet is terrific."

"Omelets are pretty easy to make and hard to screw up."

"You haven't tried my omelets," I assure him, and when he laughs I sigh and stare out the window. The city is an early morning canvas painted with a brilliant, clear blue sky, water for miles, and the jagged edges of hills and buildings speckled here and there for a complete and perfect picture. "It's like being on top of the world here, and untouchable." I settle an elbow on the table and rest my chin on my hand, adding longingly, "Sure beats my apartment and the view of the parking lot." I glance at Chris. "Does your studio have this kind of view?"

"Yes. I'll show you later if you'd like."

A thrill goes through me at the idea of seeing where he works. "I'd like that very much."

"The studio view is why I bought the place. Plenty of inspiration for my work since I love this city. It's home to me and always will be."

"When did you move to Paris?"

"My father moved us when I was thirteen."

My brow furrows as I try to recall anything I've read about his family outside of his father and remember nothing. "And your mother is—"

"Dead."

"Oh." I let my elbow drop and straighten. His one-word reply has said far more to me than many entire stories have. "I'm sorry."

"As I am about yours." His voice has softened and taken on a somber quality.

I study him, trying to read his impassive expression, and I am so hungry to understand this man, I dare to go where I probably should not. "How old were you when she died?" I hold my breath; waiting on an answer I'm not sure he will give me. He has, after all, confessed an unwillingness to share personal details with the women he . . . dates? Fucks? I'm not sure. Actually, there is a whole heck of a lot I'm not sure about at this juncture of my life.

"Car accident when I was five."

He spits out the information without hesitation, almost as if he's reciting someone else's story, but I see it for what it is—a coping mechanism. I know that mechanism all too well. You find a place to put things, to deal with them or you crash and burn.

"I was twenty-two when I lost my mother," I say, offering him no words of sympathy. I've heard them myself. I know they don't help. "She had a massive heart attack the day of my college graduation."

He stares at me and we share a moment of understanding, of loss, of knowing there is nothing more to say. We both had something sucky happen to us. We both dread the rambling sympathetic purrs of those who discover our losses. We both get it and each other. We just . . . understand.

Seconds tick by, and I think I've shared more in these moments with this man I've known only days, than I have anyone except maybe my mother. We understand each other in a way few can.

It's Chris who breaks the silence, reaching for his fork and motioning to my plate. "Eat before my masterpiece gets cold."

I nod and in silent unison, we pick up our forks and begin to eat again in silence, both thoughtful. There are so many questions I could ask, but I don't. Personal questions about his family I know I can't ask now, if ever. He's already shared more with me than I expected, as I have with him. Still, with this new revelation about his mother, I want to know this man now more than ever.

"Why painting?" I ask. "Why not a sport or the piano, like your father?"

His jaw tenses, barely perceivable, but I notice, and I wonder why. What nerve have I hit?

"My father dated a rather famous artist who decided I needed an outlet outside the schoolyard brawls I was getting into for my anger."

"Wait. You were fighting? You don't seem like a fighter." Then again, he'd all but flattened Mark, who had seemed untouchable, with nothing more than words.

"I was a teenager. I was in a new place and I didn't speak the language, and I was an outsider to the other kids. It was fight or get beat up. I don't like being beat up. The problem was that once I started fighting, I looked for reasons to keep doing it. I was pissed off about being in Paris and wanted to come back here. The result was I got kicked out of school."

"Ouch. What did your father do?"

"He didn't even know. The woman he was dating at the time—the artist I mentioned—stepped in and got me back into school. Then she sat me down and told me I had anger issues and had to find an outlet. She shoved a paintbrush in my hand and told me to create something worth looking at."

"And what did you draw?"

He laughs. "Freddy Krueger from *A Nightmare on Elm Street*. One of my best works to date, I might add. I was trying to be a smart-ass."

I laugh. "You? A smart-ass? Never."

"You think I'm a smart-ass?"

"You ordered a beer at a wine tasting."

"You have to admit, Mark's obvious discomfort was price-less."

As much as I want to take this opening to talk about the prior night's events, I'd rather him keep talking about himself. "I'm not feeding this battle between you and Mark. What happened when you revealed your Freddy drawing?"

"She said I still had anger issues but I was also talented as hell and if I didn't put it to use she'd go Freddy Krueger on me."

"And so it began," I say softly. Warmth fills me with this story, and I wonder who the artist was who'd helped him, but I've already surmised Chris does everything with specific intent, including avoiding the use of her name.

"And so it began."

He gives me a keen inspection, and I can see his mind working and my skin prickles in a prelude to whatever probing questions I've earned with all of mine.

"So, Sara," he beings slowly. "Tell me. Just how rich is your father?"

I inhale and shove aside my plate. He's told me more than I expected him to tell me, more than he claims he tells anyone. I can't shut him down, and I know he isn't interested in the money, as much as my walking away from it.

I pull my feet to the chair and hug my knees, the big robe a cloak, a shelter of sorts. "He's the CEO of Neptune Technolo-gies."

He arches a brow. "As in the cable network?"

"Yes."

He leans back in his chair to study me. "And you live in a modest apartment on a teacher's salary?"

"Yes."

"You hate him that much."

It's not a question, so I don't answer. I get up and walk to the coffeepot and come back to the table. I hold the pot up to him. He offers me his cup, and I fill it. He glances up at me, his eyes probing. "Thank you."

I nod and fill my own cup before replacing the pot and sitting down. I pour creamer into my coffee and stir, avoiding Chris's scrutiny.

"Do you talk to him?" he prods, apparently not worried about pushing me as I was with him.

I sip my coffee, in no rush to deliver my reply but finally confess, "Never, and I don't talk about him, Chris." I add his word choice for emphasis. "Ever."

He ignores my obvious plea to change the subject. "When was the last time you actually saw or talked to him?"

"I said my good-byes to them both at the funeral." I sip my coffee, and I wish it were liquid chocolate comfort, not ground brewed beans. Chris is still staring at me when I set it down.

He looks puzzled. "She died of a heart attack, right?"

I nod.

"So why do I get the feeling you blame your father for her death?"

My lips thin. "I blame him for her miserable life."

Understanding washes over him. "You didn't take a dime. You just walked away."

"Yes." A lump forms in my throat. "Which brings me to last night. I don't know what is up with you and Mark, but—"

"It's not a cockfight," he teases, and I can tell he's trying to lighten the mood.

I cringe at the memory I cannot escape. "I still can't believe I said that."

"We aren't enemies," he adds, answering what I have not asked but planned to. "I just know him and I know how he works. I wasn't—I won't—let him manipulate you."

"I'm an employee trying to earn my way into a permanent job, and one that pays more than an intern on the floor."

"And your desperateness to make that happen showed. He can't manipulate you. If he thinks you have something to offer, he'll give you the opportunity at Riptide, minus the head games he was working on you."

"My father is the king of users and I handle him just fine. I can handle Mark, Chris."

"You ended up with nothing from your father, Sara. You didn't 'handle him just fine.' Any father worth a grain of salt takes care of his fucking daughter, no matter how hardheaded she might be about letting him. You deserve to be taken care of."

Anger surges in me and I stand up. "You have no right—"

He's on his feet, towering over me. "What if I want to have a right?"

"You aren't a relationship kind of guy, Chris, and that's why I'm here. I'm not a relationship kind of girl. No white picket fences, remember? We both agreed on that. You all but insisted on it. Therefore, you get to fuck me but you don't get to fuck with my life. This is my opportunity to prove I can have my dream just like you have yours. I appreciate the commission. I do. More than you know, but it changes nothing. I still need more than money or I'd be my father's whipping dog right now, lapping up his money." My heart is about to explode from my chest. "I need to get dressed and go home." I start to walk away.

"Already running away? Can I scare you that easily?"

I stop dead in my tracks and my chest burns. "I'm not running," I hiss, facing off with him.

"You look like you're running to me. The first time I push a button you don't like you bolt."

"A few orgasms does not give you control of my life."

"You know, sweetheart, I know I'm fucked up. But if you think the guy trying to protect you instead of walk all over you is the one trying to run your life, you're just as fucked up as I am. Walking away from your father is not managing him. It's running."

He's hit every nerve I own like a lightning rod. "But you want me to walk away from the gallery and Mark, and you don't call that running?"

His expression clouds, and he reaches for me, pulls me hard against his body, his hand snaking into my hair. "Because Mark wants to fuck you, Sara, and I don't share. You're with me or you're not. Decide now."

I can barely breathe. He's jealous. Chris is jealous. It's hardly conceivable, and I want him all the more because of it, which probably means he's right. I'm fucked up. But then, I know that already. He's wrong about my being a doormat, though. I've been there, done that, and I'm not going there again. "You want me, Chris, you accept my job and you support me."

"What do you think I was trying to do by taking away Mark's control over you last night? But damn it, Sara, say what I want to hear. Tell me you don't want him."

"I don't. Just you." And suddenly his mouth is on mine, his tongue pressing past my teeth, stroking me until I'm mindless. We are all over each other, touching and kissing, and I barely register the robe falling away.

"Damn it, woman, you are making me crazy," he groans, pressing me against the wall, his fingers caressing my breasts, teasing my nipples, his mouth already devouring mine.

I can feel him shoving down his pants. "Hurry," I plead. "I need—"

He kisses me. "Me too, baby. Me too."

And then somehow, he's inside me. Oh God. Yes. He's inside me, thick and hard and I'm no longer on the ground or against the wall. He's lifted me and my legs are wrapped around his waist. He is thrusting into me, pulling me down on top of him, pushing me so that I'm leaning so far back I feel like I might fall; only he has me. His arm is around my waist, his powerful body pushing into mine, his hot gaze raking over my breasts, and he has me. He won't let me fall, and that knowledge, that certainty that comes from some place deep inside, allows me to let go. I let myself feel and not think. I am lost to the passion, to the moment, and the push of him inside me, the pleasure of him stretching me, is more than I can take. An orgasm ripples through me with a sudden, intense blast, my body clenching around his. He groans with the impact, and God, that groan is hotness personified. I feel the wet, warm heat of his release, and I am past my release, and clearheaded enough to revel in the beauty of his face etched with the pleasure I am giving him. I am spellbound by the sight of him, hanging on every second of his release, watching the tension in his features slowly ease into relaxation.

He pulls me close and buries his face in my neck and just holds me for long seconds, still standing, holding my weight and his. My gaze goes to the window, and I am aware of the blue sea and gorgeous city beneath us. Of the feeling of sanctuary I've found here and nowhere else, if only for a short while.

Slowly, Chris slides me to the ground and offers me a paper towel, which I demurely accept, feeling a wave of shyness. Yes indeed, I'm a contradiction these days. Chris fixes his pants and then grabs the robe and pulls it around me.

"I'd like to take you somewhere and show you something I think you'll like," he says. "Overnight, if you can?"

Overnight with Chris? The idea thrills me more than it should, and I remind myself this is a hot fling. Enjoy it while I can. Don't get attached. Don't fall for him. "Where?" I ask.

"Is that a yes?"

I nod. "Yes."

"Then it's a surprise, but you'll like it, I promise." He glances at a clock. "But if we're going to do everything I want to do, we have to get going."

"I have to go home and shower and get clothes. I don't even have a shirt to wear out of here."

"You can use my shower, and you leave clothes to me."

"Chris—"

He picks me up and I yelp. "What are you doing?"

"Taking you to the shower. Me Tarzan. You Jane. Do as I say."

I laugh at his silliness and think that he's the contradiction. All rough, tough manly man and a gentle bear at the same time.

We pass the coffee table. "Wait! I need my purse."

He backs up and leans down enough for me to grab it. I snatch it. "My skirt—"

"I'll get you clothes," he says, charging up the steps from the living room to the foyer by the elevator and down another hallway I hadn't even noticed, and then up a winding set of stairs that ends in his bedroom, which is spectacular. A massive black bed on a pedestal with an incredible view I only get to see in passing before I am deposited on the white marble floor of a bathroom the size of my bedroom.

"I'm leaving you here and shutting you inside, because if I join you, we won't leave anytime soon."

I open my mouth to object, but it's too late. He kisses me quick and hard on the mouth and then steps out of the room and shuts the door behind him. I am alone in Chris Merit's bathroom and all I can do is smile.

Twenty-one

I use Chris's soap and shampoo; it has a sandalwood musky smell that reminds me of him, and makes me wish he's in the shower with me. Images of the things we've done together, the conversations we've shared, pour through me as the hot water pours over me. Chris confuses me on every possible level. Or maybe I'm confused anyway. Until this past week, I'd convinced myself I had life figured out. Did I let my father beat me by leaving everything behind? Part of me says no. I escaped with my own identity. I stood up for what I believed in. My love of art had been like my mother's, a frivolous hobby, not a career. My role would have been like my mother's, that of servitude to my father, and in my case, also to Michael.

Another part of me, well, it grimly says that I ran rather than stood up to my father and demanded he accept who and what I am, not who he wanted me to be. I'd always hoped my mother would stand up for herself, and what had I done? I'd simply left. I'd run. Chris is right. No wonder I wanted to hit the man. He'd made me see the bitter, hard truth of my actions. He'd made me wish I'd been braver, made me see I'd lost five years of my life I can never get back. Still, I don't want to see my father. I don't want his damn money. I can't be certain I'd have stayed in my current state of mind, but I would have fought for my dream rather than hiding from everything. Wasn't that the entire reason I left? To be me? I inhale and let it out. Me. I don't know myself.

My stomach is officially in knots, and I turn off the water. I did run. I can't deny it. Damn it to hell, I'm furious with myself. But I can create my own life and success now that I've decided to try. Resolve forms deep in my soul, where I've not felt anything for a long while . . . until Chris. I am going to embrace what is before me, including this weekend with Chris. Chris is my escape. This new job is my hope.

Pushing open the glass doors, I wrap myself in a fluffy white towel I'd found in a cabinet and wish for my clothes. Chris might dig up a shirt for me, but I'm sure he knows I need more for the weekend. We'll have to make time to stop by my place, and the idea bothers me. My place. My little hole in the wall the size of Chris's bedroom and bathroom. It shouldn't matter but somehow it does.

Stepping to the vanity mirror, I find the hair dryer easily since it's sitting on the shiny white tiled counter. Hair products are crucial, though, and I pull open the spacious medicine chest to hunt some down. Chris's electric shaver and various toiletries, including cologne and lotion, are inside. No hair products.

He has such great hair, and it's as long as his chin, so it must require gel or some kind or product.

I start to close the cabinet and hesitate, picking up the cologne and spraying it in the air, drawing in the familiar scent of Chris, warm and wonderful and strong in ways I've never experienced before. If you think the guy trying to protect you instead of walk all over you is the one trying to run your life, you're just as fucked up as I am. Ah, yes, I think. Exactly. I am. So is he. We are destruction waiting to happen to each other; he's a drug, as Rebecca had called the man in the journal, I'm already addicted to.

I shake off the thought and return the cologne to the cabinet. Still without hair products, I decide to focus on my makeup. Grabbing my purse, I pull out the journal to get to my makeup and set it on the counter, staring at it like it's some exploding device. "Where are you?" I whisper softly, but I'm not sure I'm talking to her or me. I am lost in her life, and I wonder if I want to be found. Does she want to be found wherever she is? Has she escaped into a new life like I have?

With Rebecca on my mind, I focus on creating a soft, natural look with my makeup and I finish with lip gloss. With no hair products, I turn on the dryer and wish for some straightening serum. Ten minutes later, my hair is dry and a bit wild. I'd kill for a flat iron right now.

I drop the towel and grab the robe, wrapping it around me, ready to find my clothes. I pause at the medicine cabinet and open it again, reaching for Chris's cologne and squirting it all over me. Inhaling, I draw in the earthy scent and smile. I like smelling like Chris.

Tentatively, I pull open the door to the bathroom and Chris is nowhere to be found, but the bedroom door is open. My bare feet touch the hardwood floor, and my gaze settles on the massive bed. On top are a good seven or eight bags, all from two high-end brand-name stores I know are in the building next door. On the floor is a woman's Louis Vuitton travel case, which would sport a $2,500 price tag.

My throat goes dry, and my chest hurts. I walk toward the items, and when I reach the bags, I see they are packed with clothes, shoes, and even, yes, bath items and a flat iron. A very expensive flat iron that puts my bargain special to shame.

I'd been in the shower maybe forty-five minutes and somehow he's pulled off an entire shopping spree. Or rather, he called downstairs and the staff jumped through hoops. These are expensive items, thousands of dollars expensive.

My heart begins to thunder in my chest. These are all stores I used to shop at. Stores I enjoyed. Sure, I left the money behind, but a more humble life hasn't been easy. I've found a place to store away the hunger for more, along with everything else associated with my past. I'd convinced myself I was fine, that I don't need these things. That I didn't care. But staring at these bags, there is an ache inside me, and I know it's not simply about nice things. It's about everything I left behind, about how easily that old life forgot me, even if I didn't forget it.

"Anything you don't like we can take back when we get back to the city."

I turn to find Chris standing in the doorway, one shoulder propped against the doorjamb, looking sexy and all man. "I can't take these clothes, Chris."

He pushes off the doorjamb. "Of course you can."

"No. No, I can't." I feel panic rising inside me.

He stops in front of me. "Sara—"

"I just want to run by my place and get my things."

"I made us reservations someplace special. We have more than an hour's drive. We need to get on the road right away."

"Chris." There is desperation in my voice I can't suppress. "I can't take these things."

"Sara, baby, if it's about money, that's not an issue. I want to spend it on you." He slides his hands to my cheeks, framing my face. "You've spent five years without the nice things you grew up knowing. Let me do this for you. I want to do this for you."

"Chris—"

"You can't tell me you don't miss these things."

"I do fine with the simple life."

"That's not the point. You have to miss these things."

Denial is on my lips, but he's watching me closely, and he's too smart to not see the truth. "Out of sight, out of mind. It's how I cope, not like this."

He runs a hand through my hair. He's gentle, and I fight the urge to lean into him, aware it will lesson my position. "You think I'm going to get you used to nice things and then leave."

"I know you are, Chris."

He presses his forehead to mine, strokes my cheek. "I told you. You'll be the one who'll run away, not me."

Me? Run away from him? He keeps saying that and now more than ever, it confuses me. Mr. "No White Picket Fence," and no relationship, is sounding like he's in this to stay and I'm not. His actions and words don't compute, and there is a

deep-seated need inside me rising and taking shape. A relationship with Chris beyond sex is becoming far too appealing to be
safe. I don't want to fall for him. I don't want to convince myself there is more between us than there is. "Chris—"

He kisses me, a long, deep, drugging kiss that leaves me
panting. "Get dressed, baby." He nuzzles my neck and pulls back,
a surprised look on his face. "Are you wearing my cologne?"
And the erotic heat in his eyes burns away my objections about
these gifts.

"Yes," I whisper. "I like smelling like you."

The yellow flecks I adore in his green eyes burn nearly
orange. "I like you smelling like me." He kisses me again, his
tongue stroking mine in a deep, seductive caress before he sets
me away from him. "Get dressed before I don't let you." He
turns and heads out the door, shutting it behind him.

I stare after him, feeling dazed, and my confusion ranks
as perpetual. He really wants me to have these clothes, I realize. And more so, it feels like he wants me to have them to
please me, not him. Though I'd not allowed myself to have the
thought upon seeing the bags, deep down I'd feared he was trying to make me fit some acceptable mold before taking me to
a public place he knows well. I've been there, done that, lived
in the place where I had to meet standards to be seen in public.

But no. I don't believe Chris needs me to fit some perfect
image to be on his arm. I felt his sincere desire to do this for
me. Emotion wells inside me. This is the first time since my
mother died that I truly feel cared about. It matters to me. Chris
is beginning to matter to me. I have to take the gifts.

My gaze falls on the bags. Maybe I do need these things. They will motivate me to study and earn a place at Riptide. It's not like before, when there was no hope of extra income. Yes. I am good with this. Chris is helping to motivate me.

Nevertheless, there's a knot in my stomach as I go through the items and pack the suitcase, finding several dresses, a pair of boots, several heels, lingerie, and toiletries. The lingerie is beautiful and expensive, and my blood heats thinking of wearing it for Chris. Since we are traveling and I have no idea where we're going, I decide to go casual to match Chris's typical biker gear.

After trying on a few items and picking my favorites, I choose a pair of slim black jean leggings and a sleek camel-colored blouse with sequins. The outfit is complete with a pair of high-heeled boots that lace up to my ankles. Beneath it all, I am wearing a cream-colored jeweled bra and thong set I'd pulled a ridiculous price tag from.

The flat iron is a relief, and I quickly put it to use, and note that I also have a curling iron for later use. For now, thanks to a high-quality flat iron, and some styling products also in the bags, my hair falls in sleek, shiny brunette waves down my shoulders. I glance at the two kinds of perfume that were included, but I choose to spray on another dollop more of Chris's cologne.

Finally, I'm ready and I head to the living room with my new Vuitton bag in tow. Chris is sitting in a leather chair, legs propped up on an ottoman and a sketch pad in hand. He sets the pad aside the instant he sees me and stands up.

"You look beautiful, Sara."

"Thank you. I wasn't sure how to dress."

He walks toward me, all loose-legged swagger and hotness. "You would have been perfect no matter what you chose. You are perfect."

No one in my life has ever said that to me but my mother. That it's Chris saying it now, that he is saying it with appreciation glowing in his hot gaze, warms me in ways well beyond the words.

He strokes a lock of my hair behind my ear, something I'm becoming accustomed to his doing, but I still shiver from the gentleness of the touch. "Ready to leave?"

"Yes. Where are we going?"

His lips curve. God, he has great lips. "I told you, baby. It's a surprise."

More of the emotion I'd felt in the bedroom rises inside me. "Chris—"

"Don't thank me. Just be with me, Sara."

"I am. I want to be."

His lips curve. "Good." He motions toward the exit. "Let's blow this joint, then, aye?"

I laugh. "Aye."

We head to the elevator, me pulling my roller Vuitton and him with a black leather case he throws over his shoulder. There is a raw energy and excitement in the air, and we glance at each other and smile. I've never had that kind of energy with anyone. I feel suddenly light and free. This is an adventure. Chris is an adventure.

We exit in a garage and I immediately spot not one, not two, but three Harleys, and stop dead in my tracks. "Holy cow, they're all yours, aren't they?"

He grins. "Yeah. You ever been on one?"

I shake my head.

"We'll have to fix that soon." He clicks his key ring and the Porsche's lights flicker.

We approach the car and next to it I admire a sky-blue classic Mustang that's been remodeled. "Is this yours, too?" I ask, pausing beside it.

"I have a thing for remodeling old Mustangs."

"How many do you have?"

"Five."

I blink at him. I know he has money. I know he's sold a lot of work. But still. "How rich are you, Chris?"

He barks out a laugh, his eyes twinkling. He knows I've mimicked his words when he'd asked about my father. "My father was an accomplished musician and well paid for his craft. My mother was Danielle Wright—as in the founder of the cosmetic line that still exists today."

Holy crap. He inherited a fortune on top of what he makes himself. "Do you own Danielle Wright Cosmetics?"

"I'm not a boardroom kind of guy. I sold out years ago and reinvested in things of more interest."

Stunned does not describe what I feel. "You're filthy rich, aren't you?"

He laughs. "It depends on how you define filthy, sweetheart." He wiggles a brow and opens the door to the Porsche.

"You don't seem that rich. I mean, clearly you have money, but you don't act like it."

"I don't know if that's a compliment or an insult." He doesn't look insulted, though, more entertained.

I study him a long moment, trying to see something I've missed in him. Some hint of what makes him like my father, or Michael—who rides my father's coattails and acts like he's successful on his own—but I see nothing. He doesn't treat people like they are beneath him. In fact, when he'd given me the clothes, he'd acted like wearing them was a favor to him, not an honor he'd bestowed upon me.

I lean forward, push to my toes, and kiss him on his sexy, perfect mouth. "It's a compliment, Chris. In every way possible." I pull back and see a flicker of surprise on his face before I slide into the car, letting the soft leather absorb my weight. He said I was never what he expected. He is never what I expect. And when Chris slips behind the wheel, and revs the engine of the 911 into a soft purr, I do not think about the car's connection to my father. I revel in how utterly male and sexy Chris is as he maneuvers the sleek vehicle onto the highway.

We are weaving through several side streets and Chris cranks up the radio to the old AC/DC song "Back in Black," and I laugh. "Old-school rock? I guess it goes with a Mustang obsession."

"I use music to paint by. This one reminds me of a particular work I created not so long ago."

"Every piece of art has a song attached?" I'm thrilled to see inside his creative process.

"Some pieces I play the same song over and over. Some I have a collection of songs I use."

"And this song goes to what work?"

"A Stormy Night San Fran piece I sold at auction last year."

We begin to cross the Bay Bridge, and I am growing curious about our destination, but not as curious as I am about Chris. "A Dark Sea," I say, knowing exactly the work he means.

He casts me a sideways look. "You do know your art and artists, don't you?"

I smile and sink lower into my seat, wondering if I will truly know this artist. "It sold for an astounding amount of money, Chris." Seven figures.

"Yeah," he agrees. "It did."

I turn to face him, studying his profile. "How does it feel to have people pay seven figures for your creation?"

"Like validation."

It's not the answer I expect. "Surely you're well beyond needing validation?" He steers the car out of the city and onto a major highway.

"I create in solitude and then take whatever I put on the canvas out to the world. And not all of my work sells for big money. A lot doesn't."

"You make millions a year on your art, Chris. That's big money."

"It's not about the money. I donate most of it anyway."

"You donate your art proceeds?"

"That's right."

"To whom?"

"Some years back, I was talked into an event held at the Children's Hospital Los Angeles, and it was pretty mind-blowing. All those brave kids and the parents who were dying

241

inside right along with them. I knew I had to do what I could to help and I have since."

He donates his money to save dying children. There are so many layers to this man—deep, dark, wonderful layers. I know he's fucked up. I know he's damaged. I know this need to help children must call to some part of him that's raw and bleeding. Which part?

"Have you guessed where we're going?" he asks, before I can find the words to express how much I admire what he's doing.

I glance around and realize we are on Highway 29 North. "Napa Valley?" And it hits me: he's taking me to a winery to show his support of my career.

"Have you ever been?"

I laugh. "No. I wasn't kidding when I said I have zero knowledge of wine. Well, I guess now I can say I have some knowledge but not much."

"We'll fix that," he promises.

My lips curve. I'm going to my first winery. I've always thought it would be a neat thing to do. "I'm excited, Chris. Thank you."

He grabs my hand and kisses it, cutting me a mischievous look. "I'm looking forward to having you alone and well wined."

I bite my lip. "Chivalry will get you everywhere."

"I'm counting on it."

"You didn't sleep much," he comments. "Maybe you should rest your eyes so you can enjoy our getaway."

"What about you? You slept less than me."

"I slept enough. Rest, baby. This is the one place you can count on my letting you sleep this weekend."

My lips curve. "Sounds like I should take a nap." I let my eyes shut, the soft hum of the car vibrating through me. And with Chris at the wheel, I find I am more relaxed than I have been in a very long time.

Twenty-two

"Wake up, baby. We're almost there."

I blink and feel Chris's gentle hand on my arm. "Where?"

"The hotel."

"I barely remember closing my eyes," I admit. "How long did I sleep?"

"Half an hour, out cold."

I sigh and sit up, aware of the hollow moan of my stomach as I stretch and bring the scenery into view. I gape at the miles and miles of beautiful green mountains and countryside. "It's gorgeous. Absolutely spectacular."

"The Mayacamas Mountains. And, yes, they are."

"I'm surprised they haven't shown up in your artwork."

"I'm not a landscape guy. You know that. I can't believe you've never been here. You've lived in San Francisco since college, right?"

I nod. "Yes. I just . . . it's the out-of-sight, out-of-mind thing." And a teacher's pay, I add silently, as my eyes light on a gorgeous hotel property and the name on the sign. Auberge du Nuit, the hotel for the rich and famous, like Chris. I remember reading about it in a magazine I'd tossed in the trash because it was torturing me with all I couldn't do and see.

"I'm going to put an end to that out-of-sight, out-of-mind thing, baby. Just you wait and see." He whips the vehicle onto the long driveway, and I shove aside the tension his words create. I'm not going to think about adjusting to his being gone, and he will be gone. For once, I'm living for the moment, and for the dream I am chasing.

The instant the Porsche is under the awning at the front door, a bellman in a sharp black suit opens my door. I step out of the car, and Chris does the same on his side.

"Good to see you, Mr. Merit," the bellman says in greeting.

Chris rounds the hood and tosses the keys at him. "Don't go on any joyrides, Rich."

"No, sir," Rich agrees, grinning, and Chris slides him a tip I'm pretty sure is a hundred-dollar bill. One-sixth of my weekly pay for parking the car. "Luggage is in the trunk."

"I'll have it up right away, sir," Rich assures him. "Are you doing an event at the gallery I haven't heard about?"

"Not this time," Chris replies. "For once, it's all pleasure." Chris laces his fingers in mine and waves at Rich.

We head toward the check-in desk. "A show?" I ask, unable to douse my curiosity.

"They have a gallery on the property."

My eyes light up. "It seems wine and art go hand in hand."

"A little too much for my taste," he mumbles under his

breath, and it's not the first time I've gotten a negative vibe from him about the association.

We are treated like royalty at the front desk, or rather Chris is. I am warmed by the way he keeps me close to his side, always touching me, as if he can't stand not to be with me.

By the time we step onto the elevator, headed toward the penthouse suite, and he leans against the wall, pulling me against him, my hips to his, I am all melted butter, and dripping chocolate. Yes, it's a silly saying Ella had used when she'd first met her doctor, but it's fitting. Ella. I miss her, and wish I'd hear from her, but Chris strokes a hand down my back, molding me closer, and my mind is pretty much mush.

He nuzzles my neck. "I cannot wait to get you alone."

My hands settle on the hard wall of his chest, and I peer up at him. "I thought we had reservations."

"We do." He pulls my ear to his lips again, and I know there must be cameras and recording devices. Of course there are. "Which is why I'm going to fuck you hard and fast. We'll go slow later."

I gasp at the wicked words and my sex clenches, wetness clinging to my panties. Hard and fast. Oh yes. Please.

The doors ding a warning and open. Chris takes my hand and all but drags me down the hallway. The walk is eternal, the Alice-in-Wonderland tunnel of forever, before he slides a card through the door lock and we are inside. Before I can blink, I'm against the wall, with Chris pressed deliciously against me, his thick erection nuzzling my belly, his mouth devouring mine.

I moan into his mouth, the taste of him rich with desire, hungry for me. Me. That's what makes me hottest of all, beyond his hands stroking my body, palming my breasts and nipples. How much I taste his desire for me. How much I feel his need.

"No one has ever made me lose control the way you do, Sara." The confession is sealed with another scalding kiss, and oh yes, I am melting.

A knock sounds on the door. "Bellman."

"Fuck," Chris hisses, pressing a hand to the wall, and I sense him reaching for control, and I have this sudden, desperate need to keep him from finding it. This sudden certainty that the only way I will ever know this man as I want to is to take his control.

"Come back later," I call out, and press my lips to Chris's, my hand sliding down his hip and around to cup his shaft, stroking the thick ridge through his jeans.

He growls low in his throat and pulls his mouth from mine, and his eyes are dark pools of turbulent passion. He's mad. Holy shit. He's furious. "Losing control and you taking it from me are two different things, Sara. You won't ever take it from me." He shoves off the walk and stalks to the door and opens it, whistling to get the bellman's attention.

Frozen to the wall, I feel shell-shocked. The dark Chris, the dangerous damaged Chris I keep forgetting exists, is back. What just happened to set him off? And damn it to hell, why does it turn me on when it shouldn't?

The bellman is in the door with our bags and I haven't moved. I feel his eyes on me, and I know I must look a disheveled mess. Somehow, I focus on the room, bringing the amazing details into focus. A vaulted ceiling encases me and to my right is a living area and full kitchen. A California king-size bed is to my left, a stucco fireplace in the corner in front of it, and beyond that a private patio overlooking the mountains.

The hotel door shuts and Chris locks it. My heart is thundering in my chest. I can't look at him. I don't think he wants me to look at him. I don't know why. It's just a feeling.

He rolls my suitcase to the center of the room and unzips it, pulling out a pair of cream-colored strappy high heels he drops on the floor, and a pale yellow chiffon dress he lays on top of the case when he closes it. "Put them on."

I force my eyes to his. "You want me—"

"Yes."

I wet my dry lips. Okay. He wants me to dress up. Sounds like a good excuse to escape and regroup and boy, does regrouping sound appealing. I walk to grab the dress, intending to head to the bathroom, wherever it is.

"Right here," Chris says. "Where I can see you."

I gape and try to clarify again. "You want me—"

"Yes. I want."

He sits down on the bed, and I realize he intends to watch me undress and dress again. This is about control, about him demonstrating what he has and I do not. He needs it. He needs it on some deep level, and I am not going to deny him. For reasons I've yet to understand, giving Chris control doesn't bother me, but I know in my heart, it keeps me at a distance. This is his wall, his barrier, his great divide; I am beginning to wonder if I can ever conquer his barriers. Right now, though, I'm happy to let him conquer.

I swallow hard, my throat like sandpaper, my body wet

and wanting. I am aroused by this and everything Chris does. I reach for the dress.

"No," he orders. "Undress first."

I nod and lean against the wall to unlace my boots, and pull them and my socks off. He stares at my pink-painted toes and, good Lord, he makes even that hot. I reach for my pants and unlace the strings holding them closed before sliding them down over my hips and down my legs, leaving the expensive, gold-jeweled cream-colored panties in place.

My shirt comes next, and I pull it over my head and toss it to the floor, standing before Chris in only my bra and panties.

His gaze sweeps over me, hot and heavy, his eyes dark, hooded. "Everything."

I blanch. "But—"

"Everything. I want to be able to get to you when I want you. And we'll both know I can anytime, anywhere."

Heat rushes over my skin at the implication. He means to have me in public. I should be appalled. I should say no. Instead, I am weak in the knees with desire. I slide my fingers into the thin strings of my thong and slide it to the floor.

Chris's gaze follows the path they take, his stare traveling my skin, touching me with such heat that it might as well be his hand. I step out of the panties and have no intention to stand there and wait for his next command.

I unhook my bra and toss it at him. "Happy now?" I challenge.

He arches a brow, and I think I might see a hint of a smile on his lips, maybe. Perhaps not. "Don't test me, Sara. You won't like the results."

"Or maybe I will." Maybe I'll push his control. Maybe I'll get inside him and tear down the wall.

"You won't." His words are hard and too certain to be comfortable for me.

He pushes to his feet, though, and I silently cry out with joy. Touch me. I don't care how you do it, just do it. He saunters over to me and stops out of reach. He scoops up the dress, his eyes raking over my body. My nipples pucker under his scrutiny, tight balls of aching need and I pray for his mouth on me sooner, not later.

He hands me the dress. "Put it on."

Put it on? Without him touching me? He can't be serious. "Right now?"

"Right now."

You know I have to punish you. Rebecca's words come back to me. He's punishing me, absolutely torturing me. Making me pay a price for daring to take control. But deep down, I come to a conclusion. I came close to breaking through his wall or he wouldn't be doing this. It's this information that makes the torture bearable.

I take the dress, and I notice he is careful not to touch me. I pull the chiffon material over my head and the silk rasps over my nipples and skin. I am so ultrasensitized I think I could come with one touch of his mouth in the right place. And I believe there would be many right places at this juncture in time.

The dress falls into place, and Chris's eyes never leave mine. "The shoes."

I slip them on and he walks around me, giving me a careful,

penetrating inspection before stopping before me. "Beautiful, baby. You look stunning."

My chin lifts. "But not stunning enough to fuck right now."

"More than enough to fuck, just not yet." He leans in, his lips by my ear, but he is careful not to touch me anywhere else. "Because when I do, you'll be so hot and wet, you'll be mine to do with what I want. And believe me, baby—I want plenty."

"You're punishing me."

He looks at me and his eyes soften as he brushes his knuckles over my shoulder. Goose bumps lift all over my skin. "Does that feel like punishment?"

More like pure bliss. "No."

"Then you have your answer."

We step into the hallway and Chris takes my hand, his eyes meeting mine, and I know he can see the sweet relief washing over me at his touch. His green eyes dance with amber heat, and he leads me down the hallway, all masculine sensuality and raw power. I am insanely into this man. He pushes every button I own, in all the right ways. Every second I am with him, I feel more alive.

Another couple waits by the elevator, and we step inside behind them. Chris leans against the wall and pulls my back against his front. I soften against all his hardness, and his fingers curl around my waist, where they begin a slow caress. My nipples pucker against the thin material and I become ultra-aware of how naked I am underneath the dress.

The man across from me glances down, stroking my chest with a stare that makes me want to smack him for the woman he is with. I turn in Chris's arms, giving the man my back. "Where are we headed?"

"In light of recent events, I thought food before wine seemed a good idea."

"Yes. Please."

The elevator dings and we let the other couple exit first. Chris takes my hand, and I hit the elevator button to hold the door. "I need to go upstairs." I glance down at my dress, my nipples puckering too obviously.

His lips quirk. "I already planned to have the hotel bring you a shawl and a coat to match the dress in case the evening gets chilly."

Relief washes over me. "Thank you."

"You just let me take care of everything tonight." He pulls me under his arm and I let go of the elevator button as we step into the lobby. Let Chris take care of everything. It is a thrilling, dangerous idea, I cannot help but crave.

Twenty-three

We are escorted to a circular private dining room. Chris holds the chair for me as I settle next to an oval window overlooking green mountains and a glorious blue skyline. I slide my purse onto the chair and I am in awe of the view. "It's spectacular."

Chris claims the window seat across from me and slips out of his leather jacket he'd put on as we'd left the room. "So is the food, but since I'm taking you to a special winery that will serve their vintages along with fruit and cheese, I suggest we eat fairly light. I thought we'd visit the restaurant for brunch tomorrow before we leave, if you'd like?"

"Yes. Very much. Sounds perfect." I am warmed by the romance of this place and his actions, but I tell myself not to get carried away. This isn't romance. It's a sexy adventure. After all, I'm not wearing panties or a bra.

"Anything look good?" Chris asks after I've studied the menu a moment.

"Everything. I'm starving." It's nearly three and we haven't eaten since early morning.

A waiter appears and Chris arches a brow at me. "Ready?"

"I am. Cobb salad for me."

Chris hands both of our menus to the waiter. "Burger for me. Well done. And bring us a bottle of the recommended wine selection—the Robert Craig zinfandel."

The waiter gives a small bow. "Coming right up, Mr. Merit."

"No beer for you?" I ask when the waiter departs.

"It's never good to mix alcohol, and I have a few friends around these corners of the world who would have my hide for drinking beer over wine."

It hits me how well Chris is known here, how the waiter and the doorman knew him by name. A sick feeling hits me. I never bring women to my home. Is this where he brings them? Where he wines and dines them into pantyless submission. "How often do you come here?"

"A couple times a year." He gives me a shrewd, narrow look, and I'm pretty certain he's reading me like a book. I hate that I am transparent, that I have knots in my gut, and that I am reacting this way at all. I worry I'm getting emotionally attached to Chris and I don't want to be hurt.

Chris slides a brochure of some sort from the edge of the table in front of me. "This is why I visit."

I blink down at what appears to be an advertisement for the art gallery on-site and swallow hard at the list of featured artists, including Chris. I've jumped to conclusions and made it obvious.

"And to be clear, Sara, until now, I've never brought a woman here."

My gaze jerks to his. "Never?"

"Never."

"Then why am I here?"

"You tell me. Why did you come?"

"Because you asked me."

"I'm sure there are plenty of men who've hungered to give you an escape, even take care of you, whom you've rejected."

It's true. I've barely dated since college, and the few dates I've had were disasters. "And I'm sure there are plenty of women who've hungered for more with you."

He studies me a long moment. "Why five years, Sara?"

The unexpected probe sets my pulse to racing. "I thought you didn't ask personal questions?"

"I've done a lot of things differently with you."

"Why?"

"Because you are you."

"I don't know what that means."

"Neither do I, but I'm hoping to find out."

There is an odd tightening in my chest. Emotion. I don't want to feel any emotion but he pulls it from me anyway. "Can you tell me when you do?"

He smiles, and it's a gorgeous smile that chips away at the tension prickling at my nerve endings. "You will be the first to know." He turns serious quickly. "Who was he, Sara?"

"He who?" I ask, but I know where this is going.

"The man who fucked with your head enough to make you celibate for five years."

The waiter appears and saves me from answering. I don't want to talk about Michael. I don't want to remember him. He's the past.

The waiter settles two glasses in front of us and then pulls a bottle of chilled wine from a silver ice bucket. The waiter works the cork from the bottle, but Chris ignores him. He leans back and watches me, his eyes intense with scrutiny.

The wine is uncorked and a sample is poured for Chris. He smells the wine and tastes it. "Excellent selection," he says to the waiter. "Give your wine expert my regards."

The waiter fills our glasses, gives a small bow, and departs. "Yes, Mr. Merit. I absolutely will."

I sip from my glass, and my taste buds explode with a tangy fruit flavor with a hint of oak I quite enjoy. Chris stares at me. "Who was he?" His voice is low, taut.

I inhale sharply and set my wine back down. "The past. Leave it at that."

"No."

"Chris—"

"Who was he, Sara?"

"My father's prodigy, the son he never had." The confession slides from my mouth without a conscious decision to allow it to.

"How long were you with him?"

"Six months."

"How serious?"

"An engagement ring."

Surprise flashes in his eyes. "That's pretty serious."

I run my hand over my tense forehead, and for once, words escape me.

"Did you love him?"

"No," I say immediately, dropping my hand. "I was

infatuated. He was five years older—successful and confident. He was . . . everything my father wanted for me."

"What about your mother?"

"She wanted whatever my father wanted. I barely know the person who would do anything to please . . . him." I cannot bring myself to say Michael's name, and not because I have any emotional connection. I simply dislike remembering who he made me, or rather, who I let him make me.

"Anything?"

I nod stiffly. "Even when I hated him for it."

"Are we talking sex, Sara?"

I let my eyes shut, trying to make my suddenly thick breath leave my lungs. "Everything."

"So the answer is yes. He made you do things you didn't want to do." It's not a question.

My lashes snap open. "Because it was him and he treated me like I was his property put on this earth for his personal satisfaction."

He studies me, his expression impassive, his features carved in stone. "And how do I make you feel?"

"Alive," I whisper without hesitation. "You make me feel alive."

A warm blanket of awareness wraps around us. "As you do me, Sara."

Chris's unexpected confession does funny things to my stomach. I make him feel alive?

"Your food has arrived," the waiter announces in a far too efficient display of good, poorly timed, service.

My salad, which is gigantic, is placed in front of me, and

then the waiter sets down Chris's burger. I sip my wine, and the chill helps calm the heat burning through my body.

"They have an impressive wine list here at the hotel," Chris comments. "And they have a wine educator on staff. If you want, I can arrange for her to spend some time with you in the morning."

"I'd like that," I say, aware of how hard he is trying to show support for my job. It matters, I think again. Chris keeps doing things that matter.

We dig into our food and he launches into some interesting wine facts about the region, and I am far more interested in wine than I was when I was simply learning names and wineries.

"Part of understanding wine is understanding the regions where it's produced. Italian wine is so revered because of the soil and the climate. Napa is one of the few places that can compete in those arenas, at least in my opinion. The climate here is classified as 'Mediterranean.' Only two percent of the earth's surface is Mediterranean. Add summers and mild winters, and grapes grow all year long."

"It allows the grapes to grow but does it change the flavor?"

"Absolutely. Ten million years ago, the collision of the tectonic plates created the mountains and terrain here, along with a multitude of volcanic eruptions. The result is more than one hundred varieties of soil, and each lends a different flavor and texture to the product produced."

Impressed with his knowledge, I ask a lot of questions as we eat. "How do you know so much about wine?"

There is a slight crackle to the air, a subtle tension. "My father was a connoisseur of wine to an extreme, and as you've noticed, despite my preferences otherwise, wine and art meld together quite frequently."

His father. I sense tension in him when his father is brought up, and I'm fairly certain he is also why Chris prefers beer over wine.

"Your car has arrived, Mr. Merit," the waiter announces, appearing by our table.

"We'll be right out," Chris replies. "Charge the room for the tab."

I'm surprised by this news. "You aren't driving?"

"Easier to enjoy the wine with a sober driver to drive us back to the room." Chris pushes to his feet and walks over to me, pulling my chair out and helping me to my feet. Suddenly, I am pressed against him, his hand molding me to his body, and he adds softly, "Easier to enjoy you."

We step outside and I am reminded of how two hours of travel can drastically impact the weather. Where San Francisco has the chilly late-August wind off the ocean, Calistoga, which is the Napa region we are in, does not.

A limo is parked in front of the doorway, and it doesn't surprise me to learn it's for us. While I've never attended a wine tour, I'm aware the limo ride between wineries is fairly common. What isn't common is the bellman handing me a neatly folded and delicately beaded cream-colored shawl.

"In case you get cold, ma'am. I understand you need a coat for your trip back to the city as well. We'll have that waiting for you in your room. The city does get quite chilly."

"Thank you." Relief washes over me at the sight of the

garment, despite what I guess to be the eighty-degree temperature. Inside the winery, I fear there will be air-conditioning, and my braless state will draw unwanted attention.

Chris smirks at the look on my face, and I lift my chin defiantly and slide the shawl around my shoulders before climbing into a car with strangers.

"Ready?" he asks when I'm well bundled.

"Ready."

The bellman opens the car door, and I slide to the far window seat to find I am alone until Chris joins me. He settles in next to me and the door shuts behind him. "Will there be others joining us?" I ask.

"Just us," Chris informs me, and I wonder why I imagined he would have it any other way. He has money and self-proclaimed desire for privacy.

The window between us and the driver slowly lowers but I am behind the driver and cannot see what he looks like unless I twist and look back. I suck in a breath as Chris's hand slides under my dress and settles on my bare thigh, his fingers splaying intimately around my leg.

"I'm Eric, Mr. Merit," the driver announces. "I'll be your guide today. Are we still touring the vineyard, sir?"

"We are," Chris replies. "I'm eager to show Ms. McMillan how Chateau Cellar produces a wine to rival the best in Paris." He glances down at me, his green eyes dancing with enough heat to scorch the seat, while his reply is somehow matter-of-fact. "Chateau established Napa Valley as the wine industry it is today. In a blind test in Paris in 1976, the judges, biased to their own wineries, chose one of the chateau's wines."

A tray lowers in front of us, but all I can think about is Chris's fingers caressing lazily beneath my skirt. A bottle of wine and two glasses appear, and Eric quickly explains, "It's a 2002 Chateau Cellar cabernet sauvignon, one of our flagship wines, and a gift from our owners to you and Ms. McMillan, Mr. Merit, for your long-term support of our operation."

Chris leans forward and fills two glasses, never taking his hand from my leg. "I'll be sure and extend them heartfelt thanks."

He lifts his glass and sips the wine, before holding it to my mouth. "Try it." He gently urges my legs a bit farther apart, and I do not have wine on my mind.

The limo engine rumbles and we begin to move. My heart is thundering in my ears. "Chris," I plead, and I am not sure if I am asking him to touch me or asking him to stop. Both I think.

"Drink, Sara," he orders softly, no give in his voice. He is in control, still teaching me that lesson. The driver is close, so very close, and he fully intends to take this further than I want. He's pushing me out of my comfort zone, testing me again, I think. Testing me. He is always testing me and I am not sure what the scorecard is or even what I'm trying to achieve.

I drink from the same spot that Chris has drunk from and taste the sweet plum flavor. Chris's fingers brush my sex, and I barely manage to swallow the wine.

"How is it?" he asks.

"Good," I whisper.

"Just good?" he challenges, and his finger strokes my sensitive flesh. "Try another swallow."

There is an edge of danger in the air; the risk of the driver catching us is all too obvious. I have never done anything like this in public and it frightens me, but what is most shocking is how it excites me.

I sip the bloodred liquid, and Chris's finger slides inside me. My gaze goes to the seat in front of me, but I cannot see the driver and he cannot see me. Though I feel as if he can.

Chris drinks from the glass again and then holds it to my lips. "Another," he commands softly, tersely.

He isn't going to allow me to escape this car without having his way with me. Of this, I am certain. I don't want to stop. I don't want to be the girl who never lived in the moment. Alive, I'd told him, about what he makes me feel, and he does. I take the glass from him and down it.

He laughs low in his throat. "A little liquid courage?"

"Yes," I confess.

"Is the wine satisfactory?" Eric calls out.

Chris sets the glass down, still teasing me mercilessly. "Is the wine satisfactory, Ms. McMillan?"

I glower at him through the thralls of near orgasm, my voice throaty and affected. "It's . . . exceptional."

"Excellent," Eric approves jovially. "We're approaching the entry to the vineyards now." He begins telling us about the history of the territory, but I do not comprehend his words. It is all I can do not to moan as Chris's thumb teases my clit and he slides a second finger inside me. The ache inside me expands and blossoms. I am going to have an orgasm in a limo with the driver practically watching. This can't be happening.

"If you look to your right, you'll see an important piece of the chateau's history, Ms. McMillan," Eric says. "Do you see the pond?"

"Yes," I manage in a choked voice without looking. My body clenches around Chris's fingers and spasms. My teeth sink into my lip and I turn to the window to hide my face, for fear Eric might glance at me in his rearview mirror. He's still speaking, telling me a story. I am oblivious to anything but the shattering of my body.

"Isn't it a wonderful story?" Eric asks, wrapping up whatever he'd been saying.

"Yes," I manage again, capable of speech but barely. "It's delightful."

"Isn't it?" Chris asks, dark, heated mischief dancing in his green eyes as he strokes the slick folds of my sensitive flesh and slowly pulls out his fingers.

His eyes meet mine and hold my stare, and he brings his fingers to his mouth and sucks them dry. "Delicious," he murmurs, and my body clenches one last time at the brazenly sensual act.

"I'm so glad you're enjoying the wine," Eric proclaims.

Chris and I blink at each other, and we erupt into laughter. I do not know how I have gone from dark forbidden passion to this lighter shared moment with Chris, but I do know one thing for sure. I have never felt more alive.

Twenty-four

After a forty-five minute tour of the vineyards, I have had a glass of wine and I'm feeling a bit loose-limbed and warm all over for reasons aside from Chris's wicked ways. I've enjoyed the tour and learned far more about wine on the drive than in all my studies on my own.

The limo arrives at the chateau and it is truly a nineteenth-century castle, with green vines traveling the stone walls and massive arched wooden doors almost as high as the structure.

"It was remodeled in the seventies," Eric tells us, "and the entire two hundred and fifty-six–acre property was converted to a modern wine-making facility."

I follow Chris as he slides across the seat and pause as Eric turns to me, and I see him clearly for the first time. He is in his midfifties with graying hair and sharp blue eyes that miss nothing.

"Thank you for such a wonderful tour, Eric."

He inclines his head. "My pleasure." I cringe at the choice of words, because though his well-schooled features give nothing away, this man is too sharp not to know about the pleasure in the backseat. "Enjoy the chateau, Ms. McMillan."

Chris has long ago shed his jacket, and he tosses it onto a backseat before exiting the car. I follow him out and understand why the jacket is staying behind. It's still a warm day despite the five o'clock sun creeping lower in the sky, a complete turn-around from the chilly city on the ocean I've come to love.

I slide my hand into Chris's to allow him to help me out of the car, and I am amazed at the zip of electricity up my arm from such simple contact. My eyes meet his and I know he feels what I do, and I'm almost certain he, too, is surprised by how readily we impact each other. But then two lost souls searching for an escape should connect, I reason.

With a cautious tug of my dress, I stand up and Chris's lips quirk in a way that tells me he is thinking of what we'd done in the back of the car. I am, too.

His hand slides to my elbow, and we head through a massive wooden door that seems more movie fantasy than real life. We step inside the chilled foyer with its high ceiling and stone walls.

An employee greets us, a pretty woman in her twenties, with long blond hair and a curvy petite figure shown off in a pale pink suit. Her gaze lingers on Chris with admiration. I have a thing about blondes. I always have. Well, since high school when my best friend, who was of Swedish ancestry, caught every guy's eye with her long, natural white-blond hair and curves in all the right places. I was cute, and she was beautiful. This guide makes me feel cute.

"I'm Allison, Mr. Merit," she announces, offering him her hand, which he accepts. "Such an honor to have you here. I'll be taking you on a tour of the chateau." She flicks me a look but doesn't extend her hand. "Welcome to our establishment."

Chris slides an arm around my waist, almost as if he senses my sudden insecurity. "Thank you, Allison. This is Sara, and she's the reason I'm here today. I want her to learn why this place is special."

His hand resting on my waist is possessive, protective. My throat thickens with his actions. I feel as if no one else exists when I am with Chris, and no one has ever made me feel this way. My fear of cute verses beautiful fades away.

We begin the tour and we stop in various tasting rooms made of stucco and stone walls, and rich culture everywhere. We end the tour in a wine cellar that is chilly, and I am suddenly aware of my barely there dress and lack of undergarments.

Allison leads us toward the stairs and before we follow, Chris pulls me close, blocking her view with his back. "Cold?" he asks, molding me close, and his hand glides up my rib cage, under the shawl, to caress my breast, and tease my already puckered nipple.

"Not anymore," I confess breathlessly.

"You look beautiful tonight, Sara. I can't stop thinking about all the things I'm going to do to you when the opportunity presents itself."

When the opportunity presents itself, not when we get back to the room. Control. This is all about control, and I'd almost taken his earlier tonight. He didn't like it, and he's making damn sure I know I'm at his mercy. While I sense how much he needs this control, and I am aroused by this side of him, there is a deep part of me that screams in protest, that will not let go of what I've spent five years fighting for—my own control.

"Maybe you should think about what I am going to do to you," I challenge.

His eyes darken, heat, and he surprises me by leaning down near my ear and whispering, "I've been thinking about it since the day I met you."

I expected some power play, and maybe it is that and more, because my reaction is white-hot arousal. My heart races wildly and heat rushes through my blood. When he pulls back and draws my hand into his, leading me toward the stairs, I am aware of the raw masculine power radiating off him, of my absolute burn for this man. Yes. He has control and I cannot wait to give him more. This is a power play and he's won.

We reach the top of the stairs to be greeted by an older couple who look as if they're in their midsixties. The woman is dressed in a simple blue sheath and the man in black slacks and white button-down collar shirt.

"Chris! It's so good to see you, son," the woman says. "It's been too long since I've seen my godchild." She hugs Chris like she is a mother seeing her child for the first time in years, and without question, there are deep ties here.

The man hugs Chris next. "We don't see you enough, boy."

Chris pats him on the back and releases him. "I know. I'll work on that." He wraps his arm around my waist. "Mike and Katie Wickerman, I'd like you to meet Sara McMillan."

"It's lovely to meet you, Sara." Katie beams, offering me her hand. She is pretty, with sleek gray hair and a friendly smile.

"Thank you," I say, sliding my palm against hers. It is warm and so is she. I like her. "I'm excited to be here."

"Welcome, Sara," Mike chimes in eagerly. "About time he brings a woman around."

I blush and shake his hand, but he pulls me close and hugs me. He leans back to inspect me. "Let me look at you. No. No, you don't look like a wine virgin to me."

My cheeks heat further, and I laugh. "I guess the excellent cabernet I had in the limo saved me."

"Broke your cherry, aye?"

I laugh and so does Chris, who pulls me under his arm and leans near my ear. "I thought I did that."

"Mike!" Katie chides. "She doesn't know you well enough to get your sense of humor." She motions us forward. "I have a special tasting room set up for us, but we won't be allowing Mike a taste of the festivities."

We fall into step behind Katie and Mike. "They like you," Chris whispers.

"Godchild?"

"They were close friends of my parents and they never had kids of their own."

I inhale at this announcement, stunned to realize Chris has done more than bring me some place he doesn't bring other women. This is a piece of his past that I didn't think he would allow me to see, but he's let me inside his world, at least this tiny part.

My steps are a little more anxious as we enter a room with a huge wooden table spanning several feet, with a dozen or so chairs on each side. Fruit and cheese trays are displayed in the center of one end of the table.

Chris and I sit side by side, and Katie and Mike sit down across from us. Katie is studying me with interest, and I tie the shawl around my shoulders, afraid I'll ruin the virginal image I've been granted with too much nipple action. "Chris tells us you've recently went to work at a gallery in the city?" Katie asks.

"Yes. The Allure Art Gallery downtown, where Chris has a collection for sale. That's how I met him."

"I know it well," Katie comments. "And you were a school-teacher before this?"

I'm surprised by how much Chris has shared with her. "I was. I am. My degree is in art, and it's my true love. We'll see how the rest of the summer works out. My boss says he has high hopes but seems to think I need to know about wine to truly navigate the art world."

Mike knocks on the table. "Right he is. Everyone needs to know about wine."

"Chris doesn't think so," I dare to remark.

Katie's gaze falls on her godson. "Then why does the local gallery serve wine?"

"Because this is Napa Valley."

"Exactly," she concurs. "Wine and art go together."

Mike waves at a waiter. "Sounds like the cue to start the sampling. It'll loosen everyone up." He winks at me. "That's when you really get to know someone."

Chris looks amused. "Good thing I don't loosen up easily." He nudges me. "You do, though. Are you going to tell us all your secrets over cabernet?"

"Hold out for a good year, honey," Katie whispers conspiratorially. "Make him pay for your confessions."

I glance at Chris, and he smirks. "Name the year, and I'll gladly pay the price."

"I'm not the one who's lacking in a confessional," I remind him. "Maybe we need to get you a case of beer."

"Not in the chateau you won't," Katie assures us.

Chris leans close. "It's going to take a whole lot more than a case of beer."

Yes, I think. It will. I've opened up to him, but he hasn't to me, yet I am here, with what amounts to his only family, and again I think—it matters. I don't allow myself to think about how I've gone from an escape to looking for things of consequence or where that may be leading me.

Time becomes inconsequential as I taste wine after wine, nibble cheese, and listen to Mike and Katie tell me stories about how they got started. It only marginally surprises me to learn they met his father through the big Paris 1976 tasting that put them, and Napa Valley, on the wine map.

"Chris's parents traveled with us for moral support," Katie explains. "Danielle—Chris's mother—she was like a guardian angel. I swear that woman had a way of making a person smile, even the Paris locals who didn't want us Americans in the competition couldn't resist her charm."

It's hard to gauge Chris's response to Katie's memories of his mother with him beside me, but I wish I could. Too soon, more wine samples arrive and the conversation shifts. My window into Chris's family life has, at least for the time being, closed.

With each wine we taste, I listen to stories about how Katie and Mike crafted the flavors down to the soil, the climate, and processing. They sprinkle stories of the rich and famous who have visited the chateau and acquired each variety.

"Chris is always our number one star, though," Katie declares.

Chris snorts and sips from his glass. "I'm just—"

"A famous artist," I finish for him and kiss his cheek.

He runs his hand down my hair and kisses my forehead. "Me," he says, staring down at me. "I'm just me."

I smile, feeling the effects of quite a lot of wine. "Hmmm. Yes. Just you."

He arches a brow. "What does that mean?"

A waiter approaches, and Katie and Mike chat with him. I lower my voice. "I like 'just you.'"

Chris's eyes darken. "Do you now?"

My lips curve. "Yes."

"He's just like his mother," Katie comments, drawing us back into the conversation and we turn to acknowledge her as she adds, "Humble pie, that woman. You'd never know she was an heiress to an empire any more than you'd know Chris is an acclaimed artist."

"And his father was an arrogant ass," Mike grumbles, "but I loved the guy." He pushes to his feet. "Son, that reminds me. I want to give you something before I forget."

I glance up at Chris, searching his face for a reaction to the comment about his father. He responds to my unspoken question. "He was an arrogant ass, baby." He strokes my cheek. "Behave. I'll be back."

"Of course," I assure him. "I'll only be asking Katie to share all your deep, dark secrets."

His expression tightens. "And she won't have the answers."

"Oh, I might have a few tidbits to share," Katie pipes in playfully.

Chris does not look pleased, but he pushes to his feet anyway and slides into a good-natured grumble to match Mike's "women" comment before he saunters away with his godfather.

Katie rests her elbow on the table, chin on her palm. "You're good for him."

"I . . . am?"

"Yes. You are. The boy is so damn guarded that it's worried me, but he's different with you. Relaxed. It does my heart good to see someone finally breaking through to him. He had a hard time growing up, but I'm sure you know that."

This little jewel of information has me eager for more. I open my mouth to ask more detail, but Allison rushes forward and whispers into Katie's ear. "Oh dear. Sara, dear, I have a problem I need to attend. I'll be back soon."

Disappointment fills me. Katie is the only person I may ever know who can share Chris's secrets, besides Mike, and I don't see that happening. Suddenly, I'm alone with a tray of cheese and fruit and several glasses of wine. Fifteen minutes later, I've emptied the glasses and I know it was a mistake. My head is spinning, and I quickly nibble cheeses because, apparently, drinking makes me want to eat and calories are of no consequence. In fact, I'm pretty sure wine cancels out calories right about now.

I feel Chris's return before I see him, a tingling awareness the hum of too much wine in my blood cannot diminish. My gaze lifts to the doorway as he enters, followed by Mike, who looks confused. "Where's Katie?"

"She had an emergency with a guest, I think."

Mike scowls. "How long has she been gone?"

"Right after you two left."

"Oh crap," he grumbles. "I better go check on her."

Chris hasn't spoken, and I really can't read him. My head is too fuzzy. He saunters over to me and squats down in front of me, moving my chair to face him.

His hand settles on my leg. "You need to get some air?"

"Air would be good," I confirm, and he helps me to my feet and I study his face, cursing the wine I've drank. His happy mood has faded, and there is an edge to him I haven't seen tonight. Whatever he and Mike talked about, it's stolen my lighthearted artist.

I touch his cheek. "What's wrong?"

He pulls me close, and his hand slides behind my neck, and sets off alarms. His dark side is back in full force. "You see too much, Sara."

"And you, Chris, don't let me see enough."

He doesn't reply, doesn't move. We are frozen in place, and I am lost in his stormy stare, his turbulent mood radiating off me. When he takes my hand to lead me toward the room's back door, my footing is unsteady. Wine and Chris do not mix well, I think, and it is the one thought I cling to as we exit into a garden. Wine and Chris do not mix. Why? I intend to find out.

Twenty-five

Even with too much wine in my system, and his hand still firmly wrapped around mine, I feel Chris closing off, erecting walls around him as we exit through a side door of the chateau. We cross a small brick walkway to a wooden bridge that arches over a large pond. The night is upon us, and glowing orange lanterns dangle from poles mounted in the wooden rails, the stars above us dotting the black, cloudless canvas. I inhale the hot air; the cool breeze I'd hoped for to clear my head is nowhere to be found. The stuffy night is suffocating, as is the tension humming off Chris.

He leads me down the wooden bridge toward a gazebo, and my nostrils flare with the sweet scent of roses. These flowers are haunting me everywhere I go. I can see the greenery entwining the wooden overhang, delicate buds clinging to the leaves. I do feel ready to bloom, ready to go wherever he leads me. That is what Rebecca felt for the man she'd been writing about. That is how Chris makes me feel.

Halfway down the walkway, I stumble, and Chris reaches around and catches me, his strong arms circling my waist, my hand resting on his chest.

"You okay?"

"Yes. Fine." I don't look at him. This is the second time in as many nights he's had to right my drunken footing, and it's embarrassing. I haven't had this much to drink since the day of my mother's funeral.

Once we're under the gazebo, he leans on the railing and I almost expect him to set me away from him. Relief washes over me when he pulls me into his arms and folds me against him. I settle my hand on his chest, over his heart, the soft thrum beating against my palm. The buzz in my head irritates me, clouding my ability to gauge Chris's mood accurately.

"What's upset you?"

"Who says I'm upset?"

"Me."

"Like I said. You see too much."

I ignore the comment. "Mike seemed eager to give you whatever he wanted to give you. I expected you to return pleased, not cranky like a bear."

"Cranky like a bear?"

My lips quirk. "Yes. Cranky like a bear."

He studies me with a hooded look, his lashes thick veils hiding his eyes from my prying gaze. He is beautiful in the starlight—and the wine, or perhaps Chris himself, has washed away my inhibitions.

I reach up and trace his full, sensual mouth that I know can both punish and please, studying him. My fingers travel his face, tracing his high, defined cheekbones, and down to the light stubble on his square jaw. I imagine how the stubble could scrape my bare skin. I am infatuated with his beauty, his talent, his wit . . . his body. But I want to know the man.

"Talk to me, Chris," I plead when the silence stretches eternally.

He draws my hand into his and kisses the back. "Not an easy thing to do when you're touching me." He slides my hair behind my ear. "Especially when you've been drinking and I can't do any of the many things I planned to do to you while you're pantyless."

A slow smile slides onto my lips. "And braless."

"Thanks for reminding me, because I'm not going to push you when you've had too much to drink."

Push me? Please. I yearn to know what that means. "What happened to Mr. 'I'm No Saint'?"

"Apparently he comes with limits, namely yours."

I'm pretty sure he's not talking about the wine I've consumed any longer and the hard lines of his expression tell me I'm right. "My limits aren't as narrow as you think."

"I guess that's yet to be decided."

My brows furrow. While he's playful as usual, there is an undercurrent of tension in him that isn't going away. "What happened with Mike?"

"You're giving me whiplash, baby. That's a sudden change of subject."

"And you're avoiding an answer."

"For someone so tipsy, you're pretty damn pushy."

"I used the word cockfight the last time I was drinking," I remind him. "So yeah. I am."

His lips quirk. "Ah, yes. How could I forget?"

"What happened with Mike?" I repeat.

"He gave me something that used to be my father's. He thought I'd like to have it."

I'm shocked he's really answered. Tentatively, I push for more, "But you didn't want it?"

"No. I didn't."

"Did you tell him that?"

"No."

"What was it?"

He reaches in his pocket and pulls out a small laminated card and hands it to me. I study what appears to be a wine judge's certificate with his father's name on it.

I glance up at Chris, at the hard set of his jaw, and I feel the ache in him, the turbulence and pain. "Why didn't you want this?"

"Because Mike and Katie don't know that wine was my father's drug of choice. It's how he tried to forget the day he was behind the wheel of the car when my mother died."

Air rushes from my lunges. "He was driving?"

"Yes. He was driving and he never forgave himself for letting her die. He hid behind the tasting events and the judging tables, and slowly drank himself to death."

I feel like I've been punched in the chest. Chris not only lost his mother that tragic day, but he'd also lost his father. "Oh God. Chris, I'm sorry."

Anger crackles off him. "Come on, Sara, you of all people know sorry is not what the hell I want to hear."

"I do. You're right." Damn the buzz in my head that won't let me communicate properly. His sharing this with me is a huge breakthrough. Desperately, I fight the buzz; I try to let Chris know I'm here for him. "If this is the deep, dark secret you think is going to make me run away, it's not. I'm not going anywhere."

He barks out in bitter laughter and turns me so that I am against the rail, his hands framing my shoulders, his body no longer touching mine. Dark Chris is back, and he is harder and edgier than I have ever seen him. His voice lowers and bites like a whip. "If you think this is my darkest secret, then it tells me you have no idea just how dark life can get."

"How do you know if you don't try me?"

"You can't handle it," he grinds out. "End of story. And you're not going to get a chance to prove me right. I've broken rules with you, important rules I've lived by, and you're the one who'll pay the price. I'm not going to let that happen. I shouldn't have brought you here." He pushes off the railing. "We're leaving." He grabs my hand, and when he sees the card in my palm, he tosses it into the water. My stomach knots as I double-step to keep up and watch the small piece of his father flutter toward the water. My heel catches on a board, and I stumble again.

Chris rounds on me and catches me. "And stop drinking too much damn wine."

I'm appalled at his reprimand, my defensiveness rising to the challenge. "You gave me the wine, you . . . jerk!"

His hand tightens on my arm and he pulls me close. "Finally you get what I've been telling you. Yes. I'm a jerk. The kind of jerk you don't deserve." He takes my hand and starts walking, and like the jerk he proclaims to be, his steps are fast and my footing is painfully unsteady.

We round the building without ever going inside and head to the limo parked off by the side of the drive. He yanks open the door. "Get in."

"What about Katie and Mike?"

"Get in, Sara."

My throat thickens with emotion, and I consider refusing, but the world is spinning around me, and not entirely because of the wine. I slide into the car and over to the far window. I watch Eric scramble upright from an apparent nap and straighten.

"Is everything okay, sir?" he asks as Chris climbs into the vehicle.

"We're ready to return to the hotel" is Chris's only answer. He slams the door, and this time he does not move to sit beside me.

We are worlds apart.

The ride back is short and tense, but it is long enough for the anger to build to a near-explosive level inside me. I have let Chris turn my life upside down in a matter of a week. It's insane. It's everything I said I would never let a man do again.

When the car stops, I open my side and get out. Eric quickly does the same. "Thank you, Eric, for the tour." I turn on my heel and let him shut the door I've exited.

Chris is waiting on me as I round the trunk, a predatory gleam in his gaze, hot and filled with desire. It pisses me off. I am not prey. I am not a token to be used and played with. I tug the shawl around me and cross my arms, giving him no chance to take my hand, and head inside the hotel.

He falls into step beside me, softly announcing the obvious. "People are watching us. They can tell you're pissed."

"How very observant of them." I keep walking toward the elevator and I know I'm swaying. I'm flipping drunk and that just ticks me off more. It means I trusted Chris to take care of me. I don't need to be taken care of. I don't want to be taken care of.

We step into the elevator and he leans on the far wall, watching me. I turn and stare right back at him. His eyes slide over me, a hot caress, and damn it, I hate how much I crave his touch. I hate this power he has over me.

He says nothing. I say nothing. The air crackles with sexual tension but I cling to anger. You can't handle it. I'm so tired of men telling me what I can and can't handle.

The doors open and I head for the hallway, and I sway. Chris's hand slides to my waist and heat darts through my body. "Don't," I hiss without looking at him. "Just don't help me and don't touch me."

His hand falls away and I start walking. The hall is long and it feels like an eternity before Chris swipes the keycard to the door.

All the anger I've bottled for the past half hour explodes from me when I enter the room. I kick off my shoes for stability and toss my purse, which I don't even remember holding, to the ground.

I whirl on Chris before the door even shuts behind him and unleash on him. "You're making me crazy, Chris. No picket fences, no talking about the past, yet you ask about my past and then you take me to meet your godparents, who you know will tell me about your past. I had no expectations from you besides your whisking into my life and thoroughly fucking me before going back to Paris. I was okay with that. It'd been five years. I needed sex, not this . . . this making-me-crazy thing you're doing."

Before I can blink, I'm against him, his hand sliding into my hair, pulling my face to his, his other hand caressing my breast, my nipple. "You want to be fucked? Is that what you want from me, Sara?"

"Yes," I whisper but I know it's not enough anymore, not with Chris. "I want . . ." A wave of nausea blasts through me and my hand presses against his chest. "Oh God." I push away from him and he lets me, as I desperately seek the bathroom, and have no idea where it is. Chris guides me beyond the bed and I remotely register entering a smaller room and a light being flipped on but all I see is the toilet.

I drop to my knees in front of it without a second to spare and what follows isn't pretty. Chris approaches and I wave him off. "Go away," I choke out. "I don't want you to see me like this."

"Forget it." He goes down on a knee beside me. "I got you like this, I'm going to take care of you while you're going through it." He hands me a towel which I clutch eagerly and I can't argue anymore. I fall into eternal heaves, and he is holding my hair, stroking my back, until I collapse on some shiny white surface I think is the side of the tub.

Chris eases me off the tub, cradling me against his body. "We need to get you out of this dress. It's a mess." He tugs it upward. I am a limp noodle and barely raise my arms to help him pull it over my head.

I am naked on the bathroom floor, and Chris slides his arms under my thighs and behind my back as he picks me up. Clarity begins to come back to me. I put my trust in Chris to take care of me and he is but I am sick all over again thinking of the irony of what has happened.

He pulls back the sheets and settles me in the bed, pulling the covers up before kneeling in front of me. "Let me get you some water."

I grab his hand before he can leave. "Chris . . . my getting drunk on wine after what you told me—"

"You did nothing wrong tonight. I did."

"No," I argue, certain, for reasons I'm not clearheaded enough to analyze, that his taking the blame is a problem. "Chris." I don't know what else to say. I'm too sick and to weak. "I . . . we . . ."

"Rest, Sara. I'll be right here if you need me."

The question is, will he be here tomorrow? And should I want him to be? But it doesn't seem to matter what I should want. I just want to be with Chris.

Twenty-six

I blink against the morning sunlight in my eyes and swallow against the dryness in my throat. Awareness comes to me first with the throbbing of my head, next with the horrid taste in my mouth, and then, with the warm weight wrapped around me. I'm naked, under a blanket, and Chris's arm is draped over my body.

For a moment, I lay here absorbing the implications and the complications that have become our relationship, remembering the explosive fight we'd had. The turbulence of that battle fades away in Chris's embrace. Because Mike and Katie don't know that wine was my father's drug of choice. My poor damaged artist. He's been through so much, and though Mike had meant well with his gift; instead he'd sideswiped Chris and left him reeling. I'd been there for the aftermath, and thanks to the wine, I'd handled it horribly.

Guilt twists in my empty, aching stomach as I remember

hugging the toilet, with Chris watching me be sick on the very drink that had destroyed his father. And still, he'd tenderly taken care of me and been my hero.

"You're awake." The raw, morning rumble of his deep voice burns through me and I'm amazed at how easily everything about this man affects me.

"And embarrassed."

He nuzzles my neck. "You have nothing to be embarrassed about."

"Yes. Yes, I do."

He tries to turn me and I push to a sitting position, tugging the sheet with me and scooting against the headboard. "I'm radioactive. Unsafe until I shower and brush my teeth." I frown, noting he's wearing the clothes he'd had on the night before, a dark blond stubble thick on his jaw. He looks rough and sexy, his blond hair a wild hot mess. "You're fully dressed."

"Because you're not and I didn't want to be insensitive to how sick you were."

"Oh." Could he really want me when I've just been sick? Surely not.

"Oh," he repeats, his lips quirking.

I wet my parched lips and my head thunders as if in reaction. I press two fingers to my temple, a moan slipping from my lips. "Dear Lord, I'm hungover. Will this hell never end?"

Chris climbs over my legs and grabs a bottle of water and some pills. "I called down to the front desk last night and had them bring some ibuprofen. You fell asleep before I could give them to you."

Blown away by his thoughtfulness, I touch his jaw, letting

his whiskers rasp against my fingers. "Thank you." My hand falls from his face, and tenderness fills me. "I guess you aren't a jerk all of the time."

He nips my fingers and gives me one of his charming grins that always melt me like butter. "But leave it to you to let me know when I am."

I swallow the pills. "You can count on it." My stomach churns and I imagine I must look green and sickly. "I haven't been hungover in ..." I catch myself before I confess the five years that is so telling, "in years. If the art world requires I drink, maybe I'm not meant for this job."

Disapproval furrows his brow, and he leans back on his elbow, resting on his side. "The art world doesn't require you to drink or understand wine. It does, however, need passionate people like you. I hate that Mark's made you feel otherwise, and it's one of the reasons I'd prefer to help you get other opportunities."

"Riptide would allow me to make a solid salary, Chris. I need that if I'm going to make art my career."

"I can get you a solid salary elsewhere."

Mixed emotions wash over me. If I depend on Chris now, what happens later when he's not around? "I appreciate the help. I do. But I need to do this on my own."

"You are, Sara. I wouldn't help you if I didn't believe in you."

"Having you believe in me means more than you know, but it's like you're unveiling a new piece of work. Making it on my own gives me the confidence to know I can continue to make it in the future."

"When I'm gone."

An ache forms in my chest, and it's all I can do not to ball my fist there. "I didn't say that."

"But you thought it."

Reluctantly I concede, "I'm alone, Chris, and it was my choice, but with that choice comes the need to make smart decisions."

"Do you know how many people would jump to use my money and resources?"

"You mean how many people would use you?" I don't wait for an answer. I don't have to. Michael was one of those people. "Yes. I do."

"You continue to surprise me, Sara." He hesitates, and I think he will say more, but instead, he asks, "How's your stomach?"

"Queasy."

"I figured it would be." He glances at the clock on the bedside table. "It's already eleven. We should get up and I'll order you some tea and biscuits to try and settle your stomach."

"Eleven o'clock?" I twist to confirm the time on the clock, appalled at the hour. "I can't believe we slept this late." Regret fills me at the loss of time with Chris at this wonderful place, and all because of wine. "Wasn't I supposed to meet the wine expert? Did I stand her, or him, up?"

"Her name is Meredith, and I've known her for years. I woke up around eight and canceled, but she says she can see you at twelve fifteen, if you like."

"I do, but . . . is tasting involved? I'm not sure I can do a tasting."

"No," he laughs, and rolls away from me to stand up at the end of the bed, stretching his long, muscular body, and good Lord, sick or not, I am not blind to his male beauty. "No drinking is involved."

"I'm not sure I want to learn about wine anymore."

"Because you're hungover. You'll regret missing the opportunity when you recover. Besides, Meredith's a wine expert and yet I've never seen her at any hotel, or gallery event with a glass in her hand. You can talk to her about how she manages that."

"She doesn't drink the wine she talks about?"

He crosses his arms over his broad, stellar chest. "I asked her that before I booked the training and her reply was that she can't drink on the job and keep her professionalism."

I'm suddenly encouraged by this meeting. "She sounds like someone I need to talk to." Unbidden, a memory from the night before washes over me, and despite the circumstances, it hurts. "Last night . . . you said you shouldn't have brought me here."

His expression is unchanged, but his reply is slow, his voice softening, "I say and do a lot of things I shouldn't with you, Sara."

"Then cancel the training and take me home."

"I'm not taking you home." He glances at the clock. "And if you want to shower and have time to eat before your training session, you should get up."

"So we aren't going to talk about this?"

"Why don't we talk on the way back to the city so you don't miss your session?"

"I'd rather talk now." Leaving things up in the air, wondering if today is the last time I will see him, just isn't how I'm made.

Chris relaxes his posture and sits down beside me, drawing my hand into his. "Look, baby, we were both wound tight last night. Alcohol and emotions, they don't mix."

I recall the image of his father's wine card fluttering toward the pond and his taut features as he told me not to drink too much damn wine. Emotions. He was overflowing with them because of that card, and while I've already realized this, a new worry surfaces. Does he regret my being there during a moment of weakness?

"You told me I was making you crazy last night," he reminds me, drawing me out of my thoughts, back to a present I'm uncertain of.

"You are, Chris."

"Well, you're making me crazy, too."

"Is this supposed to be making me feel better?"

"It's not about making you feel better. It's about the truth. Sara, baby," he strokes my cheek, "this 'crazy' thing you're making me feel is the best crazy I've felt in a long time. I'm not ready to let go of you. I don't know what you're doing to me, Sara, but please ... don't stop."

Not ready to let go of me. Those are the words I latch onto, the inference he will be here with me in the future. "You're confusing me again, Chris," I whisper. "If this is just hot sex, then let's have hot sex, and leave all this other stuff out of it."

"Why don't we just take it one day at a time and enjoy each other, Sara? We'll figure this out together."

One day at time. Why does that feel so impossible now? And yet, I want another day with him. I need some alone time, some time at my home, so I can think straight. Maybe then I'll find clarity, and decide what it is I want and need.

"Yes," I agree. "Okay."

"Good." He smiles and glances at the clock. "You need to get ready if you want to make your session. Wait here a second." He walks to the bathroom and returns with a hotel robe and offers it to me. "If I see you walk naked across this room, you won't be making your session."

The primal heat in his stare defies my messy, post throw-up state, and I quickly slip into the robe. I wasn't joking about being toxic. Now is not the time for hot loving, no matter how appealing it might sound.

I scoot to the side of the mattress and my gaze locks on my shoes and purse lying in the middle of the floor. Beside them is the journal which has tumbled from my unzipped purse. Unbidden, panic rushes through me and I push off the mattress and scoop up my purse and shove the journal inside.

The sound of Chris picking up the phone tells me he isn't watching and isn't interested in the journal. I'm the only one obsessed with it, and Rebecca, but I can't calm the adrenaline flooding my system. My suitcase is a few feet away and I zip it up and drag it toward the bathroom, while Chris orders from room service.

The instant I clear the door of the bathroom, I shut it and lean on the surface. What would Chris think if he knew I'd been reading Rebecca's journal? Would he understand? Would he believe me when I told him I feared for Rebecca? And damn it, if I fear for her, why haven't I done more to find her? I've gotten so caught up living her life, I've forgotten I'm afraid for hers. Silently, I vow to do more for Rebecca, to find out where she is, no matter what the consequence to me. And deep down, I know there will be consequences to what I discover.

Hours later, I had long ago showered and dressed in black jeans and a cherry-red top with sequins, a feature that my personal shopper seemed to favor and I think I might as well. I spent several hours in the dining room overlooking the gorgeous Mayacamas Mountains, while Meredith, a very likeable thirty-something woman, managed to make the vast world of wine interesting and rather simple. And, thankfully, I'd recovered from my hangover enough that Chris had joined us for one of the most delicious meals I've ever been served.

Now, though, it's approaching five o'clock, and the time to head home has arrived. Chris helps me into the passenger seat of the Porsche and by the time he's behind the wheel, I cannot suppress a hint of sadness at our weekend coming to a close.

I sink into my seat, the grogginess of heavy food and the aftermath of being hungover weighing down my mind and body. Chris maneuvers over the back roads to the highway and we fall into a surprisingly comfortable silence.

"I have to go to Los Angeles on Tuesday morning," he announces fifteen minutes into the drive.

This news punches me in the chest. Chris is leaving and I knew he would, but not this soon. But this isn't Paris, I remind myself.

"I have a charity event for the children's hospital over the weekend, and I've committed to a series of events leading up to it. I won't be back until Monday."

Tension uncurls inside me. He's coming back.

"Come with me, Sara."

Chris wants me to go with him? I'm surprised and pleased by the invitation. "I'd love to, but you know I can't. I have a job."

"I can convince Mark—"

"No." I sit up straight. "Chris, we talked about this. Whatever is between you and Mark can't overflow into my job."

"I'll get him press for the gallery."

"No," I repeat. "Please, Chris. Do not talk to Mark. I've told you. I need to know I can earn this job on my own."

A muscle in his jaw flexes and I can tell he's fighting with himself. "I won't call him." He cuts me a sideways look. "Your car is at the gallery and I live right nearby. If you won't go, stay with me tonight. We can stop by your apartment on the way to my place if you like, so you can get some of your things."

I'd hoped for some alone time to process what is between us but the idea of not seeing Chris for days twists me in knots. How has he become such a part of my life in so short a time?

"Yes. I'd like to stay with you." I don't want to go to my apartment, though, and it's partially because I don't want Chris to see how humbly I live. No, I correct myself. There's more to it. My apartment is my old life that I've managed to escape for days, and on some level, I fear that I will never escape fully. I glance at Chris's profile, his masculine beauty, and a deeper fear emerges, a fear that I will never truly belong in this life, his life. But this isn't supposed to be about me. Rebecca. Remember how this all started. I need the information I pulled from her storage unit to properly investigate her whereabouts.

I have to go by my apartment.

Twenty-seven

The sun is setting by the time we pull up to my apartment building and Chris parks his 911 in the midst of much humbler vehicles I imagine he can't help but notice.

"I'll just be a few minutes," I say, and quickly exit the 911. Chris is already rounding the trunk when I stand up. So much for my escape strategy. "You don't have to come in."

"But I want to." There is no give to his voice and he slides his fingers between mine and motions me forward. "Lead the way."

Resigned to a battle I can't win, I head toward my redbrick building with Chris by my side and quickly find my door. I tug the keys from my purse and hesitate. The journals are lying out on the coffee table. I can't hide them from Chris. There's no possible way.

Chris reaches around me, his big body framing mine, and takes the keys. He turns the key and shoves open the door.

Adrenaline pours through me and I rush inside, darting for

the coffee table. I start to stack the journals, and the only bright side to their location, and my present state of panic, is that I have something to worry about other than my simple brown couch and my five-hundred-dollar dining-room set.

The door shuts behind me and the jolt somehow rakes my raw nerves to the point that two of the journals tumble to the ground. Chris is there, as he always is when I drop things, picking them up.

I sink to the couch and set the three in my hands on the coffee table before accepting the ones in his hands. He sits beside me, studying me, ignoring the journals that are all I can think about. "What's wrong, baby? Why is bringing me in making you this frazzled? I don't care about your apartment. I care about you."

My eyes go wide. He cares about me. It's the closest thing to truly admitting this thing, for lack of a better term, between us is more than sex. "It's a lot of things, but no, I didn't want you to see my little bitty apartment."

He continues to study me with far too much scrutiny. "What else? And don't say nothing. You already said it was more than the apartment."

My gaze falls to the journals on the table, and suddenly I desperately want to tell Chris about them. "If I tell you, I'm not sure how you'll react." I glance up at him. "Call this reveal my dark secret that might send you running."

"I won't run, Sara." He pulls my legs over his, holding me captive, and I wonder if he knows this. I suspect he does. Chris has a way of controlling things, controlling me. "Talk to me."

"The journals on the table are Rebecca's." The words tumble out of me, and it is a relief to say them. "Her personal journals, with her most intimate thoughts inside."

"Rebecca's journals," he repeats flatly, his expression as unreadable as his tone. "Did you get them from the gallery?"

"My neighbor bought a storage unit at an auction—people buy the ones that aren't paid for and then sell the items for profit. She planned to do that but her rich doctor fiancé, who she barely knew, whisked her off to Paris. She left the storage unit for me to take care of."

"You have a storage unit filled with Rebecca's things?"

"Right. I couldn't bear getting rid of her things. I wanted to find her and return the items to her. That's how I started reading her journals and there were so many similarities in our lives that I knew I had to find her."

"So you went to the gallery."

His tone isn't flat anymore. It's sharp as steel, and his expression stony, his jaw tight, and nerves explode in my stomach in response. He doesn't like what I'm telling him. I've made a mistake sharing this. "I was worried about her," I say defensively. "I still am, and . . . and my good intentions have snowballed out of control."

He sets my legs down and straightens, staring at the journals. Seconds tick by, the tension in the room is volatile, stretching tighter, and I have a sense of a rubber band about to pop.

My gut clenches when he picks up one of the journals and I can't breathe when he flips to a random page. I watch as he begins to read and his body is stiff, the muscle in his jaw flexing and reflexing. I can't move, can't think of what to do to stop the explosion about to erupt.

Seconds tick by so slowly until he looks up at me. "This is what you've been reading?"

"I'm not sure which passage you're referring to, but I've read most of the entries. I was worried about her, and I've been looking for clues to find her."

He shoves the journal at me. "Read it out loud."

"What?"

"Read the fucking entry, Sara, because I want to know you understand what's on these pages."

"I do," I whisper. My hands are shaking.

His voice is low, lethal. "Read."

I open my mouth to argue but his look, the glint in his eyes, freezes the words on my tongue. I don't understand his reaction or why I'm compelled to follow his order, but I do. Slowly, I lower my attention to the entry, and begin to read.

Tonight he punished me. It was inevitable. I knew this. Looking back, I wonder if I didn't taunt him intentionally by flirting with another man. I just . . . I don't understand how he shares me, and yet he possesses me. When I was on my knees, my hands tied to the posts of the podium, waiting for the first smack of leather on my bare skin, I knew right then, if no other time, I was his world. There was nothing outside the room, nothing but what he wanted to do to me. What I wanted him to do to me. I craved the pain I knew he would inflict, as I never believed I could. Pain. It is an escape. When I feel the leather on my skin, I feel nothing else. There is none of the hurt of the past. There is—

Chris takes the journal from me and tosses it on the table, yanking me to him, his fingers curling around my neck in the way they do when he is in control. "Is this what you're fantasizing about, Sara?"

"No, I—"

"Don't lie to me."

"It's . . . I don't know what you want me to say."

"You have no idea what you're getting yourself into."

But he does. I know it instinctively. "I'm not—"

His mouth closes down on mine, brutal and punishing, hot and seductive, long strokes of his tongue caressing mine, until I can barely breathe. When he finally relents, his hand moves roughly over my breast, and his lips linger above mine, his breath hot, and his voice a near growl.

"You have no idea how tempting it is to give you a lesson you'll never forget."

Yes. Yes, please. Give me a lesson. Every part of me cries out for him, for what he threatens me with. There is no fear. Only a white hot burn and desperation. "Do it," I challenge. "Do it, Chris."

He pushes me down on the couch, framing my body with his. "You don't know what you are getting into, Sara."

"Show me," I pant. "Make me understand."

He shoves my hands over my head. "Damn it, Sara. I should. I should scare the shit out of you and throw those damn journals away." He buries his head in my neck and then he is gone, leaving me panting and empty inside.

I sit up, my sex aching and wet, my body screaming for some unknown pleasure it's been denied. Chris is standing with his back to me, raking a hand through his long hair. "Fuck," he curses, turning to me. "What are you doing to me, woman?"

He's at the edge, and I'm hungry for what is on the other side of his control. Starving in a way I never believed possible. Pushing to my feet, I go to him and I don't give him time to react. I drop to my knees and caress the thick ridge of his erection. He wants me. He is aroused by the idea of teaching me whatever lesson he spoke of. I am aroused by the idea as well.

"What are you doing, Sara?"

"Pleasing you like you do me." I shove up his shirt and press my lips to his stomach, popping his button at the same time.

"Sara," he whispers, and I love the rough timbre of his voice. I love knowing I am affecting him as he does me. I unzip his jeans and reach beneath his boxers, wrapping my hand around the hard, warm flesh of his shaft, carefully freeing him from his clothes.

He's staring down at me, his gaze nothing short of carnal, and I like it. Oh yes, I do. He is hot and hard in my hand and liquid pools at the tip of his erection, further proof of how on edge he is. I blink up at him and hold his stare, before snaking my tongue out and licking it off.

His lashes lower, his body tenses, but his hands are by his sides. He is in control, I'm not. I swirl my tongue around him, and a soft, hard breath escapes his lips. Encouraged, I suckle him, taking only the head of his shaft into my mouth, knowing he will want more.

My tongue thrusts down the underside of him and success follows. His hand slides to my head. "Stop teasing me," he orders roughly. "Take me deeper."

My sex tightens. I like being ordered by this man. I am craving control myself, but yet when he takes it, I am hot and ready for anything. I slide down his length, drawing him deeper into the wet recesses of my mouth, craving the moment he will be buried inside me.

"That's right, baby. Take it all."

My mouth slides all the way down to where my hand grips him, and I begin to suckle and glide back and forth. The muscles in his legs are locked, and he's arching into me, the grip on my hair tightening as he does.

I've given blow jobs, Lord only knows Michael wanted me on my knees, but I have never been aroused by doing it. I am dripping wet, my nipples are tight and aching, my breasts so heavy and sensitive that I caress one of them myself, trying to find relief.

"Harder," he commands. "Deeper."

I increase the pressure and he pumps into my mouth, the salty taste of his arousal pouring into my mouth moments before a low growl escapes his throat and his body jerks. It's that growl that ripples through me, and unbelievably takes me so close to orgasm. Knowing that I affect him downright turns me on. I taste his release and for the first time ever I swallow willingly, drinking in his release, as I am his pleasure. I want . . . I want so badly it hurts.

His body stills, the tension in his legs easing, and before I completely process what is happening, I am being pulled to my feet and my shirt and bra are tugged up over my head. The next thing I know, I'm against the couch, facing it, and he's pulling my jeans down, but my boots are still on.

He pulls me back against his chest, one hand molded to my breast, the other sliding into the wet heat between my legs. "You liked doing that to me."

"Yes." The word hisses from my lips.

"Were you thinking about me inside you, Sara?" His fingers are all over me, teasing my clit, and oh God, I'm embarrassed by how close I am to orgasm.

"Yes," I mouth, unable to form words. I am . . . my body clenches and then spasms overtake me. My knees buckle and Chris's hand on my breast holds me up. Everything goes black and spots dot the inky space. Lost in the sweet burn of my body, without concept of time, I relax against Chris, and slowly become excruciatingly aware of my pants at my ankles.

His hands caress a path down my arms and he leans me toward the couch, pulling my pants up. My cheeks burn as he steps away from me but he is right back, pulling my shirt down over my head.

He leads me to the couch, and sits down, pulling me onto his lap, and resting his head against mine. How long we sit there I don't know, but I could sit there with him forever.

"You do know Rebecca was tormented and lost in that entry, don't you?"

Like me, I think, but I don't say that. I lean back to look at him. "Yes. That's exactly what bothers me, Chris. The journals are more than sex. There is this eerie feeling to them. And they tell me at the gallery that she's on vacation when her whole life is in a storage unit. That makes no sense. Something happened to her and no one seems to miss her."

"You're really worried about her." It's not a question.

"Yes. I am. If something happened to me, I'd like to know someone would care."

He tightens his grip around my waist. "Then we'll find out what happened to her."

"We?"

"We, baby. I'll hire a private detective."

I'm blown away. "You will?"

"If you really think something happened to her, then we need to find out."

I press my lips to his. "Thank you."

"Thank me by letting me stay here tonight. We'll order Chinese or whatever you like and watch a movie."

"I thought we were going to your place."

"I think it would do you good to remember this is your world tonight. And me, too."

"My apartment doesn't have the luxury you're used to."

"It has you, Sara, and that's all that matters."

Twenty-eight

Monday morning, I rush into the gallery a second before I'm due to work, and I barely contain a smile as I make a note to myself. No showering with Chris before work.

"Morning, Sara," Amanda says, and she gives me a quick inspection from behind the desk. "You look fabulous. Open your jacket and let me see the outfit."

I pull back the expensive leather jacket Chris had given me in Napa Valley to show off my simple Chanel sheath in pale pink. One of the many items in my gift bags from Chris, it is elegantly simple, and I love it. I pause outside the offices, in front of her desk.

"I love that dress. The color is beautiful."

"Thank you." I beam. "A compliment is always a nice way to start the morning."

"You look lovely, Ms. McMillan."

I glance up to see Mark standing behind Amanda, wearing

a dark pinstriped suit and looking as gorgeous and powerful as ever.

"Thank you," I manage, wondering why I feel defensive. I've been feeling that way too much lately.

Mark's eyes glint with a hint of what I believe is amusement meant to be at my expense. "Now you have two compliments to start your day."

"I hope that means it's a lucky sales day on the floor for me," I dare.

His lips quirk. "I'm fairly certain it will be. There was a certain client at the party Friday night who says you promised to get him a private viewing of Ricco's collection. Big promises, Ms. McMillan, make you, and me, look bad if they are not delivered upon."

Oh, crap. "I thought since you know Ricco and he displays his art here, we could convince him to allow a visit."

"Good luck with that one, Ms. McMillan." He glances at Amanda. "Get her Ricco's number, and, Ms. McMillan, you're approved for the sales floor, but it does not dismiss you from the testing you'll find in your e-mail." He starts to turn and stops. "If you do pull off this Ricco meeting—I'll be impressed."

I watch him depart, and Amanda peeks over her shoulder. "Ricco, Sara? Have you met him?"

I feel the blood drain from my face. "No."

She whistles. "Think Mark on acid. He's arrogant and intense, and—"

"I get the picture." I head for the office door and enter.

Amanda rolls her chair around. "Here's Ricco's card."

I accept it and she lowers her voice. "Ricco had a soft spot for Rebecca. She's the one who set up the charity event, but he hasn't given Mark another piece to show since she left. If you can win him over, you really will impress Mark."

Rebecca. She's everywhere I turn, but I feel a bit of hope in this otherwise grim situation. "Thank you, Amanda. I am going to give it my best."

She smiles. "Go, Sara. Go, Sara."

I've barely settled into my desk when Ralph appears in my doorway and holds up a sign reading GO, SARA with a smiley face and then disappears.

I laugh and decide I should dive right in and call Ricco before I talk myself out of it. I'm about to dial the office phone when my cell phone goes off. I dig it from my purse and smile when I see the text message from Chris, remembering him adding his number in my phone himself the night before.

I set down the office phone and open the message.

Taking a hot shower has new meaning today.

I laugh and type. So does a cold shower.

True. Very true. Can you do lunch?

I start to say yes, but remember Ava. I have a lunch meeting.

Cancel.

It's tempting, but my gaze catches on the rose candle and I think of Rebecca. I'm hoping Ava can tell me more about her. I can't.

I'll be starving by dinner.

I roll my eyes in good humor. I like it when you're starving.

Then I'll try not to disappoint. I'll pick you up at eight.

I shove my phone back inside my purse, and dial the office phone, and promptly receive Ricco's voice mail. I hang up knowing a message means I have to wait a respectable amount of time to call again.

The buzzer on my desk goes off and I answer. "You have your first customer on the floor, Ms. McMillan," Mark says. "Make me proud."

I'm thrilled at the challenge. "I will."

He is silent a beat. "I look forward to being right about you." The line goes dead and I rise to my feet. So far, this is a good day.

By lunchtime, I have one sale and another potential sale and I'm feeling good. Ironically, Ava has called and chosen Diego Maria's to meet me.

I entered the restaurant to find her at the same table Chris and I had occupied the prior week.

"Sara!" She pushes to her feet, looking petite and lovely in a black pantsuit, her long dark hair cascading over her shoulders. I am wrapped in a hug, and I surmise she's a hugger like I am. I feel a friendship despite barely knowing her.

We settle into our seats, and Maria appears at our table. "Welcome back, Señora Sara. I see we didn't scare you off with the hot peppers."

"No. That was Chris's fault, not yours."

"Ah, well, I assume you make him pay for burning your mouth."

I laugh. "You bet I did."

She claps. "Excellent. In that case, you lovely ladies get tacos on the house, with sauce on the side."

Ava arches a brow. "I sense a good story."

I quickly recount the events of my prior visit and we fall into easy conversation. She tells me all the neighborhood gossip, and I listen for tidbits about Rebecca, trying to find the best way to turn the conversation that way.

Ava lowers her voice. "And Diego. He's going to Paris, you know."

"Yes. He told Chris about it the day I was here."

"He's going after a woman, this exchange student he met who used to come into the restaurant. But she was just having fun, Sara. I met her. I talked to her. He plans to propose. It's really quite heartbreaking. Paris makes people get so romantic and silly."

I think of Ella, who I tried to call the night before, with no success. "You have to tell him, Ava."

"He'll kick me out of the restaurant, and I love this place."

I blink. She's serious. She's going to let the man get his heart broken over a few tacos. I have to talk to Chris and see if he can influence Diego.

"And besides," Ava adds. "Who am I to judge? I thought that hottie rich guy Rebecca was seeing was a player and would dump her in a heartbeat. I warned her off him and she got angry. The next thing I know she's off living the good life, while you're doing her job. You can't win when you warn people off the person they're dating. You just can't."

I'm dumbfounded. I've never really thought this rich guy existed. I mean, the man in the journal is Mark, right? "You met the guy she's vacationing with?"

"Once, and it was enough to see him as the hot rock he is. A player and for a reason. I'd have killed to have a night with that man. I'm not sure there is a woman on the planet who wouldn't."

"Is he an artist?"

She shakes her head. "Some investment analyst in New York she met when she was doing work for Mark. He's Mark's friend. That in itself is a red flag. Mark's as cold as ice and as hot as my coffee. Those who play together, stay together, and as singles. Or in this case, those who make money together, are . . ." She laughs. "I don't know. No smart saying comes to mind, but both those men are all about money. Two peas in a pod."

Play together? Was it a slip? A reference to sex? Does that mean this man is the man in the journal and he shared Rebecca with Mark?

The ticket arrives and our tab amounts to the generous tip we leave, while the topic of Rebecca is lost. I kick myself for not finding out the boyfriend's name. We chat on our walk back to the gallery, but it's chatter and nothing more. I agree to stop in for coffee the next day and head back to my office.

"There's a surprise for you in your office," Amanda beams.

"What is it?"

"Surprise," she repeats. "Go see."

I arrive at my office door and stop dead in my tracks when I see the bouquet of red roses. There are roses everywhere in my room, and I feel like a princess who's found her Prince Charming. My stomach churns at the sweet scent of the flowers, and I walk to my desk on wobbling legs. I can't bring myself to reach for the card, and I settle into my chair and stare at the twelve, unopened buds. Ready to bloom. Suddenly, I have to know who they are from. I grab the envelope and with a shaking hand I pull out the card.

> *Because under the rose trees I was a jerk,*
> *but a lucky one to have you there with me.*
> *—Chris*

I cannot breathe. The card, and what's on it, is perfect. My gaze lifts to the painting of the roses and I am haunted by the connection to her. I reach for my cell phone to text Chris but, unbidden, I think of another journal passage.

He's hard sometimes, demanding, but he makes me feel protected. He makes me feel special. I think I'm ready to put my fear aside of the things he wants me to do with him, and to take the next step.

I am haunted by more than the roses. I am haunted by the similarities of what she felt for the man in the journal and what I feel for Chris. But we aren't the same. He's not the man in the journal. Nothing points to Chris. The paintbrush. No. No. It's not Chris. Ava said she met the man. She knows who he is.

My office phone buzzes and I jump. "Your morning customer is back to make a purchase," Amanda announces.

I shove my cell phone into my drawer and push to my feet, welcoming an escape from what I'm thinking and feeling.

I have barely finished with my sale when Amanda tells me Mark wants to see me in his office. With my second sale of the day under my belt, I am feeling less intimidated by the summons.

"Shut the door," he commands when I enter, from behind his massive desk. "And sit, Ms. McMillan."

Okay, being comfortable with Mark isn't an easy thing to do. I figure I've used up my good luck with my new boss back somewhere around the word cockfight and my last refusal to sit, so I do as ordered and sit down in front of him. Oh yeah, and when my lover-nonboyfriend–whatever Chris is, negotiated me a fifty-thousand-dollar paycheck. I think today is a good day to do as told.

Steely eyes assess me too long and I'm about to begin talking too much, when Mark says, "I see you received flowers today."

Ohhkay. Where in the heck is this going? "Yes." I tell myself to stop there, but I can't. "It's a nice way to start the week and the roses match the gorgeous painting you've placed on my wall." Oh shut up and don't go there!

"I assume that means you're continuing your relationship with Chris."

My defenses rise despite my vow to behave. "I'm not sure why this is relevant to my job?"

"No?"

"No."

"The man negotiated a commission on your behalf and you don't know why he's relevant?"

So much for thinking I'd dodged a bullet. "If this is about money—"

"Everything is about money, Ms. McMillan, and while I have no issues paying you well, I expect to have you all to myself while you are on my territory."

"What?" My pulse hammers in my chest. "I don't under-stand what that means."

He turns his computer screen around and pushes Play and my heart almost explodes from my chest when I see the secu-rity feed. It's me and Chris by the bathroom. Chris touching me. Chris kissing me.

"Enough!" I say, pushing to the edge of my seat.

He punches a key. "Enough indeed."

"That was inappropriate and it will never happen again," I quickly vow.

"You're right. It won't. To be clear, Sara: This is my gallery, and when you are here, or attending to my business, I own you, not Chris Merit."

"Own me?" I repeat.

"Own you. You bet on it and me, not Chris. And if you think that he didn't know there was a camera, that he wasn't trying to power-play me, think again."

Chris knew there were cameras? My heart shatters with the implications behind this discovery. Of course Chris knew. This is his life, his world. I should have known. I did know. "I'm sorry." I want to tell him the wine got the best of me, but I'm afraid he'll only think it's another problem I represent. "I won't let you down again."

He studies me with those hard, calculating eyes for what seems like an eternity. "Ms. McMillan. Relax. I'm on your side. You're not getting fired."

Not getting fired. This is good. This is what I want. I nod, but I am still ramrod stiff.

"Relax, Sara." It's an order.

I want to do as he says. I want to show him I'm a good risk, a good employee, but adrenaline is lighting me on fire. I inhale and let it out, and slowly, I force the tension from my body and lean back into my chair.

"We're okay," Mark says and there is a gentleness to his voice I've never heard. "We have a bright future together."

"We do?"

"Yes. I believe in you, or you wouldn't be here, but it's also my job to protect you and this gallery. You need to understand these artists can be manipulative. They can use the prospect of a special showing, like you want from Ricco, against you. I need to make sure right now that you know that you need to do nothing to get work for this gallery but be the professional you are. We do not beg, and you do not let yourself get manipulated. Period. The end. These artists know I don't tolerate that crap and as long as they believe I own you, they won't believe you will, either. So when I say I own you, Sara, I mean I own you."

He owns me. I am not comfortable with his choice of words, but I doubt my ability to be my own judge at the moment. My gaze lifts to the mural behind Mark that I am certain Chris painted. I've trusted Chris. Has he been manipulating me? Using me against Mark? It's not the first time I've had this thought.

"Are we clear, Sara?" Mark prods.

My attention returns to Mark, to the steely strong eyes offering me protection, a good job, a future. "Yes. We're clear."

I barely remember the rest of the conversation. The minute I am back at my desk I grab my phone and text Chris. Have to cancel dinner. I turn off my phone.

318

Twenty-nine

The rest of the day crawls by and I am in knots over Chris—hurt, angry, confused—I feel all of these things and more. Nearing the end of the day, I am in my office, trying to focus on work and failing. Worse, I expect Chris to call through the switchboard to try to reach me and he doesn't. Clearly, he's not that broken up over my cancellation of dinner, and I can't help but believe he knew my humiliation was coming and has been received. I wouldn't discount Mark confronting him.

How could Chris intentionally set me up like he did? And he did. Chris is too smart to not know what he was doing and the tension between him and Mark is too damn obvious. I am a token in a game and I hate how badly it hurt. I hate that I let my little adventure turn into heartache.

When eight o'clock finally arrives, the knots in my stomach multiply, and I stay at my desk. What if Chris is outside waiting on me? What if he's not? another voice dares to whisper in my head. I am second-guessing my decision to turn off my phone, to actually talk to Chris and make it clear we are over. Right. A simple blow-off. It should be easy. Instead, I am a coward who cannot talk to him, certain I will agree to whatever he asks of me. I am too far into the infatuation I have for him. And that's what it is. Infatuation. After being humiliated by that video, I refuse it to be anything else.

At a quarter after eight, Mark appears in my doorway, his suit jacket gone, his top two buttons undone. Still, he manages to look every bit the corporate seduction king, the guy every lady wants and every man wants to be. Every lady but me, that is.

He leans on the jamb. "Isn't it time to go home, Ms. McMillan?"

"For reasons I'd rather not discuss, I'm feeling extremely dedicated tonight."

He ignores my reference to our earlier incident. "I don't like leaving you here alone."

"You have cameras."

He laughs, a rare happening, and oddly considering my behavior, he seems more relaxed around me. "Good point," he concedes and pushes away from the wall. "You are the witty one, Ms. McMillan, and I can see customers responding well to you. I'll leave you to work, but why don't you pull your car around front so you don't have to walk to the parking lot alone?"

Cab rides for staff after tastings, worries over my safety, my being manipulated. Mark's tough and demanding, but I begin to see him as a good boss, someone trying to help me get ahead in this world. "I moved my car out front before Amanda left an hour ago." And because I knew that was where Chris would look for it.

"Well then, I guess I'll depart. Remember, though, that once you exit the gallery, the security locks are automatic. You can't get back in."

"Yes. I know. I'll be sure I'm ready to leave when I exit."

"Good. Then you're all set. You had excellent marks on your wine exams, by the way. I'm impressed."

"I spent the weekend studying." And falling hard for an artist who has my insides in knots.

"It shows." He motions to the flowers, the only smirk I've ever seen on his face present. "At least he has good taste in flowers." He doesn't give me time to respond. "Good night, Ms. McMillan."

"Good night, Mr. Compton."

Unmoving, I listen to his footsteps fade, staring at the flowers that have teased my senses and reminded me of Chris all day. I reach for the card and pull my hand back. Romantic scribble on a plain white card doesn't erase what he's done. In fact, the weekend and the flowers seem more a mask for him to hide his motives. The voice of logic and the one of my heart begin battling it out in true gladiator style. But he let you into his world. He told you things he doesn't tell other people. I grind my teeth and remind myself his disclosure was created by Mike taking him off guard. I was simply there at the right—or I suspect in Chris's mind—the wrong time. But he took you to meet his godparents.

How long I sit there fighting with myself, I'm not sure, but

I feel bloody and beaten, with every nerve ending raw and exposed. Somehow, I shake myself and reach for the phone, trying to be productive. I dial Ricco for about the tenth time, hoping the evening hour plays in my favor. I receive his machine again. Hmm. I wonder if he has caller ID. I reach for my cell phone and stare at the blank screen. I've burned to turn it on, to see if Chris has replied. Why do I care if he's replied? He is playing with my life and my career. Logic raises her ugly, practical head again, and tells me I've been down this path. I can't go down it again. I won't go down it again.

Returning my phone to my purse, I gather several pieces of paper with notes I've made about Rebecca that I stuffed in a drawer earlier in the day. On one of them is a phone number for the manager of her apartment building. Or what I assume is her old apartment building.

I glance at the office phone and consider calling, but decide better. I've learned my camera lesson. Don't forget Mark is the man in the journal. Don't forget Rebecca is missing and turn him into a hero because Chris has hurt you. My Rebecca research really has to be done off-site. The building in question isn't far away and I'll go by at lunch tomorrow.

Still not ready to head home to my empty apartment and tormented thoughts, I review a stack of files I was given earlier in the day, containing information on people who have bought from the gallery in the past year. Thirty minutes later, I've filed them in order of the best prospects and made notes on each.

When nine o'clock arrives I can no longer put off the inevitable walk to my car and entry to my empty apartment filled with memories of Chris. With my purse and briefcase on my shoulder, and wearing the leather jacket Chris gave me, I pause inside at the front door of the gallery. Squeezing my eyes shut, I am uncertain if I am more worried about Chris's being outside or not being outside. Maybe he didn't do this to me on purpose. Maybe I've jumped to conclusions. I roll my eyes at myself, disgusted at my thoughts. I am so weak where that man is concerned.

Stiffening my spine, I exit into the chilly evening breeze, and make sure the door clicks behind me. Nervously, I scan the street, taking in the cars at meters, and the random pedestrians milling about, searching for Chris to no avail. Disappointment fills me, and I laugh bitterly into the wind at my misplaced hope he would be here, fighting for me, proving me wrong about him. I cut to my left and hike up the hill toward the discreet spot I'd cozied my car into, berating myself the entire time. You are so messed up, Sara. You want him after he made you a nearly X-rated video star.

Two blocks down, I round the corner of what was a busy street now turned eerily sleepy, which was not the plan. Quickening my pace, I dig out my keys. Halfway down the block, I spot my car and stop dead in my tracks, my heart racing wildly in my chest. Next to my car is a sleek Porsche 911. A wild flutter of every emotion possible goes through me. To say I'm conflicted is an understatement. The flutter in my chest becomes thunder, hard and intense, echoing in my ears.

Somehow, I force my feet to move, mentally steeling myself to be strong, to hold my ground with Chris. No weakness allowed. Chris rounds the hood of his car and heads toward me, a predatory edge to his steps. He is gorgeous, his longish hair a bit wild like the man. His jeans and biker books are so damn sexy, hugging the lithe lines of his body. I hate how much I want him.

Wicked hot anger forms inside me at my reaction to him. I don't give him a chance to confront me, charging toward him and unleashing on him. "You knew there were cameras in the gallery and still you shoved me against that wall and kissed me. He made me watch the security feed, Chris. How could you do that to me?"

He curses and scrubs his jaw. "He fucking played the tape for you?"

I don't have the denial I'd hoped for and my chest burns and aches. "Yes. He made me watch it. Am I right? Did you know there were cameras in the gallery?"

He runs a hand through his hair, the overhead light playing on the handsome, tormented lines of his face. Too tormented. He knew. I see it in his eyes.

"I wasn't thinking about the camera when I was kissing you if that's where you're going with this, Sara."

It's not enough. "But you knew." It's not a question. It's fact.

"I thought about it later, yes."

"And you didn't tell me?"

"You were worried enough over your job."

"That's not an answer. Tell me you didn't do this on purpose. Tell me, Chris. I need to hear it."

"I didn't do it on purpose, Sara." His voice is low, taut, filled with the conviction I so desperately had hoped for. "At that moment," he continues, "I couldn't think of anything but how badly I wanted you. That's what you do to me." His lips tighten and thin. "But I won't lie to you and tell you I was sorry he might see it, either. In fact, I was hoping like hell he did."

He might as well have stabbed me in the chest. "Because I'm some sort of power play with Mark?" My throat is thick, my tone choked. "Is that what this is, Chris? Or did you want me to get fired?"

"Why would I take you to Napa and help you meet his ridiculous requirements if I intended that?"

"Money to kill? A game to play with Mark?" I sound flippant and bitter. I am.

"I don't deserve that, Sara, and you know it." His voice is a hiss laced with anger at my accusations.

Deep down, I want his anger to mean something, I want to believe in him, but I don't even believe in me anymore. I don't trust my judgment. "Well, if you did want to get me fired, it didn't work. Mark has vowed to protect me and teach me the business."

"Protect you." The words are hard and flat, his body rippling with sudden edginess. "You want Mark to protect you when you tell me you don't need protection?"

"I just want to do my job."

"It isn't about the job with Mark. Not with you."

"You can't know that."

"You've read the journals, Sara. Who the hell do you think Rebecca was playing bondage games with? It sure as hell wasn't Ralph."

"It was the man she's vacationing with."

"Now she's vacationing when last night you were worried she was dead?"

"I never said that."

"You inferred it." He inhales and lets out a sharp breath. "You know what? It's time you get a reality check, baby." He grabs my hand. "Come with me."

I dig in my heels. He clicks the locks on his car. "Get in the fucking car, Sara, or I swear to you I'll pick you up and put you there myself. You are going to see for yourself who and what Mark is, and stop pretending you don't know already."

"And since you've proclaimed yourself as worse than Mark, I suppose now is when I get to see your deep, dark secrets, too?"

His jaw flexes. "Yes."

Emotion shifts and moves inside me, and my anger slides away. Dread tightens my tummy. This is the big reveal he believes will make me run.

I walk to the car and get in.

Thirty

Five minutes later, the shadowy darkness of the 911 isn't as suffocating as is the silence within. We haven't spoken a word, and it's killing me. Guilt is eating away at me over my harsh judgment of Chris. He'd been honest enough to tell me he didn't regret Mark seeing the security footage. Surely he was honest in telling me he hadn't manipulated me to create the footage.

Staring out of the window without really seeing anything, I can feel Chris next to me, far from me, but close enough to touch. My skin tingles with awareness. My mind replays the touch of his mouth on mine, and on more intimate parts of my body. The caress of his hand on my breast, the play of his fingers between my thighs.

Still the silence stretches onward and it becomes clear that we are heading toward the Golden Gate Bridge, into an elite neighborhood where trees, greenery, and mansions with insane price tags and views dominate, rather than trolleys and rooftops.

Our destination is in the elite Cow Hollow neighborhood I've heard about but never visited, where Chris stops at an expansive gated property and keys in a code. Is this his home, too? I glance at his profile, opening my mouth to ask, but his posture is rigid, his demeanor unapproachable, so I snap my mouth shut. The gate opens, and we drive down a long road to what is obviously a property spanning miles.

"What is this place?" I ask, bringing the stucco house into view, unable to bite back curiosity any longer.

"A private club," he answers without looking at me, maneuvering around a circular drive and pulling to the door.

A man in a black suit with an earpiece opens my door. Chris rounds the 911 and tosses the man his keys. "Nice to see you, Mr. Merit," the man comments. "It's been a while."

Chris doesn't appear to be feeling overly cordial. "Keep the car up front. This will be a short visit." Chris stops beside me and slides my purse from my shoulder. "Leave it in the car." He hands it to the security man, and I start to object but lose my train of thought when the man rakes me with a hot stare filled with disapproval. A smirk settles on his lips, as if he knows something I do not. Of course he does, and it's unsettling on all kinds of levels.

"And the coat," Chris adds, already pulling the leather jacket from my shoulders. I'm beyond argument at this point and let him hand it off to the same man who has my purse.

Chris folds my hand into his and the touch sizzles up my arm. I feel him tense and I think he feels what I do, but he doesn't look at me, and I am quaking inside with nervous anticipation.

We head up a dozen steps toward a set of red double doors. Halfway up Chris says, "You're not a member, which means you talk to no one and stay by my side." He cuts me a hard stare, looking at me for the first time since we arrived. "And I mean no one, Sara."

"O . . . kay." Good grief, what is this place?

We hit the top of the last step and the door opens. Another man in a black suit with an earpiece on appears in the entry and Chris doesn't bother with a greeting. "Private room."

"The Lion's Den is open."

Lion's Den? Why does that not sound good?

Chris nods and we enter the house, and I absorb the tall ceilings, the expensive art on the walls, and a winding stairwell covered in an oriental rug with some relief. This place is elegant, a place for the elite, as one would expect from this neighborhood; it's nothing scary at all.

We cut down a long hallway to our right and unease forms again as I get the feeling I am in a hotel; the fancy carpet stretching out beneath my feet as we pass door after door.

Chris stops at a doorway at the end of the hall and punches in a code on a wall panel. He knows this place and it knows him. That sense of foreboding returns with a hard jolt.

He pushes open the door and waves me forward, but grabs my arm before I enter. His eyes are hard, his jaw harder. "Two things you need to know, Sara. We leave when you want to leave, and Mark owns this place."

This is the source of their bad blood. It has to be. I swallow hard. "I understand."

"You aren't going to like what you find out."

I've heard these words before from him, and hearing them now is my confirmation. This is the secret he's been keeping, and that knowledge fills me with courage. "I guess we'll see soon."

He stares at me, unmoving, his grip on my arm tight, unyielding. "You have to let me go if I'm going to go inside, Chris." Slowly, he loosens his grip and I step inside.

Cool air washes over me as I enter a room where dimly lit spotlights color the interior in a seductive amber haze. Taking in what is before me, I'm in instant sensory overload and my hand goes to my throat.

To my right is a pedestal with a massive wooden bed sitting on top of it, and large silver cuffs attached to the headboard. On the wall beside it is a panel displaying whips, chains, and various items I've never seen in my life. To my left is another podium with some sort of arch and more cuffs.

Chris comes up behind me, his breath warm on my neck, but he doesn't touch me. He motions to a couch in front of what looks like a full-size movie screen.

"We're observing today. Why don't you take a seat?"

I walk to the back of the leather couch but I don't round to the front. My fingers curl into the soft material, and I lean in to support my weak knees. "I'll stand."

Chris steps to my side. "Have it your way. You're about to witness a group playroom feeding live from another area of the mansion." He lifts a remote he's picked up somewhere and the screen comes to life.

I gasp at what I see. There is a masked, naked woman tied to a pedestal in the middle of a stage, while an audience—all masked as well—sits in observation.

A man in leather pants is circling her, and I think he is holding a riding crop. It fits a description I remember from one of Rebecca's journal entries, but I can't be sure. He's teasing her, flipping her nipples with the leather end of the crop, back and forth. She is moaning and passion is etched on her face. Pleasure. She feels pleasure, and to my dismay I can feel my body responding, the warm heat spreading in my belly.

The crop moves lower, and I see that it is flat with some sort of leather strings. It caresses her belly and between her legs. He steps closer to her, rubbing the leather in the V of her thighs and tugging on one of her nipples. I am suddenly wet and achy and embarrassed. The woman moans and the man stiffens and does not seem pleased. He steps back from her, no longer touching her with his hand or the crop.

He walks around her and stops behind her. And then to my dismay, he smacks her hard with the crop. I jump and gasp. He keeps hitting her, fast, and oh God, it seems so hard.

I turn to Chris. "He's hurting her."

"This is what she craves, and he's trained to know her limits. If it's too much, she says her safe word and he stops."

A chill goes down my spine at his intimate knowledge of what is happening.

"Watch, Sara." It's a command, low and tight, and unforgiving. "You need to understand that this is where Mark wants you."

But this isn't about Mark. It's about Chris and it's that knowledge that makes me turn back to the screen.

Another man is onstage now, and he's holding some sort of cane. I suck in a breath as he hits the woman and her body bows forward. "Stop!" I yell and I whirl around and Chris's arms close around me. "Enough. I've seen enough." This was so much more, too much more, than the journals. "I want to leave. I want to leave now."

Chris stares down at me, but he doesn't turn off the feed. I can still hear the woman screaming. His expression is hard, his eyes cold in a way I've never seen them. "Now do you see why I wanted Mark to know you're off-limits? Why I said I was protecting you?"

I stare at him, tracing the lines of his handsome face, looking for the tender, laughing man I know, but I cannot find him, "It's Mark's club, but you're a member."

"That's right."

"Do you . . . beat women?"

"It's not beating, Sara. It's a form of pleasure. It's helping someone get the high they need to be satisfied."

My stomach knots. "And you know how to do that?"

"Yes."

"And you like to do it?"

"I understand the need."

"What need? How can you need to feel pain?"

"It's a drug. A way to feel nothing else."

"Are you saying that you like to feel pain?"

"Need Sara, not like, and not like in the past."

"What does that mean?"

"There was a time when it was all that got me to the next day."

"And now?"

"Not as often."

"You let a woman tie you up and do that to you in public."

"No. I stick to private rooms."

The calm I have managed to keep fades away. I push against him. "I want to leave."

He holds me steadily. "You mean run away?"

"Damn it, Chris, you said I could go when I wanted to."

He slides his hand around my neck, pulling my mouth to his. "And you said you wouldn't run."

"I just . . . I need out of this place, Chris. I need out of here now."

He steps back from me abruptly, and pain radiates off him and some part of me burns to go to him, to hug him. To tell him I think I might love him, but I can't compute the man I've come to know and the man who is a part of this place.

"Please take me to my car."

I watch him, his expression steel, his eyes still icy, and I feel him closing off from me. Or maybe this time, it's me withdrawing. I am a mess, shaking inside and out. He hits the remote and turns off the screen, tossing it to the ground, then motions to the door. He doesn't touch me and the walk down the hall is eternal. I don't look at the men in their suits, unwilling to see the mockery surely in their eyes. Soon, we are in the dark car again, and the silence stretches thick and heavy between us. I am numb, unable to form coherent thoughts. I'm in a haze when Chris pulls his car behind mine.

"Come home with me," he surprises me by saying. "Come home with me and give me a chance to explain, Sara."

My chest has never hurt like it hurts now. "I can't be what you need."

He turns to me, and he starts to touch me, but he hesitates and lets his hands drop. "You are what I need. You make me feel alive, Sara."

The use of my own words tightens my throat and a burn starts in the back of my eyes. I study him, search his face. "Can you truthfully tell me you will never need pain again?"

"This is new to me, Sara. That lifestyle has been my drug of choice. My way of feeling nothing. But I do feel now. I feel with you and for you. What it did for me it can't do for me anymore."

It is everything I want to hear and yet not enough. "But you can't know you will never need that . . . place again."

"Whatever I need you can give me."

I shake my head. "No. No, I can't." I reach for the door and he grabs my arm. Heat races through me and I feel a sudden need to touch him, to feel him close. It overwhelms me, confuses me.

"Please don't run, Sara."

We stare at each other and something snaps between us. I don't know who moves first but we come together in a hot, searing kiss, and the feel of his hands lacing into my hair touching me is everything I need and not enough.

I am panting when he presses his forehead to mine. "Come home with me."

It would be so easy to say yes, but I am confused and uncertain. "I can't think when I'm with you, Chris. I can't think and I need to think."

"I leave in the morning."

"I know." And I don't want him to leave, which is a

testament to how messed up my head is right now. I want space and time, but I want him with me, too. "I . . . think that gives me some time to process. I need . . . time."

He pulls back, searching my face through the shadows of the dark car. "Okay." His hands drop from me, and I am cold and lost without his touch.

Okay. He's letting me go, and I know it's what I've asked for, but it still hurts. I fumble for my purse and briefcase, and they are tangled in my feet. Chris helps me and I manage to slip both straps over my shoulder.

He reaches for the coat but I don't want it. I need out of the car before I change my mind. I shove open the door and stand on wobbly knees, closing Chris inside behind me. All but running, I rush toward my car, clicking the lock and climbing in.

Once I'm inside, I turn on the engine and tear out of the parking space. The minute I'm on the road, driving away from Chris, the tears start to fall. I swipe at them, trying to see the road.

By the time I walk into my apartment, I am a mess. I lock the door and slide down the wooden surface and explode into tears. My phone beeps with a text message, and I don't look at it. Blindly, I push to my feet and find my way to a hot shower.

I have no concept of how much time has elapsed when I retrieve my cell phone and curl into a ball in the bed. Steeling myself for a message I am sure is from Chris, I glance at the screen.

Please let me know you are home safe.

Then ten minutes later:

Sara. I need to know you are okay.

The messages continue until the final one, five minutes later.

If I don't hear from you soon I'm coming to check on you.

I'm fine,

I type and drop the phone onto the mattress, but I'm not fine at all.

Tuesday morning I barely pull myself out of bed and when I glance at the clock, I know Chris is gone, on a plane, headed to another city. I have a week to think, a week to miss him. A week to get my head on straight. I'm drinking coffee when I begin to think about what he'd said. Give me a chance to explain. The memory hits me like a cannonball, shaking me to the core. He craves pain so he doesn't feel other things. What other things? Deep down is a growing certainty that there is far more to Chris's past than I know. What has he endured, and how can I judge him when I have no idea how horrific it might be?

I walk to my bed where I've laid out my black skirt and beige blouse, but a sudden need to be close to Chris sends me to my new suitcase, where I pull out the final dress from my gift bags, a cream-colored dress with a flare to the skirt.

When I open my front door to depart, I freeze at the sight of a large yellow envelope with my name written in Chris's handwriting. My heart squeezes and I reach for it, opening it with eager, unsteady hands. I stare at the drawing inside, unable to catch my breath. It's a black-and-white draft of me, naked and leaning against the window of his apartment, the brilliant lights of the city behind me. Attached to the drawing is a piece of paper that reads—You are all I need.

I drop my head to the paper, and fight the burn in my eyes. "Oh, Chris," I whisper. I love this man. Logic is screaming it's too soon to feel such a thing but my heart has won this battle. And I am almost certain Chris is going to rip my heart from my chest before this is over, and yet, I can't wish him away.

I arrive at work, and for the first time since the club, worry about facing Mark, only to hear from Amanda that Mark is off-site for most of the day. It is the best news I can get; the space that allows me to regroup.

Needing something other than Chris and Mark to think about, I dive into my work, starting with a call to Ricco from my cell phone. He answers immediately. "This is Sara McMillan from the Allure Art Gallery."

He rambles in Spanish, and I'm fairly certain every word is not a nice one. "I do not have time for this call, Ms. McMillan."

"I have a client who wants a private viewing of your collection. He adores your work as so many of us do."

Silence. "You admire my work?"

"Immensely. I was at the charity event and hoped to meet you. It would have been an honor. I would be thrilled to do so now."

More silence. "Come to my private gallery tomorrow evening at seven o'clock. If I feel you are competent then I'll invite your client to the next meeting."

"Excellent. Yes. Thank you."

"Do not bring Mark, Ms. McMillan." He hangs up.

Mark. Not Mr. Compton. An uneasy shiver goes down my back, and I worry that he and Mark have a private club connection.

My cell phone buzzes with a text while I'm holding it and I click on the message to read, I don't want to miss you but damn it I already do. Don't run, Sara.

I inhale against the emotion in my chest and know I can't promise him I won't. I miss you, I type, and God, it's so true.

Then come here and be with me.

I can't. You know that.

I wait for a reply and wait some more. Finally I get a simple I know. I know? What does that mean? It feels important to me to reach out to him somehow, to send him the message that I am here, I am trying to understand.

I wet my lips and type: But I wish I could.

He doesn't reply, and I don't know what to think.

Lunchtime comes and I rush to the apartment building where Rebecca had lived, only to be told they can't give out private information, and Rebecca no longer lives there anyway. I'm not going to let it discourage me. I'll find another way to reach Rebecca. Visiting the club with Chris has me thinking about how easily Rebecca could have gotten into something too deep, too intense, and ended up hurt. My determination to find her is renewed with a new, fearless vengeance.

I stop by the coffee shop, hoping to find Ava there so I can just outright ask her the name of Rebecca's boyfriend. She's out of town again. I spend the rest of my lunch hour calling through random numbers I've found in Rebecca's phone directory, getting nowhere. I decide to go to the storage unit and dig around after work since it will be early when I get off.

By late afternoon, I haven't heard from Chris and it's driving me crazy. I have no idea Mark is in until he pokes his head into my doorway. "Mary is in the bathroom throwing up and I'm headed out to another meeting. I need you to work late."

"Yes. Okay."

"Good." He is gone that fast.

I check the times the storage unit is open and I'll have an hour to dig around if I leave right at eight.

I arrive at the unit at eight fifteen, and I still haven't heard from Chris. It's making me crazy. He makes me crazy, and I'm ready to throw myself into searching Rebecca's unit for answers, hoping this makes me feel like I'm doing something worthwhile.

The instant I park and stare at the concrete building with orange doors, I remember how much I hate this place, but remind myself this isn't about me. It's never been about me. Rebecca is missing. I don't believe for a minute she's on vacation and ditched her apartment and left all of her things behind. It makes no sense. Why store her items? Still, doesn't the unit infer she made an active choice to leave, and why am I still not buying that?

Remembering my last visit and the juggling act I'd pulled, I decide to leave my purse in the car so I have less to carry when I leave the unit. With my keys in hand, I step out of my car and under a flickering light, noting the absence of anyone else around. "Cue scary music," I mumble as I start walking, mocking my ridiculous nerves.

The exterior doors are open, and I make my way to Rebecca's unit and unlock it, reaching inside to flip on the light. Goose bumps lift on my skin as I stare at the neatly packaged personal items. Everything seems as I left it.

After considering shutting the door, creepy images of getting locked inside make me think better. With no time to spare, I head to a box and use it for a chair, wishing I had on a pair of jeans.

I'm digging through some papers when I hear a loud pop. I frown and still, listening. There is a sudden chill in the room, and I stand up, every nerve ending I own on edge.

Another popping sound and the lights go out. It's pitch-black and I open my mouth to scream but some instinct makes me bite it back.

Another pop.

A footstep.

Someone is in here with me.

Don't forget to look for the scintillating
conclusions to the Inside Out trilogy

BEING ME

and

REVEALING US

Available 2013 from Gallery Books